"Miss Wagner has traveled all this way believing we were looking for a teacher. But we can fix this."

Ma nodded as if trying to convince herself. "We discussed hiring a teacher for the boys just a few weeks ago."

Hank did recall. He also recalled hoping to wait another year. "Ma, if you can't handle the boys' schooling any longer, then I promise we can begin a search for a *male* teacher."

Something sparked in Miss Wagner's eyes. "If you're seeking a teacher, there's no reason why I can't be given a chance."

Her eyes met his, and she smiled, causing the tiniest dimple to emerge. Did she think she could win him over by being pretty? If so, she was in for a disappointment.

"I'll give you a week's teaching trial." There was no harm in making himself look magnanimous, to please his parents. Once Miss Wagner got a taste of the mischief his boys could unleash, she'd likely see to leaving as early as the morning.

Despite adoring happily-ever-afters, **Megan Besing** didn't unlock a love for reading until her midtwenties, which quickly expanded into writing. Her stories have won many awards, but her most cherished achievements are being a wife and mother. She lives in a pocket-size Indiana town centered around family. She's always planning a vacation with a view, yet her favorite place may just be on her front porch drinking tea. Connect with Megan at meganbesing.com.

Books by Megan Besing

Love Inspired Historical

The Rancher's Want Ad Mix-Up

Visit the Author Profile page at LoveInspired.com.

The Rancher's Want Ad Mix-Up

MEGAN BESING

LOVE INSPIRED
INSPIRATIONAL ROMANCE

LOVE INSPIRED®
INSPIRATIONAL ROMANCE

ISBN-13: 978-1-335-41894-4

The Rancher's Want Ad Mix-Up

Copyright © 2022 by Megan Besing

Recycling programs
for this product may
not exist in your area.

For questions and comments about the quality of this book, please contact us
at CustomerService@Harlequin.com.

Love Inspired
22 Adelaide St. West, 41st Floor
Toronto, Ontario M5H 4E3, Canada
www.LoveInspired.com

Printed in U.S.A.

We love Him, because He first loved us.
—*1 John* 4:19

To the best mom ever!
I treasure your love and friendship.

Also, to my awesome mother-in-law.
Thanks for loving and "choosing" me.

I'm beyond grateful for your Christlike examples.
May I be like you both when I grow up.

Chapter One

Outside Kansas City, MO, September 24, 1889

Della Mae Wagner shielded her eyes from the sun, taking in her future. Buildings lay scattered ahead. Not as many as she would have thought to warrant hiring a teacher, but whether there were ten or twenty students awaiting her, she was ready to meet them all just the same.

"Will the children still be at the schoolhouse?"

Beside her Mr. Lamson tugged on the reins, pulling the wagon to a halt in front of a cabin. White curtains decorated the windows, and two rocking chairs sat empty on the porch, creaking in the breeze. "The schoolhouse?" he replied. "Sorry to say, we don't have one of those, my dear. And anyway, they better be preparing their Sunday best, along with your fiancé."

"M-my fiancé?" Surely, she had heard him wrong. The daunting journey with its thunderous train whistles must have rattled her more than she thought. Her now *ex*-fiancé was nowhere near Missouri. No, that liar had landed in another's arms back home. One who could provide for him instead of the other way around. Marriage clearly wasn't the path for her—which was why she'd decided to dedicate herself to teaching, instead.

Mr. Lamson climbed from the wagon and patted the gray spotted mare before lifting the edge of his hat. "Of course. My stubborn boy needs a wife. And he needs you now more than ever. That's why we placed that ad."

Needed her? A wife? Panic surged in Della's empty stomach. To be sure, it wasn't unheard of for there to be newspaper advertisements for mail-order brides, but the ad she'd answered had been for a schoolmistress. The wording had been more poetic than literal, but she couldn't have misunderstood…could she? "Mr. Lamson, I'm afraid there's been a miscommunication. I am to be a teacher—"

"Teacher, cook, housekeeper, mother. Yes, yes," he said with a gentle smile. "You women folk have many responsibilities. It takes a noble woman to do them all— and do them well. That's why my Alice and I chose you. Your letter and references showed that you're a perfect match for Hank, strong where he is weak."

The cabin door squeaked open, and an older woman stepped onto the porch with her hands pressed to her chest. Her apron mirrored the pattern of the curtains fluttering in the windows. "Is this her? Oh, of course it's her. It's not like you'd pick up another Della Mae Wagner." The woman grabbed Della into a hug. "Welcome to the family."

Della could do nothing but blink, her arms locked along her sides. Her mind searched for an explanation for the bizarre situation. Maybe she was still on the bumpy train and only dreaming. Except the hug wrapped around her felt more genuine than any she'd ever received in her life.

"Come on there, Alice. Allow the poor girl room to breathe, or all this will have been for nothing."

Yes, Della needed air so she could figure out what was going on. Why did they believe she was there to be a bride?

"We're tickled you've arrived. You're an answered prayer." Mrs. Lamson squeezed Della's fingers. "I knew you'd be lovely. Your letter overflowed with your sweet spirit. Roy, isn't she lovely?"

Mr. Lamson nodded while he stroked the horse's nose. "A perfect match indeed."

The praise and approval—much more than she'd received from her own parents—made her for a moment wonder if it would really be so bad to go along with whatever they wanted. But no. She may have been desperate to leave Indiana, however Della wasn't desperate enough to marry a stranger. Of that she was certain. "Mr. and Mrs. Lamson—"

"Good heavens, that won't do. Call me Alice."

"All right, Alice. I told Mr. Lamson when we arrived—"

"This here's my Roy." Alice patted Mr. Lamson's chest.

Della smoothed the front of her dress. The wrinkles in the blue fabric only seemed to multiply, much like the problems of the morning. Really like the past few months if she was honest. "I'm sorry, but there's been a terrible misunderstanding."

"That's our fault, dear. Forgive us. We should have already made proper introductions. Blame it on our excitement." Alice pulled Della in for another embrace.

This was going nowhere.

"Ma. Have you seen the boys?" A man's voice came from behind her.

She expected to take in a breath once Alice released her, but when Della turned to greet the third stranger, she couldn't breathe for an entirely different reason as she found herself face-to-face with the most handsome man she'd ever seen.

He stood a bit taller than Roy Lamson and his broader shoulders looked ready to endure life's labor. The scruff on his unshaven face and the mud splattered across his clothes and boots somehow added to his allure. Could he be the alleged fiancé who clearly had yet to change into his Sunday best?

Della bit the inside of her cheek, stopping her mind from wandering where it shouldn't. This was not her fiancé. She was not here to be a bride. No matter what everyone else here seemed to think.

Alice pushed her fists onto her sturdy hips. "Hiram Robert Lamson. I told you we were to have an important arrival. Where, may I ask, are your Sunday clothes?"

"Ma. I don't have time for…" He glanced at Della before concentrating again on Alice. "For this."

"Please tell me I did not raise you with such awful manners."

His brown eyes locked on to Della's, and she had to remind herself she wasn't the swooning type. "Look, ma'am…"

"Her name's Miss Della Mae Wagner." Alice emphasized the *Miss* part and pushed Della closer. "She came here all the way from Indiana. You two go ahead and shake. Got to start somewhere."

Huffing a sigh, he grabbed a handkerchief from his

pocket. After wiping off his palms, he offered his welcome. Della's hand fit perfectly inside his warm and slightly calloused hand. It felt nothing at all like holding hands with Tom, whose palms were always cold and clammy.

When he let go, Della laced her fingers together, trying to keep the warmth of his touch. A shiver ran down her back. She told herself it must have been caused by the wind.

"Miss Wagner, let's cut right to it. I'm sure you're as delightful as all the other ladies, and I do hate that you traveled all the way out here. Nonetheless I'm not interested in courting you."

Finally, a matching voice of reason. "That's actually—"

"Oh, Hank." Alice's shoulders dropped as she spoke over Della. "She's not like the others."

"Ma here will feed you before you head back to Indiana." He scratched the side of his face and flakes of dirt floated to the ground. "And just so you understand, I am not looking for a wife. If you'd tell that to all your friends it would save everyone a heap of trouble."

Della straightened her back at Mr. Lamson's tone. So much for an ally amongst the confusion. Of course, she wasn't looking for a husband any more than this man sought a wife, yet she couldn't help but relive the sting of Tom's rejection all over again. "I'm not here to apply to be your wife. Nor to be someone you court."

Alice released a small gasp and Mr. Lamson crossed his arms as if he didn't believe her, either. "You're not?"

Mercy sakes. Did women fall at his feet so often he was surprised that anyone didn't wish to be his wife? What kind of women lived in Missouri? Yes, he was an attractive fellow, but so was Tom. Handsome wasn't the same as honorable or loving. She'd learned her lesson and didn't desire to re-create the past.

"But you answered our ad?" Roy ran his fingers along the brim of his hat, leaving it crooked on his head.

She recited the request for the want ad once more in her mind. Words like *marriage*, *bride* and *wife* were nowhere to be found. "I answered an ad that I thought was calling for a teacher. It's the reason I applied." After receiving the letter declaring she'd been selected, despite her lack of official credentials, she'd taken it as a blessing on her choice to pursue a teaching career.

"A teacher?" The man shifted his weight. "You're claiming to be a teacher?"

Was it so hard to imagine she could be a teacher? Della knew she could do it, even without a certificate. She had assumed the Lamsons believed in her too, and that was why they'd chosen her for the position. But now, realizing they'd been hunting for a daughter-in-law instead of a teacher, she didn't know what to think.

Hank kneaded the back of his neck. A teacher? Well, that was a first. Due to the rumors about his wealth, women had been finding their way out to him for the past three years with all sorts of stories to try to get close to him. At least this Miss Wagner was creative. But had his parents truly shipped her in all the way from Indiana? And with such a ridiculous cover story?

"The answer is no. I don't need a teacher any more than I need a wife."

"Hank, we…your father and I… Apparently there's been…" Ma wouldn't meet his eyes, proving their guilt.

"Oh, let's just get it out in the open because truth is freedom. Son, you need a helpmate."

"Pa." Hank grinded his teeth. Here they went again. Why did they keep insisting he needed more help with the boys? He thought they were all getting by just fine. Whatever care or tending he couldn't provide himself, his parents could handle. Wasn't that why his folks moved with them to Missouri when his father-in-law had inherited land?

"There's been some miscommunication over the ad we placed, and I'm afraid Miss Wagner has traveled all this way believing we were looking for a teacher. But I know exactly how we can fix this." Ma nodded as if trying to convince herself. "If you recall we discussed the possibility of hiring a teacher for the boys just a few weeks ago."

Hank held in a moan. He did recall. He also recalled hoping to wait another year before beginning the search for a *male* teacher. Preferably someone who was nothing like the cantankerous Miss Koch who'd schooled Hank when he was young.

"You know the boys will require more advanced instruction than I can provide. Let's be reasonable. We have a teacher right here. It's as if the Lord dropped her in our laps." Ma reached for Miss Wagner's hand and patted it as she gave her a smile. It made Hank feel oddly abandoned. Usually, his parents were on his side when it came to getting rid of fortune-hunting females.

What made this stranger so different from the other ladies that his folks felt inspired enough to go behind his back to get her here? They knew Hank's stance on remarriage. He'd briefly considered the idea once after Evelyn passed, yet after Miss Isabel Smith betrayed him, he'd decided it was safest for his family and heart to go on with life on their own.

A hawk screeched in the distance, making Hank's shoulders tense even more. Ma never embraced any of the ladies that made their way here, not even Miss Smith. A predator may be circling the air above the chicken coop, but it felt like his folks and Miss Wagner were circling him.

"How about we provide her a good meal, put her up in town at the boardinghouse for the night and provide her fare for a return trip home to compensate the mistake. Tomorrow she can be on the first train back. Ma, if you really can't handle the boys' schooling any longer, then I promise we can begin a search for a male teacher. However, I will be in charge of the want ad."

Something sparked in Miss Wagner's green eyes. Now that the sun highlighted her face, he noticed they were quite lovely. She stepped forward, her hands clenched around her skirt. "If you're seeking a teacher, there's no reason why I can't be given a chance. I am more than capable."

He raked his fingers through his hair and looked skyward. A useless habit. Help wasn't coming from that direction anymore. Hank dropped his hand onto his thigh and his palm landed in mud. *Right.* He took in the condition of his pants, wondering what Miss Wagner thought of him greeting her with the day's work covering the bottom half of his clothes.

Miss Wagner slipped a stray piece of hair behind her ear. Her eyes met his, and she smiled, causing the tiniest dimple to emerge on her left cheek. Did she think she could win him over by being pretty? If so, she was in for a disappointment. He had no use for pretty, useless things. And based on Miss Wagner's scuff-free boots, dainty grip and soft-spoken voice she wouldn't last a day out here. Maybe the best choice would be to stop arguing and let it all play out. Soon enough, she'd be begging to go back to Indiana.

"I'll pay for you to stay in the boardinghouse. Give you a week's teaching trial." The fewer days, the better—though again, there was no harm in making himself look magnanimous, to please his folks. Once Miss Wagner got a taste of the mischief his boys could unleash, she'd likely see to leaving as early as the morning.

Ma waved her hand at Hank. "Goodness, no. She'll stay here. We have two empty rooms upstairs."

He frowned at their cabin and shifted his weight. Despite the underhanded ad, Hank hated the thought of quarreling with his parents even at his age.

A gust of wind nearly took Pa's hat off his head. The one Evelyn had picked years ago for his birthday. The ache appeared in Hank's chest again. He wished his wife were here. She would know what to do and where to place Miss Wagner. Then again if she was still living, there wouldn't be a need to hire a teacher of any kind, and ladies wouldn't be scheming to marry him, running their wagons through his orchards, nor driving him and his sheep and cattle crazy.

But his wife was gone. And this was the life he had to live, without her. It was already filled with more than its share of troubles and disappointments. Having to put up with a city woman for a week wouldn't be that much of an additional burden.

After all, his folks may have a point in all the madness. The boys might require a teacher sooner rather than later. Even with the waning of summer's heat, Ma ran out of energy quicker these days.

Once Miss Wagner realized how rambunctious his boys were, Hank and his folks could discuss a want ad for a more suitable teacher. Then they could choose that person *together*. He would no longer be left out of decisions pertaining to his family.

Horse hooves sounded in the distance and Isaac trotted around the cabin on his black mount. He slid off and tipped his Stetson. "Boss, a rig's stalling."

If only growling would help. "Which one?" Was it too much to expect that Miss Wagner's arrival would be the worst thing to happen today—this week? He resisted the urge to glare skyward.

"The one we fixed last month."

He closed his eyes and inhaled. Had he really expected it to be the closest oil pump? "I'll be right behind you."

Isaac took ahold of the saddle horn and then glanced over his shoulder. "Sorry, Boss."

"Isn't your fault, Isaac. You know how life treats me. Plus, you gotta earn your keep somehow."

With a short chuckle and a shake of his head, his lead foreman rode away. Hank needed to head on out before one of his men hurt themselves trying to fix that problem. And yet, he had a mighty big problem standing before him, too. One with a dimpled smile.

"Leave Della to us. We'll get her all settled." Ma drew Miss Wagner against her hip as if to seal the deal. "I'm sure you're tuckered from the travel, dear. Trains always wear me out—more so than wagons. I don't know why. You'd think it would be the other way around."

Dear? Ma never used such endearments for any guest. Hank hoped his mother wasn't getting too attached. This stranger was to be the boys' temporary teacher, nothing more. No matter what "help" his folks originally had planned.

"A short rest does sound wonderful, but... I'd like to meet the children."

Hank's legs locked in place. It was a welcomed change for someone to show up for his children instead of him.

"And Roy mentioned that there isn't a schoolhouse, but what about that building over on the hill there? Could we use it for a classroom?"

Hank's heartbeat raced ahead of his reprimand. He managed to shake his head. No, he couldn't leave for the pump yet, and now he knew exactly why. "The old church is off-limits."

Ma clicked her tongue. "We'll worry about where all the schooling will take place after we find the boys."

Pa reached into the wagon, gathered two carpetbags and set them on the porch. "I'd wager they're in the coop. Caught them there yesterday when they were supposed to be weeding the garden. You'll have your hands full with them I'm afraid, dear."

And now even Pa was calling her dear?

"A new challenge is exactly what I need." Her gaze snagged on something in the distance and concern lined her forehead. "Will there be any other families who might like to have their children included in my trial?"

"My three boys and Becca are the only young'uns within miles, but the Masons' little girl isn't even knee high. Families closer to town send their children to the schoolhouse there, but Evelyn..." Hank cleared his throat. "She wanted to keep the boys near and do their lessons herself. Since her death Ma has been in charge of all that."

"Only three," she whispered.

"If such a small class doesn't suit—"

She shook her head and stuck out her hand, offering it once again to Hank. "Three students will be more than adequate. Thank you, Mr. Lamson, for your generosity. Misunderstanding over the want ad or not, this won't be a mistake."

Mistakes often found him. Though at least she hadn't called him Hank or Hiram like all the other ladies from town. He could handle a guest who was polite and formal—provided she wasn't staying for long. He knew his boys. They'd have her running for home in no time.

A worried look crossed her face, but when she saw him noticing her, she gave a smile. It was not her real one with the dimple, and it bothered him that he could already tell the difference.

His folks dragged on further behind, whispering to one another. Hank hadn't seen them do that since the day they surprised Robert with the mule the boy had named Mr. Precious for his birthday. A gift they'd failed to discuss with him, and one that caused him trouble every day. He didn't like the pattern.

Hank stopped a few feet from the chicken coop and folded his arms. "Boys."

The door cracked and two eyes blinked open wider when they spotted Della.

"That's right. Company's here." As the boys formed a horizontal line, Ma came right up beside them.

"Didn't I tell you to dress in your Sunday clothes?" she scolded.

Robert straightened his shoulders. At nine, his first-born only stood to Hank's elbows, but the boy was sprouting like a cornstalk. Growing craftier every day as well, with an uncanny ability to wiggle his way out of a punishment. "But we saw the hawks. We had to protect the hens. Papa said we didn't need to be losing anymore chickens."

Hank raised an eyebrow. "You were inside with only one chicken."

Wallie, his youngest, hugged his favorite hen to his chest, petting the top of her head. "I had to save Mabel."

"If you truly wanted to save the chickens, it's best to be outside the coop to keep the hawks from diving down and grabbing one. I'm pretty sure you were simply trying to find a way out of wearing your best clothes."

Edward pulled at his shirt as if he were dressed in his collared one. "But they're so itchy."

Didn't Hank know it? He shoved back a grin. He hadn't worn his either for that very reason. Also, he didn't see the point of wearing them to begin with. There was no one he cared to impress—not Miss Wagner or any of the other women. It didn't matter what impression he made on a temporary teacher, now did it?

Hank's horse, Pete, whinnied in the pasture, reminding him it was past time to leave. "Robert, Edward and Wallace." He gestured to each, oldest to youngest. "I'd like to introduce you to Miss Wagner."

"She here to try and marry you too, Papa?"

"No." Hank clenched his jaw.

Ma sent Pa another hopeful look.

"No." Hank repeated for good measure. Her being here as a temporary teacher was bad enough. "She's here to give you some schooling, and that's all."

"We can take it from here, Hank. Hurry on back. I'm making fried taters and ham for supper." Ma wrinkled her nose. "Change out of those there muddy boots before you enter my kitchen, be polite to our guest, and I may fix you an apple pie."

Ma knew how to win him over. Although, she better plan on fixing pie every night this week for going behind his back and sending for a bride for him. Forgiveness was easier to dish out when it came with a side of flaky crust.

Robert shuffled his feet and elbowed Edward. Seeing the looks the boys exchanged, Hank was more certain than ever that his sons would run off Miss Wagner before he had to worry about hurting anyone's feelings. She would leave no matter how attached his folks appeared to be.

Chapter Two

Once Mr. Lamson had jumped on a white horse and galloped away, Della finally managed to take a real breath. A broken rig sounded alarming, but Mr. Lamson hadn't acted surprised or appalled—the way he had to the news of her arrival. It seemed the idea of her staying with his family was far worse in comparison to whatever awaited him. She was trying hard not to take that too personally.

The boys remained in a line, glancing between her and their grandparents. The oldest was eight or nine. The next stair stepped right after, probably about seven, leaving the youngest to be around five. The age gaps were similar to those of her own three older brothers.

The oldest kicked up some dust with the toe of his boot. "If she's not here to try and marry Papa, why is she still here?"

Alice and Roy shared another glance but didn't answer. Well, Della was not going to allow the boys to get the wrong impression. If they saw her as someone who was chasing after their father, they wouldn't respect her—and if they didn't respect her, they wouldn't listen to her and her teaching trial would fail. She only had a week to make this work. And work it had to. Mother made it clear that she expected Della to fail and be on a returning train straightaway. By no means was she prepared to prove Mother right. Nor was she prepared to give up her dream.

She'd always wanted to be a teacher. The schoolmistress back in Indiana had encouraged her ambition, allowing her to come and visit the school when she could sneak away from her father's newspaper. She'd read to the children, assist the teacher, help with marking papers. But when she'd brought up to her parents the idea of attending a teacher's college, her mother had refused to consider the idea—and her tasks at the newspaper grew until sneaking away to the school was no longer possible.

She'd thought that she'd lost her chance until she'd seen the ad and had felt a new burst of hope. Hope that had only grown when Alice and Roy had asked her to make the journey. Now that she was here, she knew that this might be her only opportunity to prove that she could be a teacher. No matter what it took, she was going to make it work.

"I'm going to be your new teacher." She extended her hand, mindful of her favorite brother's advice before she left home. *Treat a boy like a man and the response will be better than if you treat a boy like a baby.* She was counting on Freeman's experience and insight, because she didn't have much else to go on besides her gut. And that rocked like a boat trapped in a tempest. "You must be Robert."

The tallest boy had freckles painted on his nose and cheeks with eyes the color of acorns. He squared his shoulders and stared at Della. His thin lips dropped into a frown, and her hope plummeted from her heart to her stomach.

Roy cleared his throat, and finally the boy placed his hand in hers.

The second in line eyed Roy before accepting Della's handshake. "Edward, is it?" she asked.

Edward slipped his hand from hers. "How come we have to go to school? Didn't Momma always say we didn't have to 'cause it was too far away?"

"That's why we got Miss Della here. She's going to stay with us," Alice said.

"In the cabin?"

"That's right."

The boys groaned. Not the response she'd pictured, but considering how their father reacted, it shouldn't have surprised her. Della squatted in front of the youngest, her eyes level with his brown ones. "I promise we're going to have fun. Learning isn't all bad."

"My name's Wallie. Don't ever call me Wallace. Never ever." He ran back for the safety of the chicken coop with his arms surrounding the hen he called Mabel.

Della hadn't called him by the wrong name, had she? She didn't believe so.

"Wallie!" Alice and Roy shouted together. The boy stopped but didn't turn around.

Goodness. None of this was going the way that she'd planned.

"Boys, you will respect Miss Della, or you won't like the consequences. No pie tonight for starters. Head straight to the garden and finish weeding. Do I hear a 'yes, ma'am'?"

"Yes, ma'am," the boys mumbled in unison.

"Now, go on. Shoo." Alice waved the boys toward the garden as if they were chickens. She twisted the bottom of her apron into her palms as a worried expression filled her eyes. "I'd hoped that would have gone over better. All our boys are too headstrong for their own good."

Roy took off his hat and kissed Alice on the cheek. "No worrying. It'll all work out. It already has."

Alice nodded, managing a weary smile.

"Why don't you prepare something for Della's stomach?" Roy suggested next. "I'll give her a tour."

Alice sniffed and then took Della back into her arms. The woman appeared to have an endless supply of hugs. "We're entirely grateful you're here."

Alice had hugged her no less than four times since she'd arrived. That was more affection than her own mother had shown her in all of the past year. It was nice to feel love in any form, yet even though Alice and Roy were wonderful, everything about her situation here remained quite a mess.

Roy slapped his hat back on his head. "We owe you a mighty big apology. We thought if we could get you here, Hank would see the light."

"About needing a wife?"

Roy gestured to the nearest barn. "Why don't we go inside? You can rest for a bit while I freshen Dorothy's stall."

Seated upon an upturned bucket, Della took a deep breath to share what she needed to say—and then immediately wished she hadn't inhaled so deeply. The smells of life around so many animals would take some getting used to.

"The ad you placed…" Della wet her lips, but it didn't erase the dryness in her mouth. "It truly wasn't for a teaching position?" As many times as she'd read the request, the words were carved into her memory.

Searching for a faithful, God-fearing woman. Teaches with patience. Balances discipline and laughter. Hands that aren't idle. Sunshine in the rain. The greatest of these: love…

It had seemed so clear to her that it was a teaching position—and the answer to her prayers. She'd been so desperate for a change, for a new chance to get her life on track, that she hadn't asked all the questions she should have. For one, she'd been too timid to bring up the question of salary. She'd just assumed the money that had been sent for her journey was an advance on that payment. Had she been bold enough to ask, could they have sorted out this misunderstanding before her arrival?

Roy rested the pitchfork against his chest and fanned himself with his hat. "No. That was not our intent. But this…yes, this is better."

An ant scurried between Roy's feet, darting here and there across the dirt floor as if it'd lost the scent trail. Much how Della felt—just as lost and unsure of where she was meant to go next.

"We were so immersed in our plan that we failed to count the cost," Roy admitted, kicking up the flattened straw. "If you had come prepared to marry Hank, and he refused you like he did, well…" He replaced his hat and sent the pitchfork into the clean straw in the corner. "Shame on us for forgetting to consider your feelings."

Roy emptied a bucket of water in a trough before grabbing a shovel. "We've been praying for directions

on how best to further assist Hank. His load as a wid-
owed father and oil rancher is heavy, and Alice and I
aren't getting any younger. We help care for the boys,
do chores, and advise when we can about the property,
but what he really needs is a helpmate that he can trust
with his heart. When we received your letter about our
ad, Alice fell in love with the idea of you becoming
our daughter-in-law. Your references from your pastor
and the local schoolteacher complimenting your abilities and personality only magnified you in our hearts.
It was as if God had handpicked you for us. For Hank."

Della's eyes watered at the notion of someone wanting and valuing her as part of their family. If they knew
what rejection she'd experienced over the past months
with Tom ending their engagement to wed a wealthier
woman, and then him becoming a partner at her father's
newspaper, as if the pain she'd suffered meant nothing
to her family compared to the business opportunity,
then they'd have known not to even bring up such a
thing. The air thickened in her chest like she needed to
cough, but all she could do was shake her head. For all
intents and purposes, she had been a mail-order bride
to a man who didn't even want a wife. And she thought
her life back in Indiana had gone sour. However, guilt
was also swimming through her, making her question
whether she'd brought this disaster down on herself by
behaving dishonorably.

"Roy, I… I worked at my father's newspaper. I was
the one who processed your ad. And… I didn't rush
to have it printed. I waited until after I had sent in my
response. So there's a high chance I got in the way of
God's true pick for—"

Popping sounds rattled Roy's knees as he crouched

before her. His expression reflected something that she couldn't quite interpret. Was it hope? Kindness? Desperation? She wasn't sure.

"No one can get in the way of God's plans. We read all the other responses after we received yours. We still choose you. My son might be blind to the fact that he needs a wife, but I know in my heart that this trial is going to show Hank that the boys do in fact need you. You thought you were coming to be a teacher. A teacher is what you can be."

"For a week." Della failed to mask the disappointment in her voice. Going home so soon would only give Mother more fodder for her unending refrain on how Della muddled everything. Wasn't pretty enough to make a good match. Wasn't clever enough to hold on to Tom. Wasn't smart enough to be allowed to pursue her dream of going to teacher's college. Wasn't capable enough to keep this position here once she'd gotten it, despite her lack of a teaching degree. Della knew every line of that horrible song—she'd been hearing those lyrics all her life.

Roy lifted her chin with his knuckles. "Ah, child. Trust, not worry. The Lord got you here. He can keep you. Now, then." At his grin, she found herself smiling, too. "You ready for that tour?"

Della curled her toes and snuggled the blanket against her cheek, breathing in its lavender scent. After one night's sleep, she was quite certain she adored the quilt, a perfect combination of warmth and softness.

A rooster crowed outside, reminding her she needed to finalize what she'd teach the boys during her trial period. Seven days. That's all she had to prove herself, and if she failed, she'd be shipped back to Indiana. Back to working in her father's newspaper, forced to interact with her ex-fiancé as he flaunted his marriage to someone who was not her. And then, at the end of each day, home to Mother, who somehow found it to be Della's fault that Tom left her for a wealthier woman.

No, she couldn't go home so soon. Not after making such a big deal about her teaching position. Her "God-given future" Freeman had called it.

A snicker interrupted her thoughts. Then another. At the foot of the bed, three sets of eyes peeped above the blanket that had given her such a restful night and then disappeared from sight.

She cleared her throat. "Good morning."

The giggles stopped.

"If I would have known you were so eager to begin your studies right away, I'd have started them last night after supper. Do we have time to eat breakfast, or shall we jump in and see where the day takes us?"

Wallie popped up and put his elbows on the bed. "Can we learn stuff about chickens?"

Chickens weren't on the top of her "must-teach list," but an interest in something was a fine place to start.

"Well…" Della fluffed her extra pillow and put it behind her back. "How many chickens do you have?"

"One. Her name is Mabel."

"I met Mabel. She's certainly a beautiful chicken, but I'm pretty sure there were more than just one, yes?"

Wallie shrugged and inspected the floor where his brothers hid out of sight.

"Robert or Edward, how many chickens are in the coop?"

The boys slowly stood. Della didn't think Alice allowed them to hide in a guest's room. However, Della didn't want to scold when she was positive that she had acres and acres to cross before the boys would begin to enjoy their studies. And her.

Robert's roll of the eyes only reaffirmed that they didn't like her yet. She clung to Roy's words from yesterday about God getting her here and trusting that this was the Lord's plan. She was with the Lamson family for a reason, and it may not simply be because she sought a new future. Perhaps the boys needed something only she could offer.

Edward squinted, tilting his head. "You look funny after you sleep."

Politeness. Yes, that was something these boys needed to learn. She must weave into the morning's studies, even if it wasn't in any of her primer books.

Della reached and found her hair had not only escaped her plait but was far puffier than usual. "How many chickens did you say you had?"

"I didn't." Robert crossed his arms.

"I see." The apple did not fall far from his father's prickly tree.

Edward followed his brother's lead, mimicking his stance. The smirk on Robert's face displayed his belief that he had won.

Ah, but he hadn't. As much as she'd prefer not to scold, letting them get away with everything would do more harm than good in the long run.

"Robert, at the start of our first lesson you will write, 'I will use my words only for good.' Ten times." When Della was younger, her teacher, Miss Esther, had given lines to write when misbehaving students required a minor punishment. Della's brothers, especially Freeman, often tried and failed to persuade Della to finish his lines for him.

Della nodded, granting herself a pat on the back for dealing with this misbehavior professionally. She could handle this teaching position just like her younger self stood against her brothers' mischief.

Robert's lips parted and shock flashed in his eyes before he tightened his arms across his chest. "We don't have nothing to write on."

"It's better to say you don't have *anything* to write on. And you do. I brought along boards and chalk. And unless you wish to begin each lesson with lines, you will treat me with the respect you should be granting all adults. That goes for the rest of you. Do we understand one another?"

The boys stared at the quilt, missing Della's raised brow. "A yes, ma'am, is required here."

"Yes, ma'am."

"Good. I will ready myself, and we'll see what lessons await us."

"Yes, ma'am," Wallie said again.

She couldn't help but smile at the child. He beamed when he observed her approval.

After changing clothes and taming her hair into a bun, Della entered the kitchen to find the boys gathered around the table. Alice held a pan of fluffy eggs. Her apron, gray this morning, was already decorated with a layer of flour.

Alice's face lit up when she saw Della. "Good morning, dear. Did you sleep all right? I hope I didn't wake you with all my piddling down here. Scoot on over, Edward, and give Miss Della some more room."

Edward did as he was told, proving the boys possessed some ability to listen and obey. They just didn't choose to obey her. *Not yet*, she reminded herself. But they would. They had to.

"Can I help with anything?"

"Oh no, you are the boy's teacher and my guest." As she spoke, she absentmindedly massaged her thumb into her hand and around her wrist.

Alice noticed Della watching her and flung her arms behind her back. "Roy! Breakfast! Robert, go and fetch your grandpa, and if your papa's outside, bring him in, too. It's time for praying and eating."

Robert's footsteps rattled a kettle on the stove as he dashed out the back door. Mr. Lamson wasn't with them when Robert returned with Roy.

"All right. I suppose your papa's eating with his crew this morning. Roy." Alice tilted her chin at her husband, who swiped his hat off his head and bowed.

"We thank You for another sunrise, for the food laid before us, and the hands that prepared it. We are blessed with the gift of family. Let us not forget how fortunate we are. You know all we need. We pray that it may be provided in Your time. Help us to trust in Your ways even when we don't like them. Am—"

At the slap of the screen door, everyone lifted their heads and focused on Mr. Lamson, standing in the doorway.

"Amen. Sorry to start without you." Alice set a pan of biscuits on the table. "Assumed you were busy when Robert didn't return with you."

He sent a quick glance at Della before thanking Alice for his food.

Della pushed a piece of egg toward her biscuit with her fork. She got the sense that breakfast would have been more peaceful without the man who didn't seem to have any expression other than scowling, but since he had chosen to join them, there was a question she wanted to ask him. "Mr. Lamson, as you mentioned yesterday, there is no schoolhouse, and I don't wish to bother Alice by having the boys barricading her kitchen."

"Oh, I don't mind one bit. That's typically where we've been having their lessons, when we do 'em." Alice finally filled a plate for herself and claimed the chair nearest Roy.

Della peeked at the boys. All three of them had forks in hand, mouths open, but eyes set on her as if they were more interested in hearing what she might say than tending to their growling tummies. "If the weather stays agreeable, might I take the boys to the trees past the smaller second barn? Have their studies outdoors?" She remembered all too well from her brothers and classmates that boys hardly sat quiet for long, especially when they felt cooped up. If they were outside, someplace they enjoyed, they might get more accomplished. Or maybe she could simply hope they'd like her better. She planned to ask for their suggestions of where to have lessons. Maybe they could end up in a different location each day. They'd only need a few places. She held back a frown, forcing her lips into a smile instead. She would not think about going home at the end of her trial.

"Fine." Mr. Lamson demolished what was left of his eggs on his plate. "Just stay away from the old church building and even further away from the bunkhouse. Don't need you distracting the men."

A distraction? Had he given her a compliment, or was he calling her lessons a distraction?

Mr. Lamson pointed his fork at the boys. "Chores first." His brown eyes took Della in, and her bite of biscuit chafed her throat. "Then lessons." Another round of obedient replies circled the table. Mr. Lamson took his empty plate, dropped it into the sudsy water and cleaned both his fork and plate. She hadn't been impressed thus far with the man's curmudgeonly attitude, but she had to admit that this surprised her. She'd never seen her father or brothers wash up after themselves.

He grabbed a rag and dried his hands. "I'll be near Lady most of the morning. Hoping she'll drop her calf by noon."

Roy released his plate in the sink. "I can watch her if you got something more pressing." He walked out the back with Mr. Lamson.

"Get to eating," Alice encouraged the boys. "You've got chores and learning to do before playtime."

After finishing her breakfast, Della marched to the sink, but Alice jumped up and knocked her hip into Della's before she managed to get the spare apron tied around her.

"You are not doing dishes. Go on and rest until the boys are finished with their chores."

There was no time for rest. If Della were a normal teacher, she'd have her own schoolhouse that she could spend time organizing and arranging. There would be a bell she'd ring to begin the day at a set time. But there was none of that structure here. No schoolhouse to arrange. No bell to ring. She was left with nothing to do but wait for her students to be ready to be taught. And given their behavior thus far, she didn't imagine they'd be in any rush to get to their lessons. Who knew how long they'd drag out their chores, eating into the precious hours that she had to prove that she was up to the task of instructing them?

"What if I went with the boys, and they showed me what they do each morning?" she suggested. While it wouldn't really count as official learning time, she could at least use the opportunity to get to know her students a little better and gain more familiarity with her new home as well. "I didn't grow up on a farm. We didn't have many animals, so I'm not sure what's involved. You boys can teach me this morning. I can be your student."

Robert nudged Edward's arm, muttering something to him. Edward grinned and nodded. "Can we start with the chickens? We can count them like you wanted." The boys raced out the door, leaving only Della and Alice in the kitchen.

"They're good boys," Alice said, sounding apologetic. "They'll just need a little time to get used to you. Robert and Edward had their momma for a teacher before she passed three years ago, but I'm afraid Wallie really only remembers having me. And I never got much schooling myself. So they do need you." She wrung the rag in her hands and flinched. "We all do."

Della found herself giving Alice a hug and receiving one in return. It was nice to be needed. After all it was the next best thing to being loved.

After Lady dropped her calf earlier than expected, Hank left the pair to their bonding, not wanting to get in the way.

Now he just needed the memory of Miss Wagner's dimpled smile to stop distracting him from the day's work.

Hank dipped his hands in the water trough and wiped them on his pants. He paused when he heard the song Ma sung to Wallie at bedtime.

"Though clouds may dim Your sunbeams, I know the Son is shining anyways." Ma must be hanging clothes on the line. He paused to listen to her sing.

When he was little, he loved the way singing the song made Ma smile. It was only as a man that he came to appreciate the way the words urged him to seek hope, to appreciate life through the trials. He still struggled with that, despite the wonderful example he had in his ma. She'd lived through her own sorrowful times, losing her father in a factory accident at a young age. Hank was jealous at how easily it'd been for her to follow the song's advice. When he'd first lost Evelyn, it became near impossible for him to even hum along to the tune.

Ma's voice grew stronger into the chorus. After she finished, he expected the song to end, but she began a whole other verse. One he didn't recall. Now that he thought about it, Ma always sang the song in a lower key. But before he could analyze that further, the words were replaced by a shriek.

"Ma?" Hank sprinted around the corner. Coming beside the chicken coop, he realized it wasn't Ma at all. "Miss Wagner? What's wrong? Are the boys all right?"

The woman's hands shielded her face while she released another yelp and ran straight for him. She grabbed him by the arm and tucked herself into a ball behind him. His heart kicked up as he looked around for what had frightened her, but he couldn't spot where the danger lay.

"Is it gone?" She gripped his forearm as her head pressed to his back.

"Is what gone?" Her ragged breaths felt like puffs of steam through his shirt, and he suddenly found it a little hard to breathe evenly, himself.

She peeked around him only to squeak and take ahold of his shirt between her fists. "The rooster."

As if he recognized his name, the rooster beat his wings and fluffed his chest, making him grow at least two inches in all directions.

"He flogged you?" Surely not. This one had never threatened an adult. He'd tried to go after Wallie once when he was a toddler, but Robert had chased him away before he landed any of his spurs. It wouldn't make sense for him to kick up his feet and attack Miss Wagner.

"He…he flapped his wings like that, and then he started for me, and he almost kicked my face."

Hank grasped the rooster and turned him upside down by his feet. "How did he get up near your face?"

She blinked at the bird hanging tranquilly upside down and took a step away as if afraid he'd lunge at her at any moment. "I was sitting on the bucket watching for the hens to lay their eggs and—"

"You were doing what?" Wasn't she here because she was going to teach the boys? If sitting was all she wanted to do, she'd accomplish that better on a train back home.

She pushed a stray piece of hair behind her ear. Her hair was a lighter brown than Evelyn's had been and seemed to be smoother looking, like the caramel sauce Ma sometimes made for apples. His fingers twitched with the urge to see if it felt as soft as it appeared. Instead of giving in, he readjusted his grip around the rooster's rough legs.

"I thought I'd help the boys with their chores so we could start on their lessons sooner. After they showed me how to open the coop's hatch and finished feeding the chickens, they instructed me to watch and gather the eggs while they went and fed the other animals."

"The other animals? I see." He failed to stifle all of his chuckle. Pa took care of the other animals in the morning. It was only day one and she'd already been had by his boys. "How exactly did they tell you to go about gathering the eggs?"

"They said I had to hurry and grab each egg right after it's laid so the hens don't step on it and smash it."

"And they told you to wait out here, sitting on the pail?" He pointed to the upturned pail with his free hand.

She nodded. "Is that rooster dead?"

It looked like Miss Wagner needed some lessons of her own. "No, he's still quite alive." Hank took a step forward, and she took an equal one away, a movement that surprised him. Women, as of late, had been doing quite the opposite. Miss Wagner made for a refreshing change of pace. "Give me your hand."

"What? Why?"

"You're going to hold it."

"But you said it's alive."

"You'd rather hold it if it were dead?"

"I'd rather go check on the children."

"The ones who told you to sit here all day and gather eggs? Follow me." He walked into the coop with the rooster still hanging upside down.

She peered inside, but didn't enter.

"Come on in, Miss Wagner. It's time for your first lesson, teacher." On the far side were evenly spaced wooden boxes attached to the wall. One of his white Leghorn hens sat in the farthest nesting area. The bird's mouth hung partly open, blinking beady eyes at nothing in particular. "This is where we gather the eggs after the hens lay them. My chickens are mostly late morning layers."

"So I won't get the eggs until later?" Her nose scrunched, probably afraid she wouldn't be able to teach the boys until after lunch.

"You won't be getting the eggs at all. It's the boys' job."

"I was trying to help so they could get to their studies quicker."

"All you managed to do was waste time and set yourself up for a flogging. The boys lied to weasel their way out of lessons. They know full well that there's no need to sit here and watch the hens to wait for them to lay." He'd have to reprimand the boys for lying. It was something he despised even if it would send Miss Wagner home quicker.

"Chickens don't smash their eggs?"

Hank shook his head. "Not often enough to warrant sitting on a bucket all morning."

"Oh," was all she said before she brushed the same rebellious strand of hair behind her ears. "I'm sorry. I promise I'll find the boys and begin their lessons right away. And I apologize for grabbing ahold of you like that. I… Well, the rooster scared me."

"Here." He held out the rooster. "Hold him."

She hugged her arms around herself and shook her head, but he refused to be swayed. He also refused to notice the way the coop's air heated warmer with her standing near. "You need to face your fear. There's no point in you being scared to go outdoors during your trial here," he insisted. "He's not going to hurt you upside down like this. The position makes him calm."

Miss Wagner studied the rooster. She reached out tentatively, then jerked back to rest her hand along her skirt. "Calm or not, I don't believe I wish to form a friendship with Mr. Rooster."

"He's not so bad after you show him who's boss. Will you trust me?" After she inhaled, she nodded, allowing Hank to take her wrist and bring it near the rooster. "I promise I won't allow him to harm you." Her eyes remained closed until he wrapped her fingers around the rooster's feet. Hank let go, and she raised the rooster up higher, inspecting his head.

"If he tries to flog you again, I'll have Ma prepare him for supper," Hank promised, hoping to make her smile. But she barely seemed to notice him, all her attention focused on the rooster. "He doesn't normally attack adults. He more than likely believed he could take you when you were hunched over on that pail singing."

Her arm began to tremble, and she shoved the rooster toward him, but Hank went out of the coop, propping open the door.

"Mr. Lamson... I..."

"Just set him on the ground."

"On his feet?"

"He'd probably prefer it that way." For a teacher, this woman had the oddest questions.

She started to squat down to release the rooster, but then rose, shaking her head. "What if he attacks me?"

"He's not going to hurt you. If he tries, I'm right here to protect you."

With one swift motion, she released the rooster and ran behind Hank. She didn't touch him, but she hovered close enough that he sensed her presence. Hank almost wished she'd step closer. Almost.

Now upright, the rooster awoke from his trance, crowed and strutted away.

Hank suddenly became aware of how close he was standing to Miss Wagner, and how alone they were. He cleared his throat. "How about those lessons you came here to teach? Unless you no longer want the remainder of your trial? I can arrange for Pa to take you into town and have you sent back on the train. It would be no trouble at all."

She stepped away from him abruptly. "It's not time for me to go, Mr. Lamson. I shall gather my teaching supplies and fetch the boys. Thank you again for…for saving me."

She picked up her skirt and marched inside the cabin.

Saved her? Hardly. Her words were more a cruel joke than a compliment. He gathered the upturned bucket and tossed it toward the coop. He was no savior. The past was proof of that.

Chapter Three

Della wanted to find the boys…but she just couldn't. They weren't on the front porch. Not by the barns or the woodshed. Nowhere near any of the places Roy had pointed out yesterday on her brief tour. After finally asking Alice for help, Della learned the Lamson property was a lot larger than she had originally thought. The quaint collection of simple structures and wide fields she'd noticed stretching into the distance was in fact all the family's, including the old church building up on the hill.

Finally, she overheard the boys huddled near a tree grouping. Before making herself known, she took a deep breath. She refused to head into battle looking defeated, so she placed a smile on her face. "Oh, good. There you all are. I've been relieved of my chicken duties, and now it looks like it's time for lessons."

Robert's body turned rigid. "You have?"

"It is?" Edward blinked.

"Hmm." Della readjusted the basket she had borrowed from Alice.

"Got all the eggs already?" Wallie picked up a stick

and swished it back and forth in the air, grinning with each new whooshing sound.

"Well, no. It seems that your hens aren't morning layers." Della placed the basket on the ground and put her hands on her hips. The two older boys stared down at their feet with a hint of shame.

Wallie dropped the stick and reached for the blackboards and chalk resting in the basket. "What's this for?"

Had he never used a lesson board for his studies? "That's for you."

He hugged it to his chest. "I've never had one of these."

"Sure you have," Robert said.

"No. You got one and Edward gots one. But I don't."

Della mentally corrected Wallie's grammar, but decided that she didn't want to start her first lesson with a correction. At the same time, she realized she wasn't entirely sure how she wanted to begin.

On the journey here, she'd pictured her own school years and how Miss Esther began each morning. Except Della didn't have a school building full of children. No, she only had three students. Three whole students who didn't want to have lessons with her.

"Can we begin? What are we doing first?" Wallie asked, while he slid the chalk along the blackboard. "Does Robert get to write his lines on this?"

Perhaps she had *one* who wanted lessons after all.

Robert swatted Wallie.

"Hey!" Wallie cried, rubbing his arm. "It's not my fault you got in trouble."

"Robert, I haven't forgotten about your punishment," Della said. "So there's no need to blame Wallie for bringing it up. You boys need to stop attacking one another and learn that you are each other's best allies. Not enemies." She unfolded the blanket Alice had placed in the basket and spread it under the shade.

Wallie squinted. "What's an ally?"

"Friend, you goof." Edward leaned over and scratched some bark off the nearest tree. "We can't be friends, Miss Wagner. We're brothers."

"My brothers are my friends," she countered. "And they are friends with each other as well."

"You have brothers?" Wallie's eyes grew as large as the cinnamon rolls rising in the kitchen.

"Yes, I have three." She patted the blanket, beckoning the boys to sit beside her. Youngest to oldest they obeyed, sitting on the far corners of the rugged blanket. It was a start.

Wallie crossed his legs and rested his elbows on his knees, chin in hands. "You don't look like a sister."

"Wallie's right," said Robert. "You're too old."

"Too old?" Della adjusted her skirt to make sure her ankles were covered. Maybe at twenty-four she was becoming an old maid, as Mother liked to remind her, but regardless of her age, she knew that politeness and manners were what she needed to teach the boys today. "Boys, it is never polite to tell a lady she is too old."

"Well, ya are. You're too old to be our sister."

Della bit her lip in an attempt to contain her amusement. While tact might not be their strong suit, the boys did comprehend what honesty was. "Here Robert, begin your lines. 'I will use my words only for good.'" Tonight she'd better search the Scriptures for verses about kind words. She had a feeling this wouldn't be Robert's only time for lines, and it would be good to have useful phrases prepared in advance.

Della handed him a chalk and a clean slate, smiling a little at the symbolism. They were going to start fresh together. "What if…we begin each lesson with a story about my brothers? They do remind me of you three." That would also help keep any homesickness at bay. Not that she expected to miss much about home except Freeman. Her oldest brothers had lost interest in their brotherly duties long before Tom came around. "However, they never tried to get me to watch chickens all day. They were kinder to me than that. The youngest of my brothers, Freeman, even used to offer me piggyback rides to school."

"Papa used to give me piggyback rides." Edward's shoulders hunched as if realizing he shared something he wasn't supposed to. He rubbed a portion of the quilt between his fingers and thumb.

How long ago had he been given a ride? He wasn't much older than his brother. "Wallie, do you get piggyback rides?"

"Nope. Robert says I'm heavy."

"I meant from your father."

He slanted his head as if he needed to think hard. "Maybe, before I was five."

"How long have you been five?"

"Since my last birthday."

He was only five and couldn't recall if his father had ever given him a piggyback ride. She held dear the memories of her own father chasing her and her brothers around the yard until they were all caught in his arms. They'd pile on top of one another, while their sides ached from the laughter. They'd been a happy family, back then—up until Father had become sole owner of the newspaper when she was a little older than Robert. After that, things had changed.

Was that what had happened to this family as well? Had a change in circumstances—the loss of their mother, perhaps—caused the joy to leave their home?

Of course, she might be overthinking things. Perhaps Mr. Lamson wasn't the type to play games and rough-house the day away. He certainly hadn't smiled a lot in the time she'd been there—except for when she needed rescuing from a rogue rooster.

A cow mooed somewhere behind them, reminding her there wasn't a moment to spare mulling over why she'd felt safe with Mr. Lamson. She only had a limited time to prove she could be a teacher. She must spend every minute possible focusing on her students. "Okay, while I tell you a story about my brothers, I want you to print your names on the board. Your full Christian names." She paused, anticipating a groan or a complaint. When none came, their quietness was almost like God shouting: *with My help, you can do this.*

Hank was long past ready for a drink of Ma's tea. The calendar was heading into fall, but the weather didn't agree. He knocked off the top layer of dirt from his pants and grabbed the latch to the back door. At the sound of Miss Vogel's nasally giggle, his legs halted him in place on the back porch. He possessed no energy nor desire to face that woman today. Or any day. Hadn't she just visited a couple days ago, hinting once again at how available she was to become the next Mrs. Lamson?

"And where is our favorite man?" Miss Vogel's voice, coated in enough sugar to sweeten a whole month's worth of tea, floated through the screen door. He pictured her batting her lashes and flaunting her dimpleless grin at Ma. Her lazy brother probably sat next to her, either eating or sleeping. Or both—simultaneously.

"Working, I'm sure." Ma was being as polite as ever, however, there was a rare shortness in her tone.

"He does seem to work awfully long hours. Between you and me, I think he needs a wife to tempt him home earlier. Though, I suppose one must work when they have as much responsibility and wealth as Hank. Might you send him word I'm here? I haven't seen even a glimpse of him in the last three of my visits."

Hank would work all day and night and twice over if it meant staying away from Miss Vogel and all the other cunning female visitors. Ma deserved a new apron or dress or whatever she wanted for dealing with the headstrong, aggravatingly persistent ladies from town. He hardly even noticed their comings and goings anymore. Ma had a routine down. Give them coffee. Provide something to fill their stomachs. Listen to their explanation on how suited they were to become her next daughter-in-law. Then she'd tell them she didn't know when he'd be in and would send them on their way. That plan was working well until Miss Wagner came along.

"Long hours, yes. Work…does keep him away from the house a good deal. But I'm afraid other things have been holding his attention."

"What kind of things? More oil drillings, I hope."

Hank rolled his eyes. Miss Vogel was one of the more blatant ladies when it came to her greediness. But he supposed he should be grateful that her motives were so clear. He couldn't bear to have a repeat of the situation with Miss Smith, who deceived him so skillfully, with him having no suspicions at all until it was too late. Hank was still paying the high price for trying to open his heart after Evelyn.

A snore filled the silence, proving yet again the indolence of Miss Vogel's brother. All he had to do on these visits was sit in a wagon and hold some reins, but still he somehow found that too much for him.

"Well, Della Mae Wagner taking up much more of his time lately."

Hank tightened his grip on the door handle.

"Della Mae Wagner?" Shock and dismay coated Miss Vogel's voice. "I—I hadn't heard of a new lady staying at the boardinghouse." That wasn't surprising. The town's most fervent gossip was Miss Appleton. Ma always appeared the most drained after that woman's visits.

"Oh, no. Della's staying with us."

"With *us*…you mean, here? In the cabin? For how long?"

"Forever would be fine by me," Ma proclaimed airily. "More bread?"

"No… I…no, I don't wish for any more bread. Wake up, Clyde. Clyde! I suppose we best be getting on home…before the rain hits and all."

Hank glanced at the clear blue sky but decided that there was no way he was going to volunteer that there wasn't any sign of rain. The chairs scraped against the floor and the front door slapping shut gave him the courage to peek into the kitchen. Empty. Maybe God wasn't always out to get him.

Ma returned inside with victory etched on her face. He didn't quite blame her, but lying was never the answer. She poured him a glass of tea and handed it to him.

"You got her believing I'm engaged—or at least courting. And you know full well I'm not."

Ma took the dishes from the table and placed them into the sink without replying.

"You gave me your word," Hank reminded her. "No matter what you think to be best. I'm going to have the final say on what's right for me, remember?" Not his folks. Not anyone else, but him. The past he may have no control over, however he could control this.

Ma wiped her forehead with the back of her hand. "You wanted that woman gone. She's gone. And I don't think she'll be back, praise the Lord. Not if I'm to judge by the expression on her face. Sheet white it was. She practically hauled her none-too-good brother up into the wagon herself. I'd imagine she's already plotting her next marriage mark, the poor man." Ma laughed as she rubbed a thumb around her wrist. "I for one sure hope the news spreads like a field fire after a lightning strike. Can you imagine what I could accomplish every day if I didn't have to entertain all your lady visitors? Why, I won't know what to do with myself. Might have to take up a hobby."

"As long as it's a pie-related hobby." Hank crossed his arms. "I hate that you lied." Lying broke trust, and trust was something he couldn't afford to lose. Again.

Ma shrugged. "I'm not sure I lied. Led her to assume, I'll admit. But Della *is* staying here. She *is* taking up more of your time than when she wasn't here. Hmm? And I'd certainly be happy if she stayed here forever. So I'm not convinced any of it can be counted as a lie if…" She turned and faced the stove.

Hank had chosen the wrong moment to take another

drink of his tea. It didn't taste as sweet as it did a moment ago. "If what?"

"Well…if you would just give the idea of marrying her a chance."

He nearly spilled the rest of the tea out of his glass. "Ma, I've decided never to remarry. And I'm for sure not marrying Del… I mean Miss Wagner. Marrying strangers is about the worst idea there is. Didn't we learn that when Miss Smith ran off with a year's worth of wages? Did you not think about the trouble you could have caused if Miss Wagner had arrived expecting to marry me?"

Ma shifted her feet, not meeting his eyes, and Hank understood where Robert got his telltale sign from.

"Ma, you gave me your word."

"And you have it." She sighed. "I won't do anything of that sort again. At the time we did what we truly thought we were supposed to do. But you are right. We were wrong to deceive you—and to put that sweet girl in such an awkward position." She grabbed the rolling pin off the table. "But Della is no stranger. Not anymore."

She sprinkled some flour and began rolling a piece of dough with more vigor than necessary. "Not that marrying a stranger is such a horrid idea, Hiram Robert Lamson." She grunted and a puff of flour dusted the air. "Not in the least."

Chapter Four

Hank halted at the sight of his boys quiet on a blanket. Even though Robert had his lips pinched and his eyebrows drawn low, he was doing his lessons—willingly. Where had he hidden his mischievous qualities that Hank was counting on to send Miss Wagner packing?

Sunshine sprinkled through the tree branches and settled on Miss Wagner. Wallie held up his board, and Hank couldn't miss the smile she gave his son, one of encouragement and genuine delight. Nor could he miss Wallie's reaction as he scooted closer to his teacher, already smitten with her and eager to please. The complete opposite of what Hank wanted. It would not do for any of them to get attached to someone who wouldn't be staying.

Miss Wagner pulled another board from a basket and began writing. When she showed it to Wallie, Edward nudged Robert's elbow before whispering in his ear. The impish grin growing on Robert's face replaced any doubt that had filled Hank. He only needed to be patient. His boys would not fail his prediction after all.

"Boss?"

Hank cringed at the volume of Isaac's voice. The man had always had a tone that carried, something Hank found useful when working in the field. Not when he was practically spying.

"Were you wanting me to ride to the Valley Ridge pump?"

Hank clamped his jaw tighter and glanced at Miss Wagner who had yet to take notice of her observers, despite Robert and Edward's side glances. Wanting to keep it that way, he patted Isaac's shoulder in hopes of directing them both back toward the barns.

Isaac, however, remained planted where he was and pointed his chin toward the blanket. "Only other times I've seen any of them that still are when Wallie-boy has that hen in his arms."

Miss Wagner hadn't looked up when the cows mooed in the distance, or the two times the rooster had crowed. Isaac's echoing voice hadn't even interrupted her lesson, but she locked her attention on Hank the moment of his muffled, reluctant agreement.

She tucked that same piece of hair behind her ear, neither smiling nor frowning, and he couldn't tell what she was thinking.

"... Boss?"

"Hmm?"

Isaac smirked. "I appear to have found my answer."

"No, I..." Hank cleared his dry throat. "I don't need you to go. I'm going. I said I would. I'll go."

"Looks to me like you're already right where you need to be."

"Isaac." First his folks and now even Isaac. Those seven days of Miss Wagner's trial couldn't be over fast enough. No, six. Yesterday counted as the first day, didn't it? "You know how I trust your insight on every-thing around here, but I really don't want you rallying against me on this."

"Hey, hey." Isaac held up his palms. "All I meant was you should check and make sure the person you've hired is doing their job. Her teaching job. That's all I was getting at." Isaac said all the right words, but the smirk on his weathered face seemed to be singing a different tune. "Like you do for every one of the guys you hire for your crew. Like I still have to do for ol' George Martin."

Hank leaned his forearm against a tree, blocking his view of Miss Wagner. "Sorry George gives you extra work, but his family needs the money. So I can't be sorry for hiring him."

"You know I'm not complaining," Isaac replied, good-natured as always. "He tries. He really does."

"Is he getting any better?"

Isaac rubbed his chin. "He's usually not getting any worse."

Not getting any worse. Yes, that was exactly how Hank rated each of his own days. He didn't rise each morning expecting the best. He only hoped to main-tain the status quo.

The noise of twigs snapping made Hank pull his at-tention to Robert and Edward as they raced toward him and Isaac. They ran side by side, elbows swinging and nudging one another the whole way.

Edward raised his arms. "I won."

Robert bent at the waist. His words rushed out more breath than sound. "You did not… Liar." He threw a punch and nearly hit his brother in the gut. "I beat you."

Before Hank could step in to prevent the battle brewing between his oldest two, Wallie took ahold of his hand and jerked. "Papa, can you give me a piggyback ride?"

"What? No, boys. Hold a minute, Wallie…"

He stepped toward his oldest boys, but Miss Wagner got there first and yanked the boys apart.

"Robert and Edward!" Hank wasn't sure how she managed to arrive so fast from her seated position.

He waited, certain that it would only be a moment before Miss Wagner would grasp both of the boys by their ears. That's what his schoolteacher had always done. She'd been a grouchy old maid whom he and his fellow schoolhouse friends had nicknamed turnip breath. Oh, how they had all despised Miss Koch. She never listened to both sides of a story. No matter how many times she caught that girl kicking him in the shin, it was always Hank's fault. If Miss Wagner was an ear-tugging teacher like that, it would prove that she was the wrong one to educate the boys, just as he'd said from the start.

"What did we discuss in our lessons?"

"That my name starts with a *w*." Wallie bobbed his head at Hank. "Did you know that, Papa? *Water* and *wash* start with a *w*, too. Oh, and *wheel*. *W*s are important."

"You are very correct, Wallie." Instead of tugging on any ears, Miss Wagner displayed her dimpled smile as if she'd wanted that answer from Wallie all along. "We also learned that our brothers are our what?"

The two oldest scowled at each another. Most days his boys got along fine. Created a mess, ignored their chores and made more of a ruckus than all of the barn animals combined, sure, but they did all of that together, as partners in mischief. It was competition that brought out their worst and triggered divisions between them.

"Allies," they both mumbled.

Wallie yanked on Hank's pant leg. "That means friends. Brothers are to be friends. But Miss Wagner is too old to be our sister."

Isaac didn't bother to disguise his amusement. "You're right, Wallie-boy. Miss Wagner is not your sister."

Wallie tilted his head and put his hands on his hips. "Does that mean we're not friends?"

Miss Wagner knelt before Wallie, not appearing to care that her pretty, pristine dress was trailing through the dirt. "A teacher can be a special kind of friend, but your family—"

Hank rested his hand on Wallie's head, staking his claim. "Family is the most important type of friendship." He agreed with the lesson she was teaching them, but he wanted it to be clear to everyone—her, the boys and even Isaac—that she was not part of their family. He'd give her the trial, and then he'd send her on her way. When the time came, he'd find another teacher—a better teacher. One with life experience and grit. Someone with the ability to prepare his boys for life's hard trials ahead. A teacher who could be counted on to stick around for the long haul.

"I agree."

Isaac wiped his palms on the clean section of his shirt. "Now that we're all agreeing…" He extended his hand. Miss Wagner took it and let him help her back to her feet. "Are you sure you don't want to stay here and have me ride to the pump?"

Robert's eyes lit, looking more like Evelyn's than ever. "I want to ride out to the pump."

Edward laced his hands together. "Me, too! Please, Papa."

"Mabel wants to go on a ride, too," Wallie said, jumping up and down.

Why was he so fascinated with that hen? "Chickens aren't allowed to go anywhere, and neither are you. You've got lessons."

Wallie froze, and Hank felt a somewhat shameful rush of triumph as he realized he'd found the wedge he sought to place between his boys and Miss Wagner.

"Why don't you take them all?" The smirk was back on Isaac's face. "You know you've been promising the boys a trip for a while."

It's not that he disliked spending time with his boys. He just didn't want the boys near anything too dangerous. And oil rigs could always be dangerous. Even ones such as Father Abraham that were nearly done producing.

The original well always made him think of his father-in-law, who had named it after the man who had willed him the land. The property had been a gift in gratitude for Hank's father-in-law saving the life of Abraham's son during the war.

Hank wished Abraham had kept his land, that it had never passed to his father-in-law. If it weren't for the land, and the oil found on it, he and Evelyn never would have moved out here to help her father run his business. And if they'd never come out this way, maybe Evelyn would still be alive. He'd still have her by his side. His sons would still have their mother to look after them and teach them their lessons.

But that wasn't how it had turned out. Evelyn was gone and he was here—with oil and money, along with heartache and motherless sons.

Hank took in his sons' pleading looks. Father Abraham would be safest to bring the boys to once it stopped pumping, or he could take them to the newly scouted site for their next well. "How about I take you with me sometime soon to a new drill site?"

Robert's shoulders drooped. "I want to see one actually pumping."

"You always say we'll go sometime soon." Edward's words tightened something inside of Hank's chest. He really had delayed keeping his promises for too long. They were soon to become broken promises, making him into a liar if he wasn't careful.

"I wouldn't mind going. I can help keep watch over the boys," Miss Wagner offered.

"That's quite all right," Hank said, shutting the idea down quickly. "You may have the afternoon off. Rest. Or prepare whatever is required for tomorrow's lessons. Come on, boys. If you promise to be extremely careful—"

"Yes!" Robert and Edward sprinted for the barn.

"I'll go get Mabel."

"No." Hank was never ready for Wallie's disappointed face, but he prepared himself best he could by curling his toes inside his boots. "You can't take the chicken."

Wallie pushed his bottom lip out. "She really, really wants to go for a ride. She told me."

"Doesn't matter what she told you, she's not coming."

Wallie scrunched up his face and crossed his arms.

"Pouting will only keep you here with Mabel."

Miss Wagner knelt beside Wallie. This time her back was to his youngest. "Hop on, and we'll go say good-bye to Miss Mabel."

His sorrow disappeared and Wallie slung his arms around her neck. Miss Wagner struggled at first to rise, but after she did, she practically galloped after Edward and Robert. When the other two noticed her giving Wallie a piggyback ride, they slowed and trotted alongside the pair, making horse sounds.

"Suppose that could have been worse."

Hank ignored the sarcasm seeping from Isaac's tone and gathered the blanket and basket that was left behind, following his crew. Miss Wagner had potentially stopped Wallie's fit before it started, just as effectively as she'd kept Edward and Robert from fighting. Yet if she believed she was going along on the trip to the rig too, she was wrong. Even if she did give Wallie that piggyback ride he'd asked him for.

Wallie slid off Della's back and gathered up Mabel, who had dashed in their direction as they approached the coop. Edward and Robert chased after Mr. Lamson's determined path to the barn.

Left with her thoughts, Della stood pondering as she swatted at a bug near her face. Why was he so determined for her not to go see the oil pump with them? She'd hoped for more chances to prove to him that she was a good fit for his boys. A rest wasn't necessary. She'd only been teaching for an hour, what with all the time wasted on the eggs and then tracking down the boys. There was no time for day one to be deemed anything but a failure.

But no, she refused to accept that. Today's school

hours were not complete. She didn't know how, but she had to visit that pump with the others. Needed to prove to Mr. Lamson that she was a suitable teacher.

Wallie petted Mabel, sharing his excitement about the oil pump and about getting a piggyback ride from his teacher. Della was cherishing Wallie's compliment when Alice came around the side of the house, singing softly with a basket of clothes on her hip. She dropped the basket beside the clothesline and headed back inside.

Della eyed the clothesline and then the empty porch. It wouldn't be wise for the wet clothes to sit long in the sun. She drummed her fingertips along her dress. Her mind did always work better when she had a task.

Yet after some towels, an apron and three pairs of the boys' pants were hung, she was no closer to a plan of securing a permanent role as a teacher for the Lamson boys. The next item Della pulled out was a shirt that either belonged to Roy or Mr. Lamson, and she hesitated.

"Della." Alice waddled down the porch steps with more clothespins in her hands. "You aren't here to do my chores."

Della lowered the shirt, her face burning hot.

"In fact, because of you, I have even more time to do them myself." Alice took the shirt from Della with a puckered brow. "Did you never find the boys? I assumed you had when you didn't return. Oh, look, there's Wallie. That boy's always with his hen."

"Yes, I found the boys. Thank you for the advice. They were in the trees beyond the swing. But it seems that Mr. Lamson's taking the boys to an oil pump. I offered to come along and further their lessons, however—"

Alice released the clothesline. The rope jiggled, causing the clothing to dance in the air. "Best pack a snack. Those boys are better behaved with full bellies. I've got some corn bread. I assume you're leaving soon? Need to get a jug of water and a good helping of jerky, too."

"Mr. Lamson and the boys are leaving soon, I suppose. But he told me to stay here."

Alice stopped. Della ran clear into her stout and sturdy shoulder. "Stay here?" Alice's blank stare changed to a scowl. "It's one thing to be difficult with the idea of springing marriage on him. It's quite another to take away your opportunities to teach. Too stubborn for his own good. I know I told you I don't need help with my chores, but would you mind, dear, gathering the food? I'll send Wallie in to help. He knows where I keep the dinner basket. I need to go have a little talk with my son. Hank needs to see you teach, and you can help watch over the boys at the rig. If that's what you want?"

"I think that sounds like a great plan."

In less time than it took for Della to prepare their snack, Alice had gotten through to Mr. Lamson. By the glare he shot Della as she climbed into the wagon, he must have assumed it was all her idea to send his ma after him. She didn't like that he was angry with her again, but what mattered was that Della was in the wagon with the boys, and he was going to observe first-hand what a fine teacher she would be for them.

Wallie changed his seated position three times before either of his brothers arrived. He reached over Della to retrieve a blackboard from the basket beside her, hugging it to his chest as if it were Mabel. Della didn't think the wagon would be the ideal spot to use the boards, due to all the jostling they'd feel once they were underway, but she was grateful Wallie took a liking to something she had provided. At least one of her pupils was warming up to her. He'd even called her a lovely teacher when describing her to Mabel. It was a pity he wasn't the one to make the final decision about her staying. If he were, she might have a greater chance.

Mr. Lamson sat on the buckboard bench, his back as straight as the boards beneath him, and his knuckles white around the reins.

"Miss Wagner…" Wallie drug a piece of chalk up and down, creating a wobbly shape that was more or less a *w*. "Is your heart hurt, too?"

Della released her hand that she'd clenched at her chest and fiddled with the basket handle. "That is a wonderful *w*, Wallie," she said to distract him from his question. Try an *a* next." She shielded her eyes from the sunshine. "Do you see Robert and Edward? They sure are taking a while finding whatever it is they were supposed to grab."

"I asked them to grab my tools from Pa's wood shop." The wagon rocked beneath her as Mr. Lamson hopped down. "I'm going to go check Lady."

Wallie lifted his piece of chalk only inches from Della's face. "Your eyes are frowning like Papa's does when he sits on the porch rocker. One time I asked him what's wrong, and he said his heart hurt."

The air inside her lungs vanished. His words, childlike but so perceptive, made it hard for her to remember to breathe. She hurt at the thought of Mr. Lamson rocking on the front porch carrying the burden of his family's future. But she also hurt for herself. Her heart ached, just as it had since Tom had discarded her. The sorrow had lessened when she received the Lamsons' letter of acceptance and boarded the train. Now at the prospect of heading back, the ache redoubled.

"You must have gotten it from Papa." Wallie blinked and then glanced at the barn. "Do you think I'll catch it, too?" He put his fist over his heart. "Will it hurt a lot?"

Della opened her arms. "Come here." He leaned in and wrapped his arms around her waist, snuggling deeper like she was a part of the family and not merely a teacher—and a trial one at that.

"Don't worry." She combed her fingers through his hair. "Hurting hearts isn't something that's caught from others." Even though they could be caused by others.

"I…" The words she planned to encourage Wallie with floated away. "Hearts are…"

Wallie tilted his head up, watching her—waiting. She forced a smile and kissed the top of his head. He was the sweetest thing, and she would miss him when the week ended and she had to leave. "Hearts are strong. So don't worry."

"You already said that."

"It's because I mean it."

"Wallie, why don't you run on and see what's keeping your brothers." Della didn't turn at the sound of Mr. Lamson's command. How much of their conversation had he heard? What if he found her responses lacking? A teacher should always have a wise answer ready.

When Wallie was out of earshot, Mr. Lamson leaned his elbows on the wagon. "He's got a softer heart than his brothers." His eyes remained focused on Wallie, who struggled with both arms to pull open the barn door. "I believe he'll grow out of it soon enough."

It was Della's turn to straighten her posture. Being attuned to another's moods was a rare and special quality for anyone to have. She couldn't sit and let Hank think one of Wallie's talents was a weakness. "I hope not."

"A man has to be strong enough to face what life throws at him."

"Showing compassion for the suffering of others isn't a weakness, Mr. Lamson. Not in any sense. And last I checked a five-year-old—"

He cut her a glare she didn't think she'd earned. "You may have taught your fair share of students, but have you ever raised one of your own?"

Her chest physically hurt as she whispered a no. When Tom's engagement ring rested on her finger, she'd dreamed of raising three. Two boys and a girl. She'd imagined the little girl, the youngest as she had been, would have Tom's coloring, and the boys' hers. She pressed her palm to her neck. Teaching children would be the next best thing to motherhood. She was grateful for the opportunity, but that didn't mean his words didn't sting at what she may never have.

"Then you'd be mindful not to teach about things you know nothing about."

Della met Mr. Lamson's stare, her heart beating faster and her hands shaking at the presumption that she didn't understand what it took to face life's struggles. If only that were true.

"Mr. Lamson, I concur that you have more experienced with parenting, but I am an expert on what my own heart has endured. And as far as my job as a teacher, it's my responsibility to share all knowledge with my students that I am able."

Mr. Lamson was the first to glance away at the sound of little feet thundering their way. Edward's arrival ended any further interaction. Robert hopped up front on the buckboard. Wallie trudged behind with both hands stretched in front of him, struggling with a bucket half his size. If Della's heart hadn't received another lashing, she may have asked why the boys made their youngest brother carry whatever tools Mr. Lamson told them to fetch. Instead she stood on wobbly legs and helped lift the bucket inside. Then, after Wallie was seated, she climbed out of the wagon.

Wallie's face lifted in concern. "Where you going, Miss Wagner?"

She gathered the basket with her teaching supplies, leaving the snacks and board and chalk that Wallie had taken out earlier. "I'm going to let you men head to the pumps."

Wallie's head bowed. "If you're not coming then I'll stay with you."

"No," Della and Mr. Lamson said in unison.

There was no point leading a horse to water if he wasn't thirsty. "Mr. Lamson, when you return, will you let me know when you might have a better opportunity to observe my teaching?" If they scheduled a time at their mutual convenience, she might gain a sweeter outcome. And hopefully the nerves dancing through her body would have time to calm.

She cupped Wallie's chin, silently praying the boy would never outgrow his gift, and hurried to speak before Mr. Lamson could. "Go on and have fun with your father and brothers doing your manly things."

Wallie raised his arms in an attempt to show off his muscles, or where they might be one day. "I already have muscles like Papa. See? I'll stay and keep you company."

She leaned in close and whispered in his ear. "Why don't you tag along and help your brothers in case they need to borrow some of your strength?" For strength he did have, even if Hank failed to see it. "I'll be here when you get back."

"Promise?"

Della opened her mouth, but Mr. Lamson cut her off. "Time to sit, Wallie." His voice held less of an edge than it had earlier with her. She was thankful for that.

Della kept her attention on the boy who looked torn, but Wallie eventually obeyed. As he should have. Mr. Lamson was who the boys must listen to. After all, he was their father while she was merely a teacher.

Wallie rested his elbows on the back ledge. "Mabel will keep you company. She's good with lonely."

Della stepped back and Mr. Lamson slapped the reins. As the horse trotted forward, Wallie waved, and the other boys watched her with neutral expressions. She remained where she was until the wagon was nothing but a blur in the distance.

Had Wallie's words meant that he knew Della was lonely, or that his hen understood his loneliness? Either way she was about to go befriend a chicken.

Chapter Five

For the fourth time, dependable Dorothy veered to the right as if to circle back home and insist on an apology from her driver. But he wasn't about to have his behavior dictated by a horse. Hank's words to Miss Wagner had been sharp and borderline unkind, however they hadn't been untrue. The childless woman couldn't fathom how to raise boys. He was doing what was best for all of them.

Dorothy released a snort and swooshed her tail as if to disagree. With a flick of his wrists, Hank reinforced the course set for the Valley Ridge pump.

Throughout their marriage, Evelyn had taught him lots about a woman's emotions. He hadn't always been as quick of a study as a man hoped to be concerning the one he loved, so how had he noticed the hurt in Miss Wagner's green eyes almost immediately? He didn't like what it had done to his chest, and that discomfort had made him lash out even harder.

He shifted on the buckboard, knocking his knee against Robert. His oldest, who resembled his mother more and more these days, faced him, and Hank could almost picture Evelyn there beside him with her arms crossed, appalled at his insensitivity.

Hank clicked his tongue for Dorothy to trot faster. He'd get to an apology, eventually. As far as a better opportunity to observe her teaching, that would probably never be. He didn't want to give her false hope. Her temporary trial wasn't a test of her abilities but a chance for her to prove how unsuited she was to this place. Once she accepted that truth, she'd leave—and life could go back to normal.

Robert wiggled, setting his elbows on his knees. "When can I steer? Grandpa always lets us have a turn."

At nine, Robert's legs no longer swung beneath him, but were planted on the wooden boards below. He was growing up strong and steady. There should be no reason to discourage him from wanting to lead the wagon. Three summers ago, he had Edward up here also, teaching them both the ins and outs. Yet that had been before he failed to keep Evelyn safe.

"Papa?" Robert stretched his hands for the reins.

Dorothy dipped her head and snorted as if to assert that she was perfectly capable of steering herself, no matter who held the reins. Hank surrendered control and extended his legs as much as possible in an attempt to relax, except his burdens remained as tight as a new leather belt.

Wallie tapped Hank on his shoulder. "Me next."

"No. I'm next." Edward stood beside Wallie.

"We're not going in order. I'm tired of always being last. I called it. It's my turn."

"Boys, sit. The wagon's moving." The boys obeyed the sternness of Hank's voice. "Edward, you can have a turn in a while."

"That's not fair," Wallie whined. "I asked for next. Grandpa says whoever voices his turn first gets it. That makes it more fair."

Edward folded his arms. "Grandpa's not here. And Papa said I'm next."

Wallie stuck out his tongue at Edward.

Hank wiped his hand down his face. He really didn't want to discuss what was and wasn't fair in life. "Wallie. Don't do that. I said your brother's next. You can sit on my lap when we get closer and help."

Wallie dug his fingers into the buckboard's ledge and rose onto his feet. "Grandpa lets me do it all by myself." He gestured to the side of the wagon where Edward sat. "And he even sits back here while Robert helps me."

That was a real surprise—and not a pleasant one. "Grandpa lets you and your brother steer by yourselves?"

"He says I'm no baby no more. And I'm not."

Hank would agree with that. All his boys were growing up far too quickly, but that didn't mean he wanted Wallie steering the wagon while his brother, a mere four years older, supervised. It was an accident waiting to happen, even if Dorothy was as tame as Mabel, if not tamer. One wrong move or too long staring in the distance and a wheel could break. How would a young boy know how to handle that situation? They wouldn't.

Hank reached over and took hold of the reins.

Robert clung tighter. "Can't I have a longer turn? Been keeping Dorothy on the straight and narrow like Grandpa tells us."

Dorothy hadn't pulled to the right with Robert like she'd done for him. But then, Robert wasn't feeling guilty over not apologizing. "You did a fine job."

"I'll do a mighty fine job too, Papa," Wallie said. "Here. I'll show ya."

Edward stood next to Wallie. "No. I'm showing him next."

With Wallie and Edward standing in the wagon and Dorothy moving at a steady clip, what if his boys fell and were tossed onto their heads? Hank yanked the control of the reins away from Robert and slowed the wagon. "I said sit down." His voice came out in an angry blast that instantly silenced all other conversation.

He regretted his outburst as soon as he'd shut his mouth. Dust wasn't the only thing filling the hushed wagon. Anger was no way to discipline a child.

The boys crouched and inspected their boots. Hank closed his eyes. Well, hadn't this turned out to be a memorable father-and-sons trip.

Wallie patted his arm. "I'm real sorry, Papa. I'll try harder to remember about sitting in the wagon. I only wanted to show you how great I can steer. Dorothy listens to me. Almost as well as Mabel. Just don't tell Mabel that. Don't want to hurt her feelings none. But I won't show you until you say so. Promise."

Now, that was a proper apology. Hank should take pointers from his son when he got around to addressing Miss Wagner.

Edward faced the west. "The sun sure don't seem like it wants to obey, either. It's hardly shining over there." If angry was a color it would look like the low, dark clouds rolling in the distance. A noise rumbled, sounding too much like thunder.

"Good thing we aren't going that way, huh?" Robert lifted his brows.

How his oldest knew the direction of the Valley

Ridge pump, Hank didn't know. He'd only brought them out there two or three times since Evelyn passed.

Robert was correct that they weren't heading straight toward the storm—but who was to say the storm wouldn't head to them? It may never get around to reaching the rig, but there was no sense in risking it. If he didn't have his boys with him, he'd consider it, but he did. And their safety was the only thing that mattered. "Think you can turn Dorothy around?"

"Are we going back to get Miss Wagner?" Wallie asked, his voice more hopeful than Hank would have liked for the temporary teacher.

Hank returned the reins to an eager Robert. "We're going home because of the storm."

Edward's face mirrored the incoming weather. "Ah, man. That's worse than having the last turn to lead Dorothy."

No, life was truly never fair. It'd be best if his boys learned that while they were young and saved themselves from the heartache he carried.

Della never would have guessed the item she'd miss most from home would be her thimble. She pricked her finger again as she pushed a needle through the elbow of a shirt Wallie had worn out. Alice had been trying to thread the needle when Della had returned inside. After several attempts and a brief moment where Alice rubbed her wrist, Della had held out her hands and Alice had reluctantly surrendered the shirt and sewing basket.

Alice hummed a hymn as she scooped out some flour. The music made the room feel cozy. Della couldn't recall a moment when her and Mother had worked in the same room feeling comfortable enough to hum or sing.

Not that Mother had ever been one to raise her voice in song, unless patronizing counted as musical.

Della secured the new patch with a knot and bit off the end of the thread. When she was young, Father used to tell her stories of her birth and how Mother had been so delighted that their fourth child was the girl she'd always wanted. Obviously, Della hadn't turned out as Mother had hoped. She'd spent far too many hours playing outdoors with her brothers. She'd never really been ladylike. Or beautiful. Or charming. By her mother's assessment, she'd never been good enough by any measure. That's what Mother had taken great pains to explain when Della told her Tom had broken their engagement.

She turned up the lamp's wick, and the brighter light revealed her stitches weren't quite even. But they did look like they'd get the job done. She tugged on the fabric along the seam and thankfully the thread remained. It'd hold for a while, especially since Wallie was sure to grow out of it soon. She remembered Freeman barely getting a new shirt, or rather a hand-me-down from either Johnnie or Grant, before it already reached too high on his arms.

Della folded the shirt and laid it on the table. "Is there anything else you'd like mended?"

Alice stopped humming and wiped her forehead, leaving a trail of white dust above her brow. "Oh, no. I shouldn't have let you do that much." She paused with the rolling pin in her hand. "But Wallie has been on me to get his favorite shirt fixed for a long while. Thank you, dear. We're both much obliged."

Della secured the needle into its pushpin, missing Alice's sweet melody in the background. The sewing box sat on the table.

Most of the box's space was filled with blue, black and white threads wrapped around wooden dowels, but a rainbow of other colors littered the bottom half, even some yarn, but no thimble in sight. "Really, Alice. I don't mind tackling more. I have nothing pressing to do." But she couldn't blame anyone but herself for choosing to climb from that wagon. Having something to keep her occupied would be a blessing if it would distract her from the clock ticking down the minutes until she'd have to leave.

Her cheeks hurt from keeping the fake smile on her face. Alice studied her for a moment before heaving a sigh. "You sure you don't mind? I hate having a guest do my chores."

Della gave her a true smile. "I thought I was more than a guest."

Alice marched over and placed her floured hand under Della's chin. "You truly are." Unshed tears danced in Alice's eyes, and she brought her voice to a whisper. "No matter what happens. All right?"

On the receiving end of another one of Alice's embraces, Della couldn't move. Couldn't speak. Nor breathe as she soaked in Alice's kindness. Della had meant that she was more than a guest because she was the boys' teacher. She had the feeling that Alice was speaking about something greater. Like the real reason she and Roy had written the want ad she'd answered in the first place. For her to be family.

Maybe marrying a stranger would be worth having the appreciation shining in Alice's eyes in her life every day. Della pulled away, making a point to focus anywhere but on Alice. The floor was the safest direction, covered in flurries of white from Alice's always abundant use of flour. Her mind switched to the need to clean instead of pondering all the what-ifs. There was no sense in wondering about marrying a stranger when the stranger didn't want a wife at all. Not that Della wished to be his bride. She dreamed of being his sons' teacher.

After Della swept, she set the broom back into its corner. "Where are the other items in need of mending?" That way she could save the rest of the house from another sweeping.

Alice wouldn't meet her gaze. "Well… I…" She backed into the washbasin and covered her cheeks with her hands, creating a new sprinkling of floury mess on the floor. "I'm ashamed to admit, there are far too many for you to do in one sitting. Let me grab a couple that the boys have asked about."

"Alice," Della spoke softly, reaching for the broom.

Alice nodded sheepishly. "You're right. I'm dressed in flour. But only pick two pieces from the pile. Three at the most. And absolutely nothing of mine." She sniffed and wiped her face with her apron, leaving a clean spot on the left pocket. "They're under my side of the bed."

Della hurried down the hallway before Alice changed her mind. Roy and Alice's bedroom door didn't squeak when Della pushed it open. She thought it would feel odd rummaging about someone else's room, but it didn't. It was as if she was back at home and gathering the laundry. She honestly felt more uncomfortable in her mother's room than in Alice's. Maybe because Alice was pleasant to be around and seemed to welcome her presence.

On the far side of the bed was a dresser with a brush and mirror resting on top, the only items announcing which was Alice's side. Della pulled up the quilt on the side of the bed, and gasped. Four piles of folded clothes were sandwiched between the under boards and ropes of the bed and the floor. Did Alice not have time to do any mending, or did she dislike it so much that she kept putting it off?

After blindly grabbing pieces from each pile, Della once again settled into the kitchen chair. The first piece of mending had a rip running along the bottom side of one of its legs as if Robert or Edward had gotten stuck somewhere and had been forced to yank themselves free.

The tear in the pants, followed by a hole in a sock didn't take Della long, especially when she hummed along with Alice. She inspected the last item in her lap for whatever needed mending. Finally, her fingertips passed over a pea-sized hole near the collar. Della searched in the sewing box and changed the thread to match the shirt.

A slap of the back door caused her to smile, but it wasn't Roy like she'd assumed. Apparently, the oil pump wasn't far from the house.

"Hiram Robert, those boots better not be mudding all over my swept floor," Alice said in between one of the verses of "Blessed Assurance."

Mr. Lamson's attention wasn't on his boots or his mother. It was fixated on Della.

"Hank. Those boots," Alice said.

He slipped out of his boots, unveiling a hole in his sock. "Is that my shirt?" He stole the shirt from Della, scrutinizing every inch as if she'd harmed it. "She doesn't need to do our chores."

Della snatched it right back and quickly shoved the

readied needle into the fabric. If he'd hold his horses, she'd have it finished in a minute.

She added another stitch. "Since I'm not earning my keep by providing lessons this morning, I offered to help Alice." And really, why shouldn't she help with the chores? Without teaching how else was she to earn her keep? It's the least she could do since Alice and Roy had been nothing but kind to her. Yes, everything had been in a tizzy upon her arrival, yet they'd all but made up for it. Everyone except the owner of the shirt.

"And she's doing a mighty fine…" Alice rested her floured hands on the table. "Goodness. Hank, your pinkie toes done run away from your favorite socks. Why don't you take those off and give them to Della?"

"I'm not handing Del—Miss Wagner my dirty sock."

Della couldn't help from wrinkling her nose at the memory of Freeman's smelly feet after he'd worked at the newspaper all day. While Della didn't mind sewing for the Lamson family during her stay with them, she was thankful Mr. Lamson refused to comply with Alice's suggestion. She didn't want to experience what a sock smelled like up close after a hard day of outside work.

The back door slapped shut again. Wallie dodged around his father and ran to Della. "There's a storm. We're going to the pumps tomorrow instead. Papa said so. Promised even. Think your heart will be better by then?"

Alice sucked in a breath, her hand clinging to a rag pressed to her cheek. With white streaks covering her forehead down to the bottoms of her skirt, she was nothing but a walking flour storm herself. "What's wrong with your heart?"

Della shook her head, but Wallie didn't let her explain. "You want to ride with us tomorrow, don't ya, Miss Della?"

"Oh, I—"

"We'll wait and see, Wallie," Mr. Lamson said.

Wallie's posture sagged. He and Della both recognized that meant a "no" rested ahead.

Della lifted his chin. "Why don't you fetch your brothers? We'll continue today's lesson."

"Miss Wagner, may I see you on the porch?" Mr. Lamson didn't wait for her answer before striding toward the door.

With the mending in hand, Della followed him through the front room and outside. He paced back and forth, neither looking at her nor at anything else in particular.

On his third trip across the porch, he stopped. "I'm sorry."

Della waited through the stitch of silence that followed, but that seemed to be all he had to say. He resumed pacing the length of the porch twice more before taking a seat in one of the rockers. The man would never earn high marks in apology class. Granted, it was more than she'd expected. Then again, she wasn't entirely sure what he was apologizing for. Being blunt about his shirt, or for making her recall that she may never have children of her own? Was he sorry for not giving her a fair chance at observing her lessons today? Or was Mr. Lamson simply sorry that she couldn't go on tomorrow's rescheduled trip to the pumps?

"May I ask what your apology pertains to exactly?"

Mr. Lamson sat in the rocker, his elbows on his knees and his hands cradling his chin. Wallie's words about hurting hearts had her making a closer assessment of his father. "I shouldn't have… What I mean is… At the wagon, my words were uncalled for. I never should have implied that my struggles were more difficult than yours."

She felt a rush of compassion. She'd lost a fiancé, so to speak, but he'd lost his wife. One who'd given him three wonderful children that he now parented alone. Mr. Lamson had been correct to say that Della didn't fully understand what he and the boys had been through. Not that it completely excused the way he'd spoken to her. Sorrow wasn't a competition. But his attitude didn't give her any right to hold a grudge. And an apology, whether good or bad, wasn't hers to judge, only to accept.

"Thank you." The breeze blew against Della's skirt, signaling the approach of the storm Wallie had mentioned. No dark clouds hovered over the trees or the valley. The old church's steeple was as clear as ever, but one didn't have to spot a storm to feel it brewing.

A cow's moos pulled her focus to the nearest barn. "Will the animals know to take cover from the storm?"

The rocker creaked under Mr. Lamson. "They know."

Della bit off the thread, finishing Mr. Lamson's shirt, then ran her thumb over her work. No one would be able to tell there was once a hole. Perhaps her best sewing to date. "Your shirt's all fixed."

He rose and took the mended shirt from her. His fingers went right to the spot Della had mended. So much for no one being able to tell where the hole had once been.

With a scan of the sky, he clutched the shirt tighter. "Thanks." His voice was softer than earlier. "For helping Ma." His gaze remained on the trees in the distance whose tops began bending in the stronger winds. His fingers kept running along the mended stitching. "And for fixing my wedding shirt."

Della settled into the paired rocker with a feeling of newfound understanding. No wonder the man grew as sharp as a needle point about his shirt. It reminded him of all he'd lost. Maybe a ride out to the oil ridges did, too?

A rustling of branches and a low howling overshadowed the faint moos now drifting safely from inside the barn. Was that what had happened to his wife? Had he lost her in a storm?

"If you're interested in the oil pumps from a teacher's standpoint…" He inspected her mending again, pinching the wrinkled collar. "We're leaving right after breakfast." He locked on to her eyes, and something inside her wanted to draw near. Was it because, like Wallie, she noticed the sadness etched on his face? Was it a teacher's instinct to offer comfort that eventually life brings more blessings, like his sweet boys?

He stepped away, breaking whatever invisible string had hemmed them together. "Wallie never stopped insisting you come along on the way home."

She hugged her arms around herself as the wind increased. Della smiled at the thought of Wallie talking about her and wanting her to come along. When Mr. Lamson rested against one of the porch's posts, his mended shirt pressed close to his chest, his previous words rang in Della's mind:

From a teacher's standpoint…

It was an odd way to phrase it. "I do want to learn about oil pumps, but what I truly wanted…"

She paused at the tensing of Mr. Lamson's shoulders and the folding of his arms.

"I just wanted to go along so you might witness how the boys and I get along. And evaluate my teaching for my trial."

He narrowed his eyes and stepped closer. "There's no other reason you wanted to see my oil pumps?"

Why else would she bump along in a wagon to see an oil pump? The only other reason she could think of was to be with the boys, and she didn't know why he wouldn't want that. Unless he was worried about them getting too attached.

"I want a real chance at becoming a permanent teacher here for your family."

He swallowed and ran his fingertip over the mended hole once more. "I must apologize again, Miss Wagner. I assumed the worst out of your genuine request. Ladies in the past have wanted to see my property for more…well, for more self-interested reasons. I promise to observe your teaching tomorrow with an open mind. You'll be given a fair chance. But bear in mind that in the end, I will make a decision based on what my family needs."

Della rose off the rocker, lacing her fingers together to prevent her from wrapping her arms around Mr. Lamson. "That's all I ask." He'd hardly appreciate a thank-you hug. She smiled and enjoyed the moment for what it was: the hope of keeping her dream. No matter how small it was.

Chapter Six

Hank set his tools inside the wagon bed. "Sparing any trouble, we'll return by noon."

Ma waved him on. "Take your time. I packed extra treats in the basket in case you decide to make a day of it."

Pa straightened his hat and wrapped his arm around Ma's shoulder. She snuggled in, and grins shined on both of their faces. They looked happy.

Hank pretended to inspect the reins in his hands to give him an excuse to look away. He missed being that happy.

"Have you lost your manners?" A warning in Pa's voice caught Hank's attention. Which of his boys was misbehaving? His firstborn relaxed in the corner beside his tools, his arm draped over the wagon's side. It wasn't Wallie in need of reprimanding. He was approaching, his hand tucked inside Miss Wagner's arm as she swung a basket in her other. Edward stood in front of Dorothy, patting her nose. All were accounted for, so what was the problem? Then Hank realized it wasn't the boys who'd won Pa's disgruntled glare. It was steadily set on him.

Ma crossed her arms over her apron, seemingly in complete agreement with Pa's mood swing. "Aren't you going to help Della onto the seat?"

Miss Wagner held Wallie's hand as he climbed over the wagon's back ledge. "I can manage on my own," she insisted. Hank bit back the urge to say that if she'd let go of Wallie he could have managed on his own, too. She walked to the side and placed her foot on one of the wheel spokes.

"What on earth are you doing?" Ma exclaimed.

Miss Wagner's cheeks reddened. "Climbing inside?" She glanced at Hank like she didn't understand why she was getting into trouble. He hadn't a clue, either.

"Nonsense. You'll ride up front." Ma pointed at the buckboard. "Right there beside Hank."

Hank wanted to shake his head, and take to pouting like his boys did when they weren't allowed their way. He settled with scowling at the sky instead. Wondering what he'd done wrong to deserve his mother's scheming to get him nearer to Miss Wagner. How could he get out of it without offending Ma?

Miss Wagner placed her basket beside Wallie. She wore a green calico dress today. Hank didn't have to look hard to know that it matched her eyes. It was the first time she had worn anything that color. Her hair caught the sun's rays, making her even more pleasing to look at than he'd like her to be. If he ever did hire a woman teacher, she didn't need to be an attractive one.

Hank rubbed his palm on his pants. Dorothy nodded her head, jostling the reins in his grip, as if she wanted to see what the holdup was. Unfortunately, Ma had a point. Why would a grown woman not take the more comfortable seat?

Hank scooted to the far left, making the wooden board groan beneath him. The wagon swayed a bit and Hank realized Miss Wagner had climbed inside right next to Wallie. Nowhere near him. "That's quite all right, Alice. This is my place. Back here with the boys. Teaching as we ride."

The reins slipped out of his fingers. Miss Wagner kept saying all the right words. She never peeked over at Hank. Not once. A part of him still expected her to be like the ladies who kept arriving, playing coy, but always batting their lashes at him.

Robert rose onto his knees. "Does that mean I can ride up front?"

Edward shoved his brother's arm. "It's my turn. You got to ride by Papa yesterday."

"That didn't count. We didn't go the whole way."

Before Hank could wade through another round of their arguments, Miss Wagner had everything fixed. "If you're riding up front while I'm giving lessons, you'll end up with a crick in your neck. It's best if every one of you boys ride back here. That way you're not half twisted around. If that's all right with you, Mr. Lamson? I'm assuming you'll be able to overhear our lessons from your seat."

"That should work out fine."

"Are we really going to have lessons the whole way?" Edward whined.

Miss Wagner moved a few items inside the basket onto her lap and pulled a small leather box out. "A new day means a brand-new story. Unless of course, you're going to continue on in that sour mood?"

The two older boys released their holds on each other's sleeves and leaned in closer to Miss Wagner. Their fight to move beside him was now all but forgotten. What was so special about her leather box? Were there sweets hidden within?

When she showed a simple photo, worn around the edges, Wallie yanked it away, squinting at it. "Which one's Freeman?"

"Can't see it, Wallie," Robert howled, dragging out his brother's name.

"I want to hold it." Edward reached, but Miss Wagner took the photo away from Wallie and rested it against her chest.

She lifted her chin. "I think we all need a lesson on who should be first."

Dorothy stomped her foot, but Hank ignored her protest. He actually wanted to see how Miss Wagner handled the boys' disagreement. Would she bring out the ear tugging this time?

Robert crossed his arms. "The oldest."

She shook her head, eyeing each of them. "Scripture says the first should be last and the last should be first."

Hank barely held on to his composure. He should have known his folks would have found someone who put God into every situation.

Wallie pressed his knees to his belly and squeezed on the toes of his boots as if they were buttons to unlock the right answers. "Does that mean Edward can't go at all 'cause he's in the middle?"

Miss Wagner smiled. Her true one with the dimple. "If you promise to share and take good care of my picture, I'll show it to each of you. I assume you'd like to know about the time Freeman got stuck in the bell tower at church? After I tell the story, I'll have Robert read about being a servant like our Savior. Deal?"

Wallie was the first to agree, but it didn't take the others long to follow. Miss Wagner handed off the photo and tucked in that loose hair behind her ear. She must have felt Hank's attention because her eyes met his. He couldn't find it in his control to focus anywhere else. The woman had not only gotten his boys to sit still, but to stop bickering. And they all seemed to be okay with continuing their studies. He'd assumed that she'd either stumble when it came to disciplining them, or that she'd resort to harshness and bullying, like his own former teacher. Either one would be grounds for dismissing her. Yet she'd found a middle ground he hadn't expected, and his certainty that she'd fail her trial was shaken.

Edward's laugh broke their connection, and after Miss Wagner turned toward Edward, Hank realized his folks were also still standing there. Pa had his hat between his fingers, and Ma had her head rested on his shoulder, taking in the scene.

Heat traveled up his neck, and he failed to rub it away. Just great. He'd given his folks more fodder to feed their appreciation for Miss Wagner.

He yah'd Dorothy into a slow canter onward to what he hoped wasn't another mistake.

"Have a wonderful time," Ma called out.

A wonderful time. Things may not go too terribly wrong if Miss Wagner kept to her lessons. And if his mind would stop wondering who that Freeman fellow was that his boys were inspecting so closely.

* * *

Turned out studying in a moving wagon was a bit harder than anticipated. At least it made reading difficult for Robert.

He stuttered on yet another word. "G-garrr…" He brought the Bible closer to his face.

Edward leaned over his brother. "Gar-ments."

Robert snatched the Bible away from Edward and read on, his finger chasing each word at a turtle's pace. A few phrases later and he stuttered again. His brows were drawn together with defeat written in his expression, and it occurred to Della that there might be more to his troubles with reading than the simple sway of the wagon.

"Edward, I believe it's your turn. Why don't you pick up at verse fifteen?" Della chose this passage to teach the boys it wasn't necessary to be first in everything. Jesus's example of washing his disciples' feet would give the boys a mighty fine lesson that would help not only with their attitudes, but also the bonding relationship they should have as brothers. However, Della was unsure how well one could apply a lesson if they'd lost interest two miles back.

Wallie rolled an apple in his hands—one of the ones they would soon use in their math equations. He held it in front of his face, and then shined it on his shirt, before gazing into the apple like a mirror.

"Wallie, did you hear that? Edward, would you re-read verse sixteen, please?"

Unlike Robert, Edward had very little trouble reading with the movement. "'Verily, verily, I—'"

A flash of pink coloring caught her attention and she scanned the brush along the path behind them. Wasn't it too late in the year for roses? "Can we please stop for a moment?" Della said, but the only thing that stopped was Edward's reading. "Sorry, Edward. I didn't mean you."

Della supported herself on the side of the wagon to gain a better view of what she believed was a rosebush. "Mr. Lamson. Would you please stop?"

Dorothy kept clipping along, the wheels crackling against the ground. Mr. Lamson clearly wasn't listening. So much for him observing her teaching skills. The roses provided an extra opportunity to remind him of his promise to observe, but if they didn't stop soon, she'd miss her favorite flowers. Ones she hadn't seen since Freeman placed two on her desk after the ordeal with Tom.

Surely, Hank wouldn't mind a little rest. The boys could stretch their legs. She squinted and barely located the pink spot nestled among the weeds. "Mr. Lamson, please stop!"

The wagon jolted to a halt, and Della fell on top of Wallie while the apples rolled to the front, probably earning enough bruises that they may not even be fit for Dorothy to eat.

Mr. Lamson set the brake and flew off the buckboard, his gaze searching his boys, the wheels and the underbelly of the wagon in quick succession. Finally, they landed on her.

He gripped a corner where the wood edges met, just above where her teaching basket had been prior to sailing toward the middle. "What's wrong? Did someone pinch their finger?"

"I… I saw some roses."

"You saw some…" He blinked his eyes wide and

glanced skyward like he'd never seen clouds before. He heaved out a breath. "You scared me half to death. I feared one of the boys had toppled out."

"I'm sorry." Her voice, though a whisper, still carried. The entire outdoors quieted to be an audience to their conversation. She was very sorry indeed. Not that she'd made him stop, but that she'd caused him to look so shaken, like he'd lost a beloved pet. "I—I didn't realize I'd yelled quite so loudly. You didn't hear me the first two times and I…" She braided her fingers together, knowing that her fidgeting betrayed her anxiety but unable to stop herself. "Roses are my favorite flowers, and I was excited to see them. And then I realized you weren't hearing me ask you to stop, meaning you also couldn't hear me teach."

Della inspected her fingernails.

Hank turned his back and ran a hand through his hair. "I could hear you teach. Your lessons have been appropriate. My mind drifted to something else…" He cleared his throat. "Why don't you take the boys to stretch their legs? Make it a quick stop."

Wallie didn't need any further permission. He hopped down and headed in the direction they'd traveled. "Are they pink? I think I see 'em." He started running with Edward and Robert close behind.

Hank offered his assistance to Della. And when her foot missed the wheel spoke, his hands remained steady as he helped her reach the ground without falling. "I've got you. I promise I'm still paying attention."

"Thank you. I appreciate that." Before she could wonder how the smell of cedar was entirely more appealing on his clothing than in the air, he released her and marched away, his heavy footsteps matching her heartbeat.

Mr. Lamson's hushed conversation with Dorothy and his tightened jaw made his lack of interest in seeing the flowers abundantly clear.

She was almost to the boys when Wallie turned and grinned. "These them, Miss Wagner? I'll pick you a big bunch." Wallie reached at the bush with both of his hands and on contact hollered out in pain.

Della picked up her skirt and hurried for the boys. She should have warned them, but she'd assumed they'd have recognized the thorns. What child didn't know that roses had thorns?

Wallie's bottom lip quivered, and Della wished she could bare the agony for him.

"Oh, stop, you big baby." Robert grabbed the stem of a rose. He jerked his hand away, shaking it, and then put his finger into his mouth. "It bit me harder than the blackberries," he said around his fingers.

Wallie had his hands squeezed together against his chest. Tears stained his dusty cheeks and Della's heart settled in her stomach. She dropped to her knees, feeling suffused with guilt. If she hadn't demanded they stop, neither Wallie nor Robert would have been hurt.

"Honey, can I see?" She licked her lips. She had never dealt with blood particularly well, ever since the day her oldest brother, Johnnie, got his finger stuck in the press at work.

Della blinked away stars. A thorn surely wouldn't produce that much blood, and she had yet to see any on his little hands. She could handle Wallie's wounds.

She touched Wallie's wrist. "I'm so sorry, Wallie.

I should have warned you that roses have thorns. Are you all right? Please let me see."

He allowed her to move his clenched hands away from his chest, but didn't open them. His fingernails were pale from the pressure he used to keep his fists balled. "Why do you like them mean flowers?"

She skimmed her fingers along his knuckles. "I think they're beautiful."

Edward squatted beside her, inspecting the flowers instead of his brother. He pointed at the fullest pink blossom, its petals as bright as the ones Freeman had picked to cheer her up. "They don't have those thorns everywhere. Just in spots."

"Well, I found a thorn, and I don't want to find another." Robert examined his finger, angling it in the sun. "I think a piece of it is stuck in me." It was possible, but Della doubted it. There was no blood to be seen on Robert's skin.

"Wallie?" She rubbed his shoulder. "Can I make sure you're okay? Open your hands. Please."

Wallie looked at the flowers and back to her before slowly unclenching his hands.

Unlike Robert's wound, there were puddles of red gathered in Wallie's palms. Della inhaled, thankfully smelling the slightest rose scent rather than the coppery aroma of blood. It kept her mind on helping Wallie and not on the wounds themselves.

"It's only scratches like mine." Robert held up his finger near Della's face.

Della turned her head. "Okay." Okay what? Robert's finger bore a shallow scratch with no thorn stuck in it, but his brother's hands needed bandaging. "Wallie, why don't you put your hands back together until we make it to the wagon…to clean them off with some…" What was used for cleaning again?

"Grandma packed a water jug," Edward offered.

"Right. Good idea, Edward. Yes, we'll use some water. Then if it's still…" She put her hand on her forehead and squeezed her eyes shut. "If it's still bleeding. I can… Cloth. Yes, cloth. To um, press on it."

"Grandma also packed towels around our snacks we can use."

Mr. Lamson's silhouette created a shadow over them as he walked over and stood with his hands on his hips. "I know Grandma said to make a day of it, but I'd much rather get going. Roses or not."

Edward showed off the three pink buds he had plucked, carefully avoiding the thorns. "The thorns got the better of Robert and Wallie. Not me. I was watching what I was doing. So I won." He stuck one rose up to his nose. "Don't they smell better than our washing soap?" He ran the petals down his cheek. "Softer than any flowers around the cabin, too."

Della took in a deep breath that failed to slow her galloping pulse. When she reopened her eyes, everyone was staring at her.

"I'm sorry I caused such a stir. We best get to the wagon and clean up Wallie's hands."

"And mine, too."

"Right, Robert." Why did her corset feel so tight? The breeze finally took pity on her and danced around them. It wasn't as cooling as it had been traveling in the wagon. But that made sense, didn't it? Wind was stronger while they were moving. She fanned herself with her hand and licked her lips.

"What happened? Let me see them," Mr. Lamson said.

Wallie hesitated, but exposed his palms.

"Got you pretty good." He flipped Wallie's hands over and a drop of blood landed near Della's boots. "Though I think you learned a valuable lesson."

Robert picked at his tiny scratch. "Don't pick flowers?"

Mr. Lamson tousled Robert's hair. "Don't rush. Go in prepared from the start. A man's got to discern what he's up against. Even pretty things can hurt you or let you down."

Della scowled. The boys needed to learn their letters, arithmetic, to have a servant's heart, or to count on their brothers and be a good brother back. Not that pretty things let you down. What sort of lesson was that?

"I think we should plant these by the front porch." Edward spun a stem in his fingers, the pink petals twirling around in a spiral. "They're real nice, and they smell good, too. Reckon Grandma would love them. Here, smell." He put one under Wallie's nose. "Think she can make our soap smell like that?"

"I think I've smelled those before," Wallie said.

"Have not," Robert huffed.

Wallie's nose flared. He closed his fists and then flinched. "It doesn't hurt too bad, Papa. Except this bigger cut in the middle." His pointer finger, scraped and covered in a bit of dried blood, was suddenly placed in her line of sight.

Della knew it was Wallie's finger stretched before her, not Johnnie's. Not the one that remained bent at the tip from being smashed, but that didn't help settle her churning stomach or racing heart. She took a step back. How long could someone remain standing when they had no feeling in their legs?

"I'm sorry." Della blew out a shaky breath. That horrible day at the newspaper was the first time she'd ever fainted on account of blood. Her mother had found out and added it to the list of things to belittle her about. So Della had tried to excuse herself when other accidents had occurred, but that wasn't possible right now, when it was all her fault.

"Miss Wagner." Mr. Lamson was close enough for her to notice he hadn't shaved today. She pressed her fingertips against his shoulder, right next to a small hole starting in the seam of his shirt. She had meant to move away from him, but all she could think about was how another piece of clothing was going to be shoved underneath Alice's bed. For how long would it live there, discarded because of its flaw?

"Miss Wagner, can you stand?"

Wasn't she?

She stopped inspecting Mr. Lamson's shirt and realized she was leaning against him. How humiliating. "Right." She pushed away and brushed off her skirt, before resting her hand on her stomach. "I—I believe a snack would do everyone good. After, of course, we wash Wallie's wounds."

"Did you see the spot between my fingers?" Wallie held up his hand to show her.

Della squeezed her fingers together. "Edward, could I carry the roses and you run on ahead to fetch the water jug for Wallie?"

"Don't forget about me," Robert added, sounding sulky.

"Both of you are fine," Mr. Lamson said.

Yes, what had she been thinking? The man was all about his boys becoming adults at the age of five. Well, even adults often needed help, especially when they were bleeding.

Edward looked between Della and Mr. Lamson before handing over the roses. He took off with both brothers right behind. Maybe Mr. Lamson was partly right. The boys didn't need coddling. Which was good, because her stomach remained queasy.

She paused and reshuffled the roses so the thorns wouldn't prick her. The largest one fell to the ground. She stooped to pick it up, but instead of grabbing the rose, she was the one who was grabbed.

Mr. Lamson held her constrained against him. The heel of his boot smashed onto the fallen rose, as if to hold it captive as punishment for Wallie's injury.

"Mr. Lamson, I'm afraid you're stepping on the flower I dropped."

His body went rigid against hers. "I thought… Weren't you about to faint?"

That wasn't exactly how she was feeling right at the moment. "I simply dropped one of the very things that created the mess to begin with." No, that wasn't fair. It had been her fault—the roses weren't to blame. Poor Wallie. And Robert. She blinked to rid the picture of their scrapes from her mind.

Mr. Lamson released her and stepped away, rubbing the back of his neck.

"I am sorry for making you stop the wagon," she said. "I just enjoy them so."

"The flowers?" He finally glanced at her, confusion clearly written on his face.

What else would she be talking about? "I know the thorns make them difficult to pick, but they remind me of…life." She stroked a petal between her thumb and middle finger. "The beauty of the roses outweighs the pain of the thorns."

He grunted and turned for the wagon. "Try telling that to those the thorns hurt." His tone implied they were no longer speaking of flowers.

"Everyone has to deal with their own thorns. It's what we do when we've been pricked by life's trials that demonstrates our character." She no longer regretted falling for Tom or enduring their failed engagement. Despite the embarrassment she'd experienced at the time, she was glad she hadn't married someone who didn't love her. Now she was starting to look back on the painful process with a portion of encouragement because it had brought her to here, teaching the most precious three boys. To a place where she could see the beauty in a dream she'd always wanted.

Chapter Seven

The morning clouds, not quite ready to wake, hung low and thin. The rocker complained beneath Hank, joining in with the rooster's announcement of daybreak. He took a sip of coffee and hurried to swallow. He'd never grown accustomed to the bitter taste, drinking it out of routine, not for pleasure—just as with so many things in his life.

While he rubbed his thumb along the lip of the mug, the front door opened, revealing Pa dressed in his work clothes, a grin on his freshly shaven face.

"Mornin.'" Pa walked over and rested his hip against a porch post. "Another chance to enjoy the beauty of the sunrise."

The rocker creaked louder as Hank fully rested against the wooden back. The mention of beauty brought Miss Wagner's words from yesterday to mind. *The beauty of the roses outweighs the pain of the thorns. Everyone has to deal with their own thorns. It's what we do when we've been pricked…*

Hank stifled a grunt before it released. Enduring the loss of Evelyn and also his father-in-law, and then Miss

Smith tricking him and running off with his money…if those events weren't thorns, what qualified? And what had he gotten in compensation? Where were the so-called beautiful parts of his life? Sure, he had wonderful sons, but it wasn't fair they'd never gotten to appreciate and love their mother as he had.

Pa eased into the other rocker. He whistled a tune, some hymn Hank hadn't thought about in a while. "Unless you have something pressing for me to work on, I'm going to spend some time in the wood shop today," Pa said.

Hank thumped his knuckles on the armrest. One of the many products from Pa's wood shop. "We need another rocker, do we?"

Pa stared down into his coffee. "The Johanssons stopped me in town last week, asking how much it'd be to make them a matching set. So I reckon a rocker may be in another porch's future."

"Guess that means they liked their wedding gift." He'd never doubted it. Pa's woodworking skills outdid anything on either side of the Missouri River. "I'm sure you quoted them a price that's far lower than fair."

"Life isn't about making money."

Hank hadn't forgotten. Money had brought more troubles to him than it was worth. If only they hadn't moved to Missouri… "You're right." Hank stood, tossing the rest of his coffee in the dirt beside the steps. "We have all we need and then some."

"Rushing off? You're going to miss my favorite part of the sunrise. There's just something about how the sunlight makes little rainbows on the dew. Like tiny promises from the Lord."

Hank didn't need anything from God. Not when the

Lord had only handed him thorns. The smell of grease gave him an excuse to ignore Pa's comment about promises and rainbows. "Breakfast's cooking. I'm going to see if Ma wants help."

Except inside it wasn't Ma who was standing at the stove, flipping bacon. Miss Wagner had one of Ma's aprons tied around her slim waist. Her hips swayed back and forth in rhythm to the song she hummed. She turned, and as she noticed him, she grabbed the pan of biscuits with her bare hands, and dropped them suddenly on the table, nearly toppling the cup holding her roses.

One biscuit landed at her feet as she gasped and waved her hand in the air, shock and pain clearly written across her face. "Oh! That was hot. What was I thinking?"

"Are you all right?" Hank found the lard container and scooped some out. He spread it on her fingertips, careful to be gentle near the blister already forming. "Any better?" The expression on her face made him want to track down a doctor himself.

She slipped her fingers away before he finished examining her wound. "You probably think I deserve that." She glanced at the roses next to the disheveled biscuits. "I'm so sorry about yesterday. About the roses. The boys' hands."

"Miss Wagner…" He should have finished all his coffee, maybe then his tongue wouldn't be struggling to wake up. "Pain is never enjoyable no matter who's living through it."

Aside from the flower incident, their trip had gone smoothly. The boys had listened while Miss Wagner gave lessons. Her interest in the oil rig proved to be centered around learning how everything worked, incorporating the mechanics into her lesson. Never once did she hint at how much wealth his pumps brought him. She appeared to be a sufficient teacher. Which may pose a problem.

Despite her apology, compassion and teaching ability, she still wasn't what he and his boys needed, especially not with her long lashes and green eyes and soft touch.

Della readjusted her grip on the books in her arms. It proved to be quite a hike to where the boys had chosen to have their studies today. On the bright side, she didn't even have to prompt them for a location. Progress. That's what it was. As if God had provided her with encouragement to lift her spirits after the rose incident and burning her fingers this morning.

The farthest old barn lay to the left of the bunkhouse. A stoned well sat equally spaced between the two and a sheep pasture beyond. Alice called the old barn one of the sheds, but other than needing a fresh coat of paint, it stood as tall as the newer barns closer to the house. With the Lamsons only keeping hay inside, Della agreed with the boys that it was more than suitable for lessons.

As two hawks screeched overhead, Della paused at the barn doors in case she should run back to the coop and protect Mabel. Their dark feathers made it easy to follow the predators' course against the backdrop of the clouds. They circled before traveling on, not seeming interested in stealing any of their chickens, for the moment.

The top book in Della's arms fluttered open, and she

struggled to keep it balanced. "Boys?" The wind tickled the hairs around her neck, that for once remained in their directed bun. Mostly. "Could you get the door for me?"

A sheep bleated from inside the fence and the rooster crowed. But no boys made a single sound. They should have beaten her here after the way she'd spent far too long gathering the right books. She hoped that if she could spark Robert's interest in a character, he might come to enjoy reading, and then perhaps the fact that he was slower than Edward may not bother him as much. After digging through her trunk, she'd decided on bringing nearly all of them along.

Della walked around to the other side of the barn. Its smaller door was cracked open. She toed the door, wedging it wide enough for a view of the inside. Hay wasn't the only thing in the barn. Between the piles of hay, the three boys stood in a line, much like they had when they'd first met. Robert held a hand over Wallie's mouth. Edward's eyes were as large as little Lizzy Greene's had been when Freeman used to tease her with snakes. Something was wrong…but what?

"Did you not hear me call for you?" They could have at least told her to go around to the side.

They blinked at her. Were they frightened about something? What if there was a snake in the barn, and they'd been struck silent due to fear? Wallie remained focused on a spot above Della's head. Was there one slithering up onto the archway?

"Wallie? What is it?" Maybe it wasn't a snake but a beehive or wasp nest. That would make more sense, and would be, in her opinion, a greater problem. A single snake she could remove with a long stick. An entire angry hive was another matter.

She used her elbow to further open the door, but when Della stepped through the threshold, she wasn't met with a hiss from a snake or a sting from a bee. Instead, a rush of cool water splashed on her head and seeped into the front of her dress, drenching the books she'd spent so much care and energy gathering.

She sucked in air as the boys' laughter filled the barn, echoing off the beams. Her hair lay plastered to her forehead. So much for looking like a respectable teacher. She wanted to wipe her face, but her hands were still full—and her arms were shaking. She squeezed them tighter around the books to try and stop the unwanted movement.

Had she really thought she'd made progress with the boys? Clearly, she'd been wrong. Completely wrong. God had confirmed that she must prepare herself for her return home.

"Robert, Edward… Wa…" She struggled to say Wallie's name. This kind of prank wouldn't really have surprised her from Robert or Edward, but that Wallie should be party to such a thing… He seemed to have shared Freeman's personality, a tender and loving heart. One that cared about others. She thought they had formed a bond, but she'd been wrong yet again. That seemed to be the theme of her life over the past few months. She'd failed to see the real Tom. She'd believed that he loved her, but when he ended their engagement, Tom claimed he'd only ever pretended to care for her. Much like the boys before her.

Della shouldn't feel disappointed. Mr. Lamson had only given her a trial. It wasn't as if she'd ever truly had a place here. But she held on to the hope that she'd pull the boys over to her side, that they would come to want her to stay and teach. Well, their vote was as clear as the water dripping from her sore fingertip.

"Wallie. Take these books. Lay them in the sun. While they're drying, you will all take turns reading from the one that is least soaked."

The boys stopped laughing, but they didn't follow her directions. Wallie puffed out his bottom lip.

"Do you understand?" Not waiting for an answer, Della turned, catching sight of an upturned bucket tied with a rope above the doorway. She marched for the sunshine, letting the light guide her wobbly steps. The Lord had at least provided a way for the books to dry. She too needed a chance to wring out her feelings.

She set the stack of books on the grass and wiped any puddles off their covers. Most of her hair had fallen and hung around her shoulders. The ends, as a sort of cruel joke, sprinkled even more water down. The boys tiptoed through the barn's doorway, their eyes wide.

Addressing them, Della pointed to the books and water droplets rained off her sleeve. "These pages require warmth, and they need it now." And so did she.

Tears welled in her eyes. She refused to allow them out, yet she couldn't stop herself from wondering how long the boys had been planning such a prank.

"I'm going on a walk. You will be reading when I return. Do you understand?"

Wallie lowered his head, placing his bandaged hands behind his back. "Yes, ma'am." At his hushed response, Edward and Robert nodded.

Della bit the inside of her cheek. A teacher did not

cry in front of her students. "We will continue with the lessons when I return."

Keeping her pace steady and even, she rounded the side of the barn, blocking their view of her, and took what felt like the first breath since the cold water made her gasp. What Robert, Edward and Wallie had done was the kind of thing her brothers had done to her often—simple pranks. But it was entirely different having it happen to her as a teacher and not as a younger sister.

She struggled with delivering a punishment not molded by anger. Della knew how Mother would have responded, but her fury had only ever fueled her brothers' passion for more mischief. What Della wanted to teach Robert, Edward and Wallie was not that playfulness was evil, but that there should be a place and time for it and to choose their audience wisely. Their teacher was not a grand target.

As she neared the cabin, she heard banging from inside the small barn closest to the smokehouse. Roy was probably working on another wood project. The wash fluttered on the line ahead and Della shooed the rooster away with a wave of her hand. Another chicken squawked as Mabel ran up beside Della and flapped her feathered wings. Wallie was correct, his chicken was a treasured friend. She was certainly skilled at recognizing when something was wrong.

Della stopped. She couldn't go into the kitchen. Receiving another hug from Alice wouldn't make things better, only worse. Because in a few days she wouldn't be here to lean on Alice anymore, she'd be back home.

To the right of the cabin's roof, the old church building's steeple rose high in the clouds. Della picked up the front of her dress and headed up the hill. The smell of honeysuckle mixed with pine drifted through the air, soothing her. She expected the building to be half crumbling from Mr. Lamson's strong reaction to the idea of using it as a schoolhouse, but to her surprise, it stood as straight and true as all the other buildings.

The front door was blocked off, but around the back, the door opened with hardly any effort. The inside, however, was quite a mess. Pews, or what was left of them, lay broken in odd directions against one of the walls like someone had used the area as target practice and the benches as weapons.

Leaves and dirt stirred around her boots as the outside air circulated not only through the open back door, but also from a broken window on the side. Della shifted a piece of wood to clear a path, half expecting rodents and bugs to reveal themselves. Instead, something unexpected caught her attention. A tree.

In the corner, a sapling grew inside the abandoned building. Floorboards by its trunk bent upward around the hole in the floor. The tree was currently about as tall as Wallie, a well-achieved height for an indoor plant. Its leaves and branches arched toward the window, searching for the light.

She ran her hand along the pale green leaves. Life was blooming in a place that had been left to die.

Stepping farther forward, she reached the worn podium. It was slanted on its side with a mess of papers circling its base. She gathered a few of the pages, ones that had once belonged in a hymn book. The song "Take My Life and Let It Be" was on the top of the stack, the words still legible, barely.

The front of the sanctuary contained the only remaining intact and upright pew. Della sat, no longer caring that the wetness from the boys' prank clung to her, or that it would mix with the dust all around her to dirty her dress. With her elbows on her legs, she let her face rest in her palms and offered the words from the hymn as a prayer and plea for guidance.

She sang softly, "Take my feet and let them be…" Wherever God wanted her, that's where she'd go. When had she forgotten to focus on what God wanted in her life? Had He wanted her to flee from her embarrassment with Tom, or had she created new trouble by not trusting God enough to take care of her back home?

"That was real pretty, Miss Della."

Della opened her eyes and found Wallie standing outside the doorway, his chin tucked to his chest.

"Grandma sings that, too." He inched over the threshold. "Sorry about the water. Robert and Edward said it would be fun." Wallie peered at Della through his lashes. "It didn't look like you had much fun."

She sighed. "It wasn't exactly the lesson I'd prepared for the day."

"I'm not doing what you told us to do, but I can't read much. When I asked Robert to read to me, he yelled. My heart hurts… And I'm sorry I hurt your heart, too." He took a step into the church. "I like you for a teacher, Miss Della. I agree with Grandma, you're a keeper. I like having chalk. When do we get to write with chalk again?"

Della placed the marred hymnal pages on the pew, wishing she could set aside her scattered thoughts and hurt feelings so easily. It was a blow to realize that Wallie didn't actually like her—rather her chalk. "I will make sure you have a board and chalk in case it takes a while before your father hires another teacher. That way, you'll still be able to practice your writing."

Wallie tilted his head. "We need two teachers? Then will you be the one to teach me, and Robert and Edward can have the other one?"

"No. I don't believe your father intends to have two teachers," she explained patiently. "You'll just have one—someone who isn't me. I'm not sure I'll be staying here much longer."

"Is it because of the eggs or 'cause of the water? 'Cause if it is, then I promise I can be good. And no more tricks. Will you stay, then?"

Della crouched in front of Wallie and waited until he met her eyes. "Those things didn't scare me away." She took his wrapped hand in hers.

"Are you leaving 'cause I hurt my hand? It wasn't your fault that the roses had those thorns. God made them that way. And now I learned my lesson. I know how to pick 'em."

Della shook her head. The edge of Wallie's bandage grazed her blistered finger, but she didn't release his hand. "That's not the reason."

"Good. I want you to stay." His smiling face fell into a frown. "But we can't stay here. Papa says if he catches us in the old church then we'll get in a heap o' troubles. Not sure what kind of work heaping is, but even Robert doesn't go near here and it was his idea to put the water bucket on the barn door."

Della tried not to smile. Wallie could pack a lot into a sentence, but she didn't want him to think she was laughing at him. Not when the church seemed to be a serious issue. "Did your father ever give you a reason as to why you weren't to come here?" Did he not believe in attending church, or was it because he thought the building wasn't sound? As far as she could tell, the only thing not solid about the structure was the mess, but maybe there was a flaw she wasn't adept enough to notice.

Wallie pointed. "That's a tree." His arm remained outstretched. "It's growing. Inside." He took a step and stopped. "And it's as tall as me!"

"It is for now," she agreed. "But I'm sure it's still growing, just like you are. I wonder how long it will take to reach the ceiling?" If it managed to remain rooted for that long. Like her, its time here was likely limited. A tree wasn't meant to grow in a church.

Wallie dropped his arm. "We won't find out. 'Member, Papa don't want us here." He crunched a leaf with his boot. "Momma died."

Della hugged him against her side. "I know, honey. I'm sorry." She wasn't sure what had suddenly made him think of that, but she was sure the situation called for comfort.

"That's why Papa don't let us come inside."

"Because your momma died?" So it did have something to do with God. Perhaps Hank blamed Him for his wife dying so young.

"Robert says a snake bit her. But I don't remember no snake. Don't really remember Momma, either. But don't tell Papa. It makes him sad. Robert says she was praying when the snake bit her and Papa didn't know she was hurt, and then it was too late."

"Your momma died in here?"

Wallie shook his head. "She died in Papa and Mama's room. From the poisonousness pew."

"A poisonous snake?" Della said more to herself than to Wallie.

"Yep. A coppertop." He pulled up his pant leg. "That's why Papa makes us wear tall boots, in case we run into one." He let his pant leg fall back down. "But we're not supposed to kick at or chase after it if we see one. We're supposed to run far away and yell for him."

"I think that sounds like a good plan." Trailing after her brothers, she'd come in more contact with snakes than most girls, though she'd never heard of a coppertop. Was that a type that only existed out here? Or did he mean a copperhead?

"Robert says Momma was sitting up front when it bit her. Do you think the snake's still in here?"

Since his mother died years ago, Della doubted it. "Probably not. But since your father made the rule for you not to come in, we shouldn't go hunting around to find out."

Wallie looked at her, his eyes big and pleading. "You going to tell him?"

"You were only searching for me, so as long as you promise not to come back inside like he said, I think you won't have to find out what a heap o' troubles are."

Wallie wrapped his arms around her. "And I won't tell him about you. I don't want you to find out neither. It doesn't sound good."

She patted his back, and he leaned his head against her. "It sure doesn't." But her heap of trouble was that this boy beside her was stealing her heart.

Chapter Eight

Hank kicked off his muddy boots at the back door right under the kitchen window. The aromas of sugar, cinnamon and apples greeted him through the screen. His mouth watered. Yes, pie had to be on the menu tonight. Good. Pie fixed pretty much everything.

He patted his pants, brushing off a layer of dirt. "Smells—" A towel landed on his face, stopping him in the door frame. He removed the towel to find Miss Wagner stirring something on the stove.

"Shh." She waved toward the corner before snatching another towel and lifting a pot away from the heat.

Ma sat in the corner, resting in Evelyn's favored rocker—the one that Pa had given her when Robert was born. Her head sloped and a snore bubbled from her lips.

"She was asleep when I walked in," Miss Wagner whispered as she peeked inside the warmer, and then used the edge of her skirt to remove a larger pan. "Sorry I threw something at you. I couldn't rush over to warn you to be quiet because I didn't want the gravy to burn, and I also didn't want your voice to wake her. I assumed if she was tired enough to fall asleep preparing supper, she was tired enough to need to remain asleep."

Hank folded the towel he'd caught and positioned it on the table.

Miss Wagner followed his lead and placed the hot pans in her hands on top of the towel. "Thank you."

Hank nodded, softening his voice to match Miss Wagner's volume. "Are your fingers feeling better?"

She looked at him as if she'd forgotten she'd even had fingers. "Can't say they ruined my day."

Another of Ma's snores rumbled through the kitchen. Hank tilted his head, straining to hear any footsteps or wrestling matches he needed to break up upstairs. Instead silence reigned—aside from Ma's snores. "Where are the boys?"

"Front porch. Doing their arithmetic."

"It's a little late to be doing lessons." Even he was done with his work. His feet had nearly rejoiced when he relinquished his boots moments ago. Mr. Precious was more trouble than he was worth. The mule was nothing like hardworking, obedient Dorothy.

But Hank wasn't ready to give up on him. One day Mr. Precious would be trained enough to help with the harvest crop. Hank could out-stubborn his mule.

Ma's sewing kit lay beside a pile of clothes on the table's corner. A needle and string poked through one of the boys' shirts. New stitches zigzagged halfway through a hole in the sleeve. Hank wiggled his toes away from yet another hole in his sock. His skin pulled tight over the sore on his big toe. Perhaps he should have let Miss Wagner fix his socks—his clean ones, at least. Blister-free toes would be worth the tradeoff. If Ma needed help with the mending for a few days, and

Miss Wagner volunteered, maybe it wasn't the end of the world.

Miss Wagner reached for the pile and laid it on the hutch out of the way. "Sorry, I rushed in with all this when I smelled something burning."

Hank crossed his arms. "How much longer till the boys are finished for the evening?"

"They'll keep working for as long as you'll allow them, I suppose." Miss Wagner added a scoop of sugar to the pitcher of tea and mixed it. "I won't push them this hard every day. But today…" She poured a glass of tea and left it at Pa's normal seat. "Today they deserve to work longer."

Miss Wagner leaned against the table. Her thumb found a grain in the wood and circled around it twice before straightening the butter dish. She'd never had this much trouble meeting his eyes, even when the rooster tried to flog her, and she'd grabbed ahold of him. Had his boys become the handfuls he expected them to be? Why did that thought no longer sit well with him? "Were the boys troublemakers?"

She stood straighter and pushed her shoulders back. "Not anything I couldn't handle." Miss Wagner checked another pot on the stove. "Everything's ready. Do you know where Roy is?"

Ma's snoring ceased, and she stretched, opening her eyes. "Supper!" She sprang up, sending the rocker thumping against the wall, but she didn't make it far before she noticed the table. Plates and filled glasses at each place, two steaming pots on either side of the butter dish with the cup of roses in the center. Ma took Miss Wagner's cheeks into her palms. "You saved my gravy. Bless you, dear."

"Why don't you sleep in tomorrow?" Miss Wagner suggested. "I can get everyone fed."

Ma made a face. "Nonsense. I don't need any rest. I…" She rubbed her wrist. "I only needed a moment. And I got it. Thanks to you. Did someone call Roy, and where are those boys?"

"Still on the porch," Miss Wagner said.

"And being so quiet. I only planned on resting my eyes for a second, knowing how they usually carry on. I would have thought they'd have woken me up in plenty of time to check on my gravy. You must be getting through to them. As I knew you would."

Miss Wagner sighed. "Something like that." She stole a quick glance at Hank. Then untied the apron around her skirt and disappeared onto the porch.

"Are you feeling bad, Ma?" Hank asked when they were alone.

"I've got more blessings than complaints," she insisted, scurrying to the cabinet and stove and back. She stopped and rested her fists on her hips when she realized that Miss Wagner had already taken care of everything for supper.

"You'll tell me if you need a break," Hank stated firmly. "We're more than capable of hiring someone to help in the kitchen." They might be placing two want ads instead of just the one for a teacher.

"Don't be fussing over me. Della's picking up my slack."

"Ma, that's not the work she's hired to do. And she won't be here forever. Her trial…" He could talk the crew's cook into helping Ma some. That would solve some of his problems, wouldn't it?

Ma closed the kitchen hutch harder than necessary,

and the salt canister toppled over. "Her trial is proving how blessed we are to have her—and why we should keep her."

"I only promised her seven days and an honest decision based on our needs."

Ma opened her mouth, but then closed it. She patted his hand instead, and he relaxed his grip on the back of a chair.

"There's pie tonight. Ahh." She winked. "See? There's that handsome grin. It's been too long since I've seen it. That's all that was needed to get you out of your grouches. Let's get everyone seated so we can eat this meal Della saved."

"I'm not grouchy."

Ma raised an eyebrow, but didn't vocally agree or disagree. After the family gathered and Pa prayed, the boys ate without saying a word. Pa filled the unusual silence with updates on his latest woodworking project.

Ma scooted her chair back. "Hope everyone has room for pie."

Hank sure did. He spooned a generous bite into his mouth and an explosion of sugar and cinnamon mixed with the flaky crust briefly erased his burdens.

He pointed his spoon at his slice and back at Ma. "This is your best pie to date." He scooped more into his mouth, chewing slowly, enjoying the richness. Yes, pie made everything better.

"The crust is perfect. How did you get it so flaky?" Pie had always been his favorite dessert, but tonight it was extra glorious. Just like Ma had known he required a little extra to get over the rough day. Rough week. Rough three years.

"Mmm." Pa placed both elbows on the table and dug in for more.

Ma dished herself a piece and sat. "I didn't." She took a bite and closed her eyes in clear satisfaction.

Hank took a sip of water. Ma *didn't*. Didn't what? What was she talking about?

Ma opened her eyes and licked her lips. "Oh, good glory, it is a perfect crust. Isn't it, Roy?"

Pa shoved the last of his helping into his mouth. "Perfect indeed." At least that's what Hank assumed he'd said.

Edward scooted his empty plate forward. "Can I have another piece?"

Wallie scraped the last of his onto his fork. "Me, too."

"Sorry boys, the pie's all dished. And where might your manners be?" Ma shook her head, her warning fading as she savored her dessert.

"Will you make another for tomorrow? I'll even fetch the canned apples from the cellar. Or peel fresh ones if they're ready," Robert offered as he licked his already clean spoon.

"Well, that's kind of you, but I'm not the one you must ask. Della made the pie. It was all her idea."

Hank's fork slipped through his grasp, and he stared at Miss Wagner, who was picking at her dessert. Hank had half a mind to ask if he could finish off her piece since she didn't seem all that interested in it.

"Your pie was mighty good, Miss Della." Edward rolled the end of his spoon in his hand. "And I promise I won't play no more tricks on you tomorrow. Please... and thank you. Ma'am."

"I won't neither." Robert smiled. "Please and thank you, ma'am, too."

"Pie in exchange for a fine day of lessons? Is that the deal?" Miss Wagner said. Her expression looked stern at first glance, but Hank noticed the way her eyes sparkled in the lamp's light.

All three boys nodded, and Hank caught himself nodding too, before he stopped himself. What he should uncover was what they'd done to Miss Wagner. However, Hank's eyes sought Miss Wagner's barely touched slice again.

She laced her fingers together, resting her chin on top. Miss Wagner balanced the boys' need for discipline in a way he hadn't predicted. Nothing like his schoolteacher had done. Never would Miss Koch have entertained the idea of making him pie in exchange for better behavior. Too bad for her. He'd have taken the deal.

Letting Miss Wagner go after seven days was supposed to have been easy. She wasn't supposed to bond with Ma over mending and helping in the kitchen. None of the other ladies who came around these past few years had done anything like that. Not even Miss Smith.

Hank never would have guessed that Robert and Edward would willingly agree to do lessons, either. Though the most troubling surprise was why did she have to go on and make pie that topped Ma's? He didn't want anything clouding his decision concerning his family. But it took a stronger man than him to be indifferent to anyone who could make pie like that.

Hank quietly closed his bedroom door behind him and stopped in the hallway. Why was there light coming from the kitchen? No wonder Ma was falling asleep while preparing supper. She was rising too early.

The cabin windows remained dark, but a lone candle produced enough light for Hank to see it wasn't Ma seated at the table. Books were stacked around Miss Wagner and a letter lay folded by the pot of ink that she must have brought with her.

She hadn't moved when he'd walked in. Her steady breathing remained heavier than normal. Her elbow was up and her head rested in her palm. If she hadn't been dressed in something different from yesterday, he'd assume she'd been out here all night and had fallen asleep. But this morning she was in her green dress again. The one that matched her eyes.

He shifted his weight and gained a better view of the material his boys would soon be learning.

Sunshine in the rain.

Love.

He reread the words he could make out over her shoulder. The first line reminded him of another one of Ma's songs. The one that made him feel gloomy in spite of the uplifting message. The last word on the page made it obvious that this wasn't something on the boys' learning list, but rather some type of poetry, maybe even of the romantic sort.

Miss Wagner hunched a bit more in her position, and a few strands of her hair drifted down, covering part of her face. Hank made a fist, resisting the odd urge to push back her hair. He had tried some romantic sorts of things when courting Evelyn. Had brought her candies. Even packed a picnic. But never had he resorted to creating poetry. She accepted his proposal long before he'd had to get desperate enough to do so.

He leaned over Miss Wagner's chair a bit more. How did a man go about expressing things hidden inside his heart? Was that what he was reading? Some man's tender words to Miss Wagner? Had she rejected the writer's proposal? The poor man. Perhaps it was the Freeman fellow she'd mentioned in the wagon.

However, she'd not been upset when she spoke of Freeman. She had smiled at the picture, holding it close, protecting it from his boys' eager hands. That dimple had appeared on her face.

If a man was after Miss Wagner, and if their affection was mutual, why was she here? Hank didn't want to hire anyone who would soon be leaving to go home and get married. And why was he looking at something personal of hers? Ma and Pa already meddled in his private matters, and here he was being a hypocrite.

Stepping back, he forgot about the third board to the right of the hutch. When it creaked beneath his weight, Miss Wagner jolted awake.

Hank swallowed. "Umm…sorry?" He hadn't realized how out of practice he was at apologizing. Evelyn had always said it was one of his flaws.

Miss Wagner took in a deep breath. "No, it's quite all right." She touched around her bun. Everything was in place besides the little hairs by her ears that always seemed to have a mind of their own. A little like Miss Wagner. "I'd come downstairs to get a jump on the day. So thank you. I hadn't meant to fall back asleep."

She thought he was apologizing for waking her and not for reading her personal things. Yes, he definitely was out of practice. Now that he thought about it, he probably *should* apologize for waking her as well. Before he could reword another apology, she stood, revealing more of the paper he'd been reading.

What kind of man looked at someone else's romantic letters? One who no longer recognized when a woman loved him for himself or loved what he owned. He obviously had failed to decipher the difference in Miss Smith's attention. Likely, that made him the exact type of man who needed to read someone's poetry. To see what love looked like. He'd known it with Evelyn, but not anymore.

"Miss Wagner, I apologize. I shouldn't…" Hank rocked on the balls of his feet. He couldn't bring himself to glance at her, acting similar to his boys when they've been caught in mischief.

She picked up the page and held it out. "I guess you hadn't ever seen the ad your folks sent in?" She jiggled the letter. Its creases were worn, proving the page had been refolded several times. "You should read it. It's what brought me here after all."

"You're certain it's not a…" Hank cleared his throat. "A love letter from Freeman?"

Miss Wagner tilted her head questioningly. Hank's face warmed and the hairs on his neck lifted.

"From my brother? Never. This was the letter for the ad that I…" She took a stride away, bumping into the chair. "I mean, that your parents sent to the paper. Hopefully, you'll see why I thought it was a want ad for a teacher. Please."

The ink was smeared in a few places and the bottom corner torn. Whatever words were on the rest of the page, it was apparent Miss Wagner had given it more than a passing glance.

After he took it, her hand flitted to her neck and then back to the books that were stacked on the table. The candle flicked with the movement, creating shadows around the room. When her eyes locked on to his, he jerked his attention back away, silently berating himself for being so easily distracted. He should have already read the letter by now. Examining it, he noted that it was addressed to the *Hoosier Recorder*, requesting a printing of the words below.

> *Searching for a faithful, God-fearing woman*
> *Teaches with patience*
> *Balances discipline and laughter*
> *Hands that aren't idle*
> *Sunshine in the rain*
> *The greatest of these: love*
>
> *References required. Finer details once selected.*
> *Contact: Mr. Lamson. Kansas City, Missouri*

Hank read the letter three times and each round his heart raced faster. Yes, he understood how Miss Wagner might have thought his folks had been calling for a teacher. He folded the page back up. More than that, he felt the words. It bore Pa's name, but he knew that Ma was the one who'd toiled over each and every word. A letter that they hoped would bring him the perfect helpmate. The woman they were after would make an ideal bride and a cherished daughter-in-law.

However the desired woman could never be Miss Wagner. She was a teacher. She'd not only made that clear upon her arrival, but also with her interactions with the boys.

He handed the letter back. Rubbing at the spot where Miss Wagner's fingers grazed his hand. What wasn't clear was why that bothered him now.

At the sight of Mr. Lamson's tightened jaw, Della sank into her chair at the table. Did he truly not see how she'd misunderstood?

"I can show you the other letter I received from them—the one that told me I'd been chosen and included the money for my ticket." Della dragged a fingertip along a seam on her dress. "It too held no words about—"

He raised a hand to cut her off and almost hit her on the nose. "You can stay as the boys' teacher."

She opened and closed her mouth, unsure what to say. Eventually, she settled on a smile. She was going to get to stay? Roy had been right. God worked everything out.

She rose and stepped closer with her arms raised to hug him, yet when her foot knocked against his, she stopped. Alice gave her hugs. Wallie, too. Never Mr. Lamson. And now she'd gone and made things awkward in her excitement.

Thankfully, Mr. Lamson didn't cringe or move back, he only blinked. "You can stay…" His voice hushed as his focus dipped to her mouth. Was he waiting for her to say something else? He squeezed his eyes shut and shook his head. "That is until you find a more permanent position. It's clear that the ad my folks placed… I see how you could have mistaken…" He rubbed his thumb up and down the middle of his forehead as if pained by the miscommunication and all the confusion it had caused.

"You probably had lots of offers to teach, and you chose to come here." He sighed and leaned against the hutch. "To make up for the trouble we've put you through, you may remain until the end of the month or possibly through the next. But only if you've shown commitment in trying to find a more suitable position elsewhere. You are good with the boys, a gifted teacher, but I hope you understand we'll still be looking for someone…else."

Della bit the inside of her cheek. Stay, but leave. God was only providing her a little extra time. It wasn't what she'd hoped for…but wasn't it better than nothing?

"Do you understand, Miss Wagner?"

All Della could manage was to nod, so she did so until Mr. Lamson picked up his boots and left the kitchen.

Roy and Alice peeked from around the hallway wall, grins on their faces. Alice opened her arms and swallowed Della into a hug. "You get to stay."

"Only for a month," Della replied, then squeaked when Alice's response was to snuggle her deeper into her arms. How in four days she'd come to depend on this woman's strength and comfort was baffling. She'd lived her life without such embraces from her own mother, why did she suddenly find them so essential?

Because she felt loved here.

Alice took her by her shoulders and put some space between them.

Space. Right. She shouldn't get too attached.

Roy lifted Della's chin. He wore a grin. "Didn't I tell you God would take care of everything? Trust, not worry. One day at a time." With a wink, he put his cap on his head and whistled all the way out the back door.

Alice patted Della's cheek. She set Mr. Lamson's cup in the basin, humming and tapping her foot as she started breakfast.

Della placed the letter that started it all under the cover of her Bible. She stacked her books on top of each other and headed for her room. Roy's words flowed perfectly with Alice's melody: *Trust, not worry. One day at a time.*

If only "one day at a time" wouldn't stop at the end of the month. How long would Mr. Lamson allow her to stay if no one else would hire her?

Chapter Nine

Della fanned her face as she stooped over the broccoli plants. Edward read aloud while Robert and Wallie listened, or at least they were seated on the blanket. The listening part remained undetermined.

The chosen spot for the day had actually been on the inside of the chicken coop. However, being huddled with Mabel, the used straw, and the stale air wasn't a very pleasant option, especially when the rooster kept climbing in and out. The silly creature only entered to flap its wings and stare Della down with one eye before turning his head, allowing his other the same opportunity. The fact that the coop's air was nearly hot enough to fry the laid eggs made them all agreeable to the outdoor change.

Wallie perked up when he realized he was being watched and waved. Della stood and placed her fists on her hips. Wallie rested his chin on top of his knees. His focus didn't settle on Edward, but on Mabel as she pecked and scratched in the dust.

A sudden breeze arrived and Della swished her skirt back and forth, taking advantage of the coolness. While the boys did their morning chores after breakfast, she had finished writing her application letters, per Mr. Lamson's request. Though she tried not to think of how many would likely respond. She held no teaching certificate and very little classroom experience. Hopefully being willing to learn was a sought-after quality. One that may save her from returning home to confirm her mother's low expectations.

She cut off a bundle of broccoli like the boys showed her and tossed it into a bucket by her feet. She caught herself wanting to sigh, but instead sent up a brief prayer. Roy and Alice served as reminders for her to focus on faith instead of doubt. She was grateful for their example. Her parents only stepped foot in church on the holidays, never stopping to think how they were stunting the family's spiritual growth.

By contrast, Roy's genuine faith and deep wisdom brought her as much comfort as Alice's hugs. She believed him when he told her that God had provided this job to get her away from Tom at the paper. She hoped that meant that this was truly where she belonged— maybe even where she'd be allowed to stay, long after the end of the month.

Della uprooted some weeds, then opened her palm, allowing the wind to carrying the troublesome weeds away, much how she wished God would eliminate her problems. With one swift answer that would settle her situation.

The barn door slammed shut and the noise made the boys sit straighter. Wallie yelled a greeting to his father, who turned in a full circle before locating Della.

Mr. Lamson marched over, stepping over the small fence, and coming to her side. "You do understand that the extension of your stay isn't dependent on you performing additional chores. This should be the boys' duty."

"I don't mind helping in the garden." She carefully lifted a bloom and grasped more weeds near the budding pumpkins. "And I offered them a deal."

"Besides pie?"

In any other teaching position, bribery would be frowned upon. However, this job came with special circumstances, and she was willing to be flexible in her approaches.

"I want them to learn more," she explained. She wanted to make a difference in their lives before having to leave. "And work will always be waiting for them."

He pointed to the boys. "Boys must grow into men. Men must work hard. My boys do chores so they will be able to survive later on their own. You have enough on your plate just teaching lessons. You can leave the farm chores to my family."

Della shifted her feet, hearing what his words meant. She wasn't family.

She understood that, but she also knew that she was more than capable of helping in the garden. The boys were having their reading time, and she'd made Edward the leader. He was the better reader, but required practice in leadership. He wouldn't always have his brothers around to follow. Edward would have to discover his own way.

The boys had only been working together for five minutes. They needed another five to work on Edward's skill. "It may not look it, but I am working on my teaching skills. Edward is practicing his leadership skills. He allows Robert to make too many of his decisions. He requires encouragement and opportunity to put himself forward. And since I don't like to be lazy as the Bible advises against, I offered to work the boys' garden chores for the time being." Bribery was also included somewhere in there, but all she stated was the truth.

Mr. Lamson's forehead creased and his arms dropped to his side. "That actually sounds like a good plan for Edward. Why haven't I noticed that Robert is too bossy? I should have." He ran a hand over his face before gesturing at his boys. "Everything I do…"

"Everything you do, I imagine, is dedicated to the care and protection of those you love. You are their father, Mr. Lamson." She walked to the row of peas and snapped a few off without checking to see if they were ready like the boys had told her. "A good father takes his entire family into consideration." Unlike her father, who ignored her desire to be a teacher simply because it was inconvenient to him to give up the free labor she provided to the newspaper. "Everyone needs help now and again." Her voice was almost overshadowed by the snap from the beanstalk. "Shouldn't a good teacher also take her students into consideration? I am doing all I can to make my students become the best versions of themselves. I cannot always be with them, so I must seize every moment to instill these lessons."

As he silently nodded, sorrow drained from his eyes and something else replaced it. Before she could figure out the clouded emotion, he lunged for her. She didn't know how to react or have time to do anything more than produce a soft squeal as Mr. Lamson scooped her into his arms.

He cradled her to his chest and leaped backward. If his eyes had been fixated on her, she'd have thought this was some sort of unexpected and clumsy courting gesture. But the idea of Mr. Lamson being romantic toward her was entirely foreign.

He took another step, this one even more urgent. As he hopped the fence, his grip on her wavered, and she flung her arms around his neck to keep from getting dropped. "Mr. Lamson?"

The pulse on his neck matched the speed of her own. She followed his gaze. Peas lay scattered on the dirt. The bucket of broccoli was upturned. "Mr. Lamson?" she whispered.

He glanced at her then, his eyes full of concern. Concern and…fear? He licked his lips and broke their connection, frantically sweeping his gaze along the garden rows. Was he trembling? She pressed her palm to his chest.

"Papa?" the boys called from their learning blanket. Obviously, the sight of her in Mr. Lamson's arms was unexpected. It certainly was doing unexpected things to her mind.

"Stay back!" Mr. Lamson hollered, his voice oddly strangled and hoarse.

Robert disobeyed. "Why are you holding Miss Della like you did Momma?"

In response, Mr. Lamson only tightened his hold. "Don't come any closer," he ordered. "There's a snake in the garden."

Della inhaled a sharp breath. A snake? Like the one that bit his wife? It must be a deadly snake, because Mr. Lamson's legs were shaking. What could she do to help him?

"Robert, why don't you go find your father's gun? Edward, take Wallie to the porch." She touched Mr.

Lamson's chest again with her fingertips, his heavy breathing moving her hand. "Mr. Lamson, you can put me down."

He squeezed her closer. His attention remained on the garden while pearls of sweat lined his brow.

"You can't shoot the snake if you're carrying me."

It took a few seconds, but Mr. Lamson finally did as she suggested. He set her feet on the ground, and then stood in front of her, attention aimed at the pea plants.

She stepped beside him, knowing she could help. Thanks to her brothers, she'd been around too many snakes to count. She could hold her own against most of them. The only time she remembered being afraid of any snake was during one of their rare family picnics. On that day, she learned the difference in a snake that can do a rodent harm versus the kind that could harm a person. And most importantly, how to remain calm when faced with the type that would attack humans.

"Stay back." He grabbed her hand and laced his fingers through hers, halting her in place. She shouldn't be concerned with the warmth of his touch, or the way it fit hers better than Tom's cold hands ever had.

A movement at the base of a plant refocused her. "Is that it? I think it's curled right under the third bush. There." Before she could grab a stick or something, the snake slithered out, weaving a zigzag path for the shade of a pumpkin plant.

Mr. Lamson scooped her back up and ran in the opposite direction.

Della wrapped her arms around his neck, straining to see the snake over his shoulder. The snake raised its head and stuck out its tongue, giving Della the view she needed. "Mr. Lamson, you can put me down."

* * *

No matter how inappropriate it was to cradle Miss Wagner, she was crazy if she thought he'd let her down. "I'm going to drop you off at the porch. You'll be safe there."

"But I'm safe right here."

His heart all but jumped from his chest. Was she saying that she felt safe with him? Her green eyes didn't sway from his. He swallowed slowly, noticing the heat from her fingertips at the nape of his neck. Was he reading her correctly? It wouldn't be their first miscommunication.

Somehow, she smelled of roses and fit effortlessly in his arms. Her lessons and attitude had earned a chance to stay a little longer as the boys' teacher, and her words earlier of him being a good father had been encouraging. She was a kind and generous woman.

He gently released her on the steps, making her near to his height. His gaze slipped to her lips, inches from his own. They looked as soft as the petals of the roses on display on the kitchen table.

She pulled the bottom tip of her lip in between her teeth, making him wonder if she was thinking about kissing him. Maybe she was. She said she felt safe with him, and she'd been in his arms.

Hank tucked his chin, the desire to protect his family pulling at him. They were so close. He wanted to protect her too, hold her. Make sure she was safe.

"Papa?"

Hank blinked at Della then spun toward the door where his boys stood. Robert lifted his gun, and the reminder of why he needed it hit Hank abruptly. What kind of protector forgets about the danger? He should be focused on the snake that could steal someone else he cared about.

After checking the chamber, Hank marched to take revenge on the species that caused him and his boys so much suffering. If God hadn't created such an evil creature, it would have saved the world a lot of heartache.

Footsteps pounded on the porch steps, and Hank put out his hand to stop whichever boy wanted to help. This was his fight. He would win the final battle.

Looking back over his shoulder, Hank expected to warn Robert back, not Miss Wagner. "Della. Stop!"

She did, her eyes wide. It was then he'd heard his mistake. "Miss Wagner." Her proper name was harder to force out. "Please stay with the boys." He shook the gun at the garden. It felt heavier than normal. He wiped his palm on his pants and readjusted his aim. "I'll take care of the snake."

This time she didn't listen. "We don't need the gun. We're safe. It's only a bull snake."

His shoulders tensed, and Hank squeezed his fingers around the butt of his rifle. The snake he'd seen was a copperhead. Wasn't it? It wore triangle markings along its back. It had darted under one of the pea plants right near Miss Wagner. Unwilling to take any chances, he'd scooped her up. He failed in keeping Evelyn safe, but he would protect Miss Wagner. At least that's what he'd thought he'd done. Had he only made a fool of himself?

When she'd said she was safe, perhaps it had nothing to do with his protection, but was only because there was no real danger. He'd misinterpreted things again. He rubbed the back of his neck and glared at the sky. And for a moment he thought about praying for help. His gaze shifted back to Miss Wagner's parted lips.

"It had…" Her hands clung to the front of her dress. "Round eyes." She released her hold and smoothed the fabric before marching around him for the garden.

He ran and stopped in front of her, shielding her from the potential danger. She based her safety on rounded eyes? He hadn't noticed the eyes—and he wasn't sure that was really an indicator he could trust, either way. He wasn't going to let her step any closer. His boys didn't need to witness another woman with a snakebite, whether venomous or not.

"Mr. Lamson." The touch of Miss Wagner's hand on his arm was even softer than her voice. "A rounded head or rounded eyes means it's not poisonous. I'll get a stick and lift up that leaf and show you where it's hiding. Once we're sure it's not dangerous, we'll simply give it a new home."

Hank shook his head and clenched his teeth together. He wasn't putting her life in the hands of a brief inspection of a snake's head. She was worth so much more than that.

"I'm not afraid of snakes. I know—"

"I said stay here!" His tone came louder and harsher than he'd planned.

Wallie's face on the porch expressed how regrettable Hank's tone had been. His entire family had watched him yell at their beloved teacher.

Pa wrapped a protective shoulder around Wallie while Ma patted her chest, shaking her head. Even Edward and Robert grimaced.

Why had he gotten so upset? Yes, he was concerned with her safety, but was it more than that? Was he attempting to redeem his past by being the rescuer? Or was there something about her that affected him in ways he couldn't understand? When he'd held her in his arms, he'd forgotten his stance against remarriage. The desire to search for a woman that he could grow old with began pumping through him. The thought of a helpmate who loved him for him, and not for his money.

Hank hung his head. Miss Wagner didn't need his protection. She wanted to march right in there and prove how wrong he'd been.

"My mistake. It seems you don't need my help after all." With a flip of her skirt, Miss Wagner headed for the cabin.

Except he had wanted her help. Had wanted her to stand beside him and face the trouble at hand, and that was scaring him even more than the snake.

Why was getting what he supposedly wanted not making him feel any better? It didn't matter. Right now, he had a snake to move, and he couldn't need her help. He sure didn't need her distracting him from what he must do—protect his family, which also included shielding his heart.

Chapter Ten

Everyone else had retired to bed, but Della had stayed up to continue working on her secret project. She wrapped the yarn around the long needles and knitted a row on the sock she was making for Wallie. Only a few days ago she'd learned Wallie's birthday was coming at the end of the week. Socks wouldn't be a child's ideal gift, but she hoped it would be the thought that counted.

Rain on the roof was a constant drip. It hadn't relented since yesterday's sunset. Growing up, rainy days meant she'd have to remain indoors. Mother was never thrilled about allowing her to traipse after her brothers in any weather, and she drew the line when it came to playing in mud puddles.

When Mother would catch Della watching her brothers through the windows as they'd stomp in the puddles, she'd huff. *Girls cannot be ladies if they're covered in dirt, Della Mae Wagner. How can you expect to find a decent husband when all you do is act like your brothers?*

Of course, that didn't mean that Mother approved when Della showed interest in more ladylike pursuits, either. She'd asked Mother to teach her how to knit when she was eight. She'd thought her mother would be pleased that she wanted to learn something that was widely considered women's work, yet Mother only mumbled how she needed her extra time to prepare tea for her friends. While she enjoyed berating Della for not being sufficiently feminine, that did not mean that she was willing to sacrifice any of her own time to engage Della in more appropriate pursuits. At the end of the day, she'd rather criticize Della than help her. Thankfully Pastor O'Ryan's wife taught her how to knit when she started attending their church by herself as a teenager.

Della knotted off the final row and balled the remaining loose yarn. Whether Wallie wanted them or not, his birthday gift was complete. She ran her finger over the rows on the first sock and felt an irregular loop. She pulled it closer to the lamp and sure enough, she'd missed a stitch. Della sighed. She should be used to doing things incorrectly. Rainy days were reminder enough.

A noise interrupted the pitter-patter melody of the rain and Della paused, straining to distinguish the sound. She put the socks in the sewing basket and carried the lamp outside, shutting the front door gently behind her. The noise came again, almost resembling a meow. Had one of the barn kittens wandered outside and gotten lost?

Off the porch, the ground squished beneath Della's boots and fat raindrops landed on her shoulders, sending a chill down her spine. She shielded the lamp's glass chimney and called for the kitten, looking around carefully to spot the small animal. However, no animal needed rescuing tonight. Instead Wallie sat curled against the house with his knees pressed to his chest. Another muffled sob—sounding remarkably like meowing—came as he wrapped his arms tighter around his legs.

Della dropped beside him. Water seeped through her skirt and she suppressed a shiver even as she resolved to ignore the cold and wet. This sobbing child was far more important. Lifting Wallie's chin, she searched his face. "Honey, what's wrong? Why are you outside?"

The drizzle drowned out the lamp, easing them into the gloom of night. She set the now useless lamp on the ground and scooped the sniffling Wallie into her arms.

"Are you hurt?" She carried him up the steps and placed him onto the first porch rocker. Squatting in front of him, she patted his arms, his legs, searching for any injuries.

He whimpered while his eyes remained squeezed shut. She couldn't see him clearly in the dim light trickling through the windows, especially with his face turned away, but as far as she could tell, there were no stains on his clothes. No opened cuts. Nothing appeared broken. She stroked his soaked hair. "Wallie, honey? Now would be a great time to tell me why you're outside, all wet, when it's bedtime."

He hiccupped and wiped his nose. "I'm…going to become a rabbit."

Della rested her hand on his knee. Of all the scenarios she'd imagined the moment she'd found him—ranging from him falling from an upstairs window, to him wanting to play more in the rain like she'd encouraged them to do after their lessons—she'd never once came close to thinking about him becoming…a rabbit.

"You're out of your bed because you want to be a rabbit?"

"No." He sniffled again. "I never want to become a rabbit."

Right. That cleared up absolutely nothing. She dabbed a runaway rain droplet off his forehead, waiting to see if he'd say more. When he didn't, she prompted him gently. "Why are you outside?"

He used his other sleeve to wipe his tears. It left a smear of mud on his cheek. "Because that's where rabbits live."

Della stood; her fingers dug into her hips. "Okay, I think it's time to get you tucked back in."

He shook his head so hard the rocker fell forward. "I can't go inside no more."

She gathered Wallie on her lap, the rocker creaking under them. "Why don't you start at the beginning?"

Wallie leaned against her and she rested her chin on his wet head. He inhaled a shaky breath. "I—I... My teeth are making me turn into a rabbit." He took a piece of Della's fallen hair that had drifted to her shoulder and rolled it between his fingers. "But I don't want to live outside and eat grass. Grass makes my belly hurt."

Della rubbed his back, trying to sort through his answers and make some kind of sense out of them. His teeth made him a rabbit? That's why he was outside at bedtime, a nightmare? "Why don't you pretend your teeth make you into a boy, and then you can live inside and eat your grandma's cooking. I really like how she makes her eggs so fluffy. You don't want to miss out on those in the morning, do you?"

Wallie gripped her shoulders, turning his head into her chest. His body shook with a new round of sobs.

"Shh." Wallie's cries kept rhythm with the dripping rain that had gained energy in the stillness. She rocked and hummed a melody, hoping to soothe Wallie, but he kept crying. "Wallie, whenever you're scared, you can always pray. Anywhere and anytime. God's there. And you can also always hold my hand, too."

He slipped his hand into hers, yet his tears didn't stop. Should she pass this over to Alice? Or Mr. Lamson? They wouldn't mind being woken for this—and they'd probably have a much better idea of what to do. She felt totally lost—and more than a little ashamed of herself for not being able to fix this. Yet why would she expect to know what to do? She had no professional teacher training. No motherly experience. Was God providing this moment to show her that she deserved the childless future that awaited her back at her father's newspaper?

She scooted forward to stand, ready to hand the child off to someone better equipped to soothe him, but Wallie only tightened his grip, keeping her in the chair. "Wallie," she whispered. "You're going to have to help me understand. No one is going to make you stay outside and become a rabbit."

He took her thumb and placed it under the top of his front tooth. It wiggled back and forth. She smiled. Finally, they were getting somewhere.

"You're upset because your tooth is loose? Honey, that just means you're growing up. You're going to lose your baby teeth and get bigger teeth."

"Yeah, great big teeth like bunny rabbits have." He wrinkled his nose and Della refrained from telling him what a cute bunny he'd be. "Edward and Robert told me all about it."

Della rubbed his chilled arm. Ah, it was all starting to make sense. "Did they now?"

Wallie fell against her once again. He nodded as he wiped his nose on her shoulder.

"So they told you how they lost their front teeth, too? And how they never ever turned into rabbits? That they're still boys who get to sleep inside in warm beds and eat eggs and gravy and drink milk for breakfast? Wallie." She tilted his chin. The tears pooling in his eyes shined amongst the shadows. "They were only teasing. But it was wrong of them to get you so upset. I promise you, though—you're not going to turn into a rabbit. Not tonight or any night."

Wallie pulled back, squinting. "Does that mean they were wrong about you, too?"

"About the prank on me? Well, you guys really didn't need to be pouring buckets of water on anyone's heads, especially when I was holding lots of books that I wanted to share with you—"

"No." His eyes were swollen and he was shivering from the wet and cold. How long had he been outside, in the rain? His brothers had taken the teeth nonsense too far. "About you leaving us."

Della stilled her rocking. The week of her arrival she hadn't wanted to leave the Lamson boys because she didn't want to face what was waiting for her back in Indiana. But now? She ran her fingers through Wallie's hair, biting her quivering lip. "I'll be here for a little while longer." She looked over his head, seeing only the bleak night, hoping it wasn't foreshadowing her future. Now, her leaving would be a struggle because she cared for this family.

"Do you not like us anymore? We promised not to

be mean. And—and if Robert and Edward plan another trick, I'll tell you before it happens. I promise I will."

Della met his concerned gaze. "I will always like you. That's not why I have to leave."

"Is it 'cause Papa yelled? It was the snake that made him upset. Grandma said he wasn't mad at us. Or you."

"Your grandma's right." It wasn't anger that Mr. Lamson had displayed that day, but fear. The look he had given her had dug a hole into her heart and left her wanting to help him through his memories of his wife's death. If she was honest, he'd hurt her feelings by not accepting her help.

If only there was a way for her to bring him comfort as quickly as he'd whisked her away from the so-called danger. "But your father thinks you boys need—"

"For you to be our new mother?"

"Oh." Della placed her hand near her throat. "He… That wasn't…" Had Wallie or one of the other boys overheard Alice and Roy talking before her arrival about their plans for her to marry Mr. Lamson? Children had a knack for overhearing conversations out of context. "I came here to be your teacher, but your father believes you boys need a different teacher. That's why I can't stay."

Wallie glanced at the porch ceiling. "Okay." He jumped off her lap. Finished with his crying, and all done with his desire for her to remain with them, apparently. Someone else who so easily cast her aside. Della's heart stung as much as it had when Tom broke their engagement.

Wallie pushed his sleeves to his elbows. They were too wet to stay put, and they fell back to his wrists almost immediately. He twisted the fabric around his wrist and water sprinkled onto the porch. "Then you can stay and be our new mother. Grandma says my old momma was pretty, and funny, and made pies for Papa."

He switched to his other sleeve, ringing it out too, unaware of the squeezing he was doing to Della's chest. "You do all that. So Papa's right. We'll probably need another teacher when we move you to the mother spot."

Wallie hugged her, taking her common sense with him. "You'll make a great momma. Papa said your pies were better than Grandma's."

He hopped over the puddle he'd created and tromped to the door. Unlike the footprints he left on the wooden planks, the ones marked on her heart would never disappear.

Wallie was inside and stomping up the stairs to bed before Della had gathered herself enough to try and explain why she couldn't stay and become his mother. She rested her forehead in her palms and closed her eyes. If Wallie's plan could never work, then why was the possibility of staying forever with him making hope pound in her heart?

The icing around Wallie's mouth made his grin look even wider. The hat and boots Hank had given him had immediately been forgotten when Pa brought out his and Ma's gift. Wallie threw his hands in the air, sending a dab of icing to the tip of his nose. Who knew a bag of chicken feed would make a now six-year-old happy?

Wallie plunged his hands through the feed, spilling some of the grains onto the floor. Ma and Pa nodded and smiled, trying to keep up with another story of Mabel. Edward ran the toy train Isaac had carved and sent along for Wallie across the top of the table, and

Robert tiptoed over to the stove, lifting the towel over the leftover cake. Hank noticed that the scene was unfolding about the same as last year's birthday, except with one new addition.

In the corner, Miss Wagner stood with her hands clasped in front of her as if giving his family their space. She'd served the cake, served the sweet tea, even served the candied pecans. Ma had swatted her hands away at first, but Miss Wagner whispered something near her ear. Ma had frowned, making the creases around her eyes blend together along their edges.

"That ain't true. No matter what. Hear me?" Ma had said loud enough for Hank to catch over Wallie's excitement; however, the meaning was lost without more context.

Miss Wagner had apparently won because Ma sighed and went and sat beside the birthday boy, leaving Miss Wagner to serve. She'd been taking over quite a few of the household chores lately, on top of her teaching duties. She'd probably jump at the chance to leave when another teaching offer arrived since her position here had been anything but easy or typical. So why wasn't that comforting him?

Wallie opened the present from his brothers. "Wow!" Wallie's word was followed with a bit of a whistle. Hank couldn't believe his youngest was old enough to lose a tooth. Weren't the older boys closer to seven before they'd lost any of theirs? Hank sighed. Evelyn would have remembered—but Evelyn wasn't here, which meant that all the responsibility rested on his shoulders. He needed to outgrow his weaknesses and become a better parent. His boys only had one parent to rely on, so they deserved the best he could be.

Wallie squinted at the gifted stick and pulled at the attached rubber bands.

"It's a slingshot," Robert said.

Edward scooted his chair away from the table, bumping his arm against Pa's coffee mug. "All you gots to do is pull that band back. No. Here. Let me show you." He wiggled his fingers at Wallie.

Wallie pulled the stick closer to the bag of chicken feed. "I ain't a baby. I'm six now."

"Not like that." Robert reached over Ma and tried to take it from Wallie.

Wallie jerked it farther back and nearly stabbed himself in the eye.

"Boys," was all Hank could manage before Miss Wagner replaced the slingshot with a small fabric-wrapped bundle.

"Here's one more gift. I'm sorry to say it's not as special as the slingshot Robert and Edward made." By taking it away, she probably saved the room from witnessing another argument from the boys—one that might have ended with someone losing an eye.

Why couldn't Hank be as quick and adept when it came to handling his boys?

Miss Wagner inspected the slingshot. "This is fantastic, boys. Way to work together. I knew you'd come up with a wonderful gift."

Edward and Robert had full grins when they gave each other a high five, but the praise made Hank realize he was falling even further behind as a father. Shouldn't he have already instructed his boys to make each other gifts?

Wallie unfolded the fabric and lifted what appeared to be a pair of misshaped socks. "What are these?"

"Wallie." Ma gave him the stare down.

Della put her hand on Ma's shoulder. "It's all right, Alice. They do look a little strange, don't they?" She knelt beside Wallie. "They're socks. Freeman always wore wool ones when he went to bed on the extra-cold nights. I thought maybe you'd like a pair, too. But…" She took them and fitted her fist inside. "I messed up some of the stitching, so they're a bit crooked. If you don't want to wear them, we can always make them into hand puppets, instead."

She pointed at the top. "I can stitch eyes and a mouth. It would have to be in a different color besides red. Otherwise you wouldn't be able to see it."

Miss Wagner handed the gift back. "What do you prefer? Do you want to wear them as socks, or you want me to make them into puppets?"

Wallie rubbed his fingers along the crooked stitches. "Both. I want socks that are puppets."

Pa chuckled. "Best of both worlds."

Miss Wagner swept Wallie's hair off his forehead, combing it out of his eyes. Hank needed to cut all the boys' hair. If only they'd sit long enough to get it done.

"Sounds perfect. If you give them to me, I'll finish their faces tonight, and they'll be all ready for your inspection at breakfast. Does that sound all right, Wallie?"

Wallie placed the socks in Miss Wagner's hands, keeping his fingertips in hers. "I think you should call me Wallace now."

Wallace? The entire room fell silent. Even the train froze in Edward's grip.

"Oh…um…" Miss Wagner glanced at Ma, who wore a wobbly smile. Hank wasn't sure what lined his own face. Shock? Confusion? Wallie hadn't wanted to be called by his full name since he was old enough to understand that his mother had died.

Hank buried his nails into his skin. Once Wallie had learned Evelyn had called him Wallace, he'd not wanted to be called by that name anymore, thinking of it as just his mother's. He'd only answer to the nickname Hank had spoken when he'd first laid eyes on the roundest baby cheeks he'd ever seen. Evelyn, who'd chosen Wallace because it was her pa's middle name, encouraged everyone else to use his full Christian name, and everyone did until a few years ago.

Hank rested his palm on his knee, stopping the bouncing motion he hadn't noticed was shaking the table. Had Wallie gone through Evelyn's trunk again? Were there red socks inside that reminded him of his gift from Miss Wagner? Why was Wallie giving Miss Wagner, and only her, permission to use his full given name?

Miss Wagner's gaze clearly asked for help, but Hank couldn't even move enough to nod or shake his head. "Well…thank you. For letting me call you Wallace."

She touched the end of Wallie's nose, removing the icing without him even realizing it was there. "Do you remember the day we met?" She wiped her fingers on her borrowed apron. "You told me never to call you by that name. And you know what? I hadn't even called you Wallace yet."

Wallie nodded. "The sun made your hair shiny, and Robert asked if you were here to marry Papa. Remember that?"

Miss Wagner blinked quickly, her cheeks turning red. "I do." Her voice softened as she stood. "Do you remember what I told you yesterday morning?"

Instead of answering, Wallie tunneled his fingers through the feed bag.

"Don't forget. Okay?" Miss Wagner's voice sounded hoarse.

Wallie hugged the bag of Mabel's chicken feed into his lap. "Will you tuck me in tonight and sing Grandma's song but with your words instead?"

"If it's all right with your grandma…and your father."

Ma rose from her seat, gathering the dishes from the table. "Only if you scurry on up those stairs. Even birthday boys need to be fully rested to see those finished puppet socks. Edward. Robert. You head on up, too. And best be leaving that slingshot downstairs."

Edward tugged on Miss Wagner's skirt. "Can you make me a pair of puppet socks?"

"Is that what you'd like for your birthday gift as well?"

Edward nodded.

"And you, Robert," she said, turning to his oldest. "Are you too old for puppet socks?"

"No, ma'am."

Miss Wagner smiled. "You're right. No one's too old for puppet socks. Okay. Tomorrow during lessons we'll go over the calendar. You can each tell me when your birthdays are so I'll know when I must have your socks ready by. Be thinking about what color you'd like."

Edward pointed to the red socks in her hands. "They'll need faces like Wallie's getting."

Hank thumped his knuckles against the table. Time to get the boys upstairs. Miss Wagner didn't need to promise the boys socks for birthdays that were still months away when she'd more than likely have another job lined up long before then. "Enough dallying. Go change. I'll be up in a minute."

Wallie groaned. "Miss Della's tucking me in. You said she could." He wrapped his arm around Miss Wagner's, staking his claim.

Actually, Ma had implied she could. Hank considered pointing out that *he* hadn't given his permission... but it was Wallie's birthday. He supposed there was nothing wrong with Miss Wagner singing his boys a song before bed once or twice. Was there?

"It's all right, Mr. Lamson. I don't have to—"

Hank held up his hand. "You sing. Then I'll do the final tuck-in."

"You have to wait until she's done, done. I want her to pray with us after she sings. Then you can come up." Wallie nodded as if he'd been used to handing out orders all his life.

Hank crossed his arms. Fine. Birthday boy could get his way one night a year. Hank didn't feel the need to pray anyways. "Just for tonight."

Miss Wagner shooed the boys into action, while Hank and Pa helped Ma clear the table. Ma sent him to the stairs before the sink was empty. Miss Wagner's voice drifted along the upstairs hall. Her version of the song was a little higher than Ma's, just as he'd noticed on the day the rooster had tried to flog her. The verse he wasn't used to ended, and her prayer was filled with words all about his family, sincerity displayed in her tone.

He swallowed. She prayed like Pa, Ma... Evelyn. Like he used to when he believed God listened.

Hank pressed against the wall, resting the back of his head. There was more than enough space for Miss

Wagner to walk past and find the staircase, but when the boys' door opened, she stopped in front of him.

She twisted the red socks in her hands. "Will you…" She tucked that stubborn piece of hair behind her ears. Her gaze met his in the shadowed door frame. "Will you meet me on the front porch once you've finished?"

Hank grunted, more stunned than anything. Miss Wagner's smile didn't quite make her dimple shine, but it made Hank want to draw closer to her. To rest his hand on her jaw to see if he could make her dimple appear. The one he hadn't seen since before the garden fiasco. He shoved his hands into his pockets. She must have taken his nonresponse as an agreement because she moved past him and walked down the stairs without another word.

The heat where she'd touched his elbow moved up his arm and settled in his chest. He stood there staring in the direction she'd gone. She wanted to speak to him alone?

"Papa?" Wallie called from inside their room.

Hank shook his head. Time to tuck them in and make sure the boys felt safe for bed. He kissed each of the boys' foreheads as they snuggled their blankets to their chins. He shouldn't have been so surprised by Miss Wagner's request. She probably wanted to meet to discuss his boys' schooling. That's what teachers did. It didn't matter that she wasn't a typical teacher who made thoughtful and time-consuming gifts for his boys, sewed for his ma, or made him pie—well, not just him. Anyway, at the end of the day, she was still his boys' teacher, and it was perfectly natural for her to want to discuss their progress with him.

Or had she already heard from another school? He

couldn't let himself forget that she was seeking a position elsewhere. As soon as she found it, she would leave—just as he'd known she would all along, even if no one else in the family seemed willing to acknowledge that. He must remember he couldn't allow himself or any of his loved ones to get too attached. She wasn't staying, and that was that.

Chapter Eleven

The moon's glow silhouetted Miss Wagner's slim figure near the steps. At the sight of her, Hank tripped over the threshold and the screen door slipped through his fingers, rattling more than the door frame.

"Are you okay?" Her touch was on his arm again, doing odd things to him.

He stepped away, his back hitting the door. "I think I must be tired."

"I'm sorry. This will be quick. I decided you should hear what I told Wallie yesterday. I mean Wallace." There was a question in her voice as one of her hands cupped her cheek while the other arm wrapped around her stomach. "I think I prefer to call him Wallie."

Hank rocked on the balls of his feet. He preferred that, too.

The sound of dishes clanking in the sink mixed with the cicadas' chirped call. A sugary smell from Wallie's birthday treats hung in the air as if the celebration planned to continue on past bedtime.

"Wallie, he…well, he…" She walked to the farthest rocker, the one Ma always claimed. "During the rabbit incident—" Miss Wagner had told him about that, and he'd had a stern talking-to with his two oldest about teasing their little brother "—he asked if I was leaving soon." She looked at the empty seat beside her, then at him. No words exchanged, yet he understood what she asked.

He eased into the first rocker Pa had made once he and Ma moved over from Kansas. Originally it was meant to be placed in the parlor of their house. Hank had every intention of building Pa and Ma their own cabin in the valley near the old church building. But when his father-in-law passed, Evelyn had suggested his folks stay in the big house with them for a while longer. And after they'd lost Evelyn... Hank wasn't sure how he and the boys would have survived those following weeks if Ma and Pa hadn't been so near.

They'd been a life saver with his boys, his land, the chores, and especially with strengthening him.

Miss Wagner rocked beside Hank. "I told Wallie that you still wanted a different permanent teacher for them."

The waver in her voice made him grip the wooden handles. Was he right in thinking she wasn't the right fit, or was he just being stubborn?

A coyote howled in the distance, and Hank arched his feet in his boots. He should check and make sure the boys had locked up the coop. No need in having Mabel disappearing before she had a chance to try Wallie's birthday feed.

When he glanced at Miss Wagner, her eyes were closed. He cleared his throat. "Was that all?" If it were, then why had his stomach done flips upstairs when she'd suggested they needed to talk? Was it because he needed to apologize—again?

"Mostly." Her fingers flexed on the arm of the chair, and her rocking slowed. "I told him to enjoy the time we have left together. He…" She shook her head. "The rest were silly things from a five-year-old's mind. Oh, six. He's six now. Either way, nothing to worry over."

Miss Wagner had only been with them for a few weeks, but for some reason he was able to read this woman better than Ma. "What has Wallie come up with this time?"

She patted the apron flat against her lap. "Nothing you need to concern yourself with. I just told him to enjoy the time we had left together."

Hank studied Miss Wagner's profile, waiting for the punch line that never came. "What did he say to make you say that?" Hank pressed. "Was he upset about getting another teacher?"

She pushed her lips together. "Not exactly."

Hank was admittedly surprised to hear that. Of all the boys, Wallie appeared the most attached to Miss Wagner. Maybe her *enjoy the time we had left* was said more for her own benefit than Wallie's? It was possible his boys weren't as fond of their teacher as he'd imagined.

"Did you finish your application letters?"

"Hmm? Oh, yes. I left them on the desk for Roy to take to town days ago."

Hank nodded, appreciating her quick action—a trait that he prized. In this, and in many other ways, she'd been an excellent employee. He thought they'd all be at least a little sad to see her go. But his family had survived without Miss Wagner before, and they would again.

A mosquito buzzed near his ear, and he swatted at it. "How long do you think until you hear back?"

She stopped rocking and the insects quieted, too. "I'm not sure." She lifted an edge of her apron, twisting it into a ball. "If no one wants me after the end of the month, then I'll… I guess I'll…"

Maybe this was why she called this meeting. She was worried over the unknowns of her next position. She'd admitted that this was her first teaching post. Perhaps she needed reassurance that she'd find the right fit with her next posting. "They'll be plenty of jobs opening their doors for you. When they inquire, I'll be able to send a glowing report of your abilities. You have done quite well with the boys. In fact, I'm surprised Wallie wasn't sadder about the idea of seeing you leave."

She bit her lip, and stared down at her fingernails.

"Is something else bothering you? Have the boys done more than make Wallie believe he was turning into a rabbit?"

Miss Wagner rose, walking to one of the porch posts. "Wallie doesn't mind that you're going to hire another teacher because he believes that I will be…staying." She folded her arms around herself, looking out at the night. "Just moving to another position."

Another position? There hadn't even been an official teacher opening when Miss Wagner arrived. "What other position is there?" Had Ma talked about her staying on to handle the household chores—cooking and handling the mending and such? Having Miss Wagner around to help with those things had shown that Ma needed some help. However, hiring someone—anyone—should be discussed with him before any offers were made. Like it or not, this was his home, and he wanted control over the decisions for his family.

Miss Wagner exhaled loudly. "Mother."

"I'm sorry?"

"It isn't your fault, nor mine, but that's the new position Wallie believes I'm moving to."

Wallie wanted Miss Wagner as a…mother?

"Please don't worry." She waved her hands in front of her like a white flag. "I—I set him straight. And that's when I told him to enjoy the time we had left together."

Finally, she met his gaze and faked a smile. From the first day, he'd been able to tell which smiles of hers were real and which weren't. He'd done a fair job in the past year of ignoring the features of all the other women who'd shown up at his house, until Miss Wagner and her dimples. He didn't want to be so aware of her, but he didn't know how to stop, other than sending her away. And his family wasn't making getting rid of her any easier.

She blinked and muttered something about socks, leaving him on the porch. Alone, like he claimed he wanted to be.

Life's burdens and the stress of parenting alone hunched his shoulders, and he rested his forehead on his fist. He couldn't let emotions get in the way of his decisions like he did last time, with Miss Smith. He squeezed his fingers into a tighter fist. If he was to allow Miss Wagner to stay and be a permanent teacher for the boys, he'd have to be one hundred percent sure that she was the right choice.

* * *

Della glanced up when Mr. Lamson came around the chicken coop.

"Miss Wagner, if you don't mind, I must steal the boys for a while." He shielded his eyes from the sunshine with a bunch of empty flour sacks.

"Awww." Wallie scrunched his nose and tapped his piece of chalk against his blackboard. "I want to do lessons."

That boy sure knew how to lift her spirits. If only she could remember to call him Wallace as he'd requested a couple days ago.

Edward pointed at the sacks. "I don't want to do whatever those mean."

Mr. Lamson tossed a sack to each boy. "Means we're picking apples."

With a groan, Robert crumpled the material into a ball. "Can't we pick them later?"

Did she need to clean out her ears? Since when was picking apples worse than lessons?

"Later the sun will be hotter. Come along."

Wallie used the bag to wipe off his board. "I'd rather not do apples at all."

"Wallace." Miss Wagner gave him the eye.

"Fine." Wallie huffed and pushed to his feet. "But will you come, too?"

Mr. Lamson stopped, and Robert almost rammed into the back of him. "I didn't mean for you to have to help as well," Mr. Lamson explained.

"I don't mind." Della collected the chalk and boards and placed them into her basket of school supplies. There was no need leaving the chalk out to allow the chickens to get a taste of it—her supply was running low enough as it was. She'd considered ordering more, but it hadn't seemed worthwhile if she was going to be heading back to Indiana eventually.

Wallie threw his bag into the air. On the way down, it slipped through his fingers and he nearly toppled over trying to snatch it before it hit the ground. "Can we play the game, if Wallie gives an apple to Mabel how many does he have left?"

"Yeah or if Wallie loses one more tooth, how much longer until—"

Della raised her brow, and Robert's smirk disappeared.

"Sorry, Wallie," he mumbled as he stretched the bag out of its crumbled form just to squish it down again. "Boys don't really turn into rabbits."

"It's okay. Plus, if I turn into a rabbit and have to live outside, I can live inside the coop with Mabel. Right, Miss Della?"

Della shook the leaves and dust off the blanket. "Sounds like a perfect plan." She smiled, but stilled when she caught Mr. Lamson's stare. She touched her face around her mouth and cheeks, worrying that something from breakfast was hiding there. But the boys, always ready to point out someone's misfortune, would have let her know if that was the case, wouldn't they? She folded the blanket in half. Was he upset over what Wallie had told her? It wasn't like it was her fault.

Mr. Lamson cleared his throat. "I had only meant to recruit the boys."

She reached for one of the bags in Mr. Lamson's hand, her fingertips meeting his skin. "I can handle gathering apples." And she wasn't ready to give up all her time with the boys yet.

His shoulders pushed back, but he didn't release the bag or move away from her touch. Warmth spread from their connection, trickling up her arm. Her breath caught in her chest and she licked her lips. Did he really not want her to go? "Unless I'll only get in the way?"

He looked at her mouth. "What's in the way?"

Della dropped her hand. "Will I be in the way picking apples?"

Hank shook his head. "Just didn't expect you'd want to come along and do more work."

Wallie slipped his hand into hers. "Of course she wants to come with us." Wallie pulled her forward. "Last ones there have to throw the rotten apples to the cows."

Della ran with Wallie until his hand disappeared from hers when Mr. Lamson lifted him onto his back.

Wallie twirled a fist in the air. "Yee-haw!" He leaned into Mr. Lamson. "Faster. Faster, Papa. We got to beat Edward and Robert. I don't want to touch the squishy apples."

Robert passed Della in a sprint. "Hurry, Miss Della. The rotten ones have worms. You won't like those."

Della laughed along with the boys, the race bringing back memories of chasing after her brothers. They bolted past Roy's wood shop and Della waved as he stuck his head out through the door.

He tipped his hat, shaking his head, a grin on his tanned cheeks.

Mr. Lamson slowed a bit when they passed another barn. A momma and baby sheep called to them as they jogged beyond the fence. At least ten apple trees lined the field in two rows. Smaller trees than she would have thought to produce such a harvest.

"Looks like a tie." Mr. Lamson eased Wallie to the ground. "Guess we'll all have to feed the cows the rotten apples."

Edward picked an apple off the ground. "Not Miss Della." He flipped it over twice, checking for rot, before taking a bite. "She shouldn't have to touch the yucky ones." He wiped his mouth with his elbow. "She won't want worm guts on her hands."

"Why thank you, Edward. You're a true gentleman." She stepped closer to him. "But do you want to know a secret?" All three boys leaned toward her. She cupped her hands around her mouth, whispering loud enough for them to hear. "I'm not afraid of worms."

Wallie stuck out his tongue. "You would be if you bit one in half." He shook his whole body. "Don't like worms. But Mabel eats them. Papa, can I give a few apples to Mabel, too?"

"If you work hard without complaining."

They made quick work of the task, placing the apples in different bags based on their quality. The boys gathered the ones already on the ground while Della and Mr. Lamson picked the reachable ones off the lower branches. Flies and bees buzzed around. Roy's whistling was heard before he came into view with Alice holding on to his elbow. Robert tossed an apple toward them. Roy caught it and shined it on his shirt.

"My, my, that was quick," Alice said, inspecting the bags and the near-emptied grass.

Mr. Lamson wiped his brow. "Had some fine helpers."

Roy took a bite from the apple, crunching through its red skin. "That you did. Good job, boys. And Della." Roy winked. "We'll enjoy some apple butter soon." He rubbed his stomach while directing his grin at Alice. "That is if we get ourselves on into town. Ma needs sugar. Can't believe she's done near runned out. You've never let it get so low before."

"Am I not allowed to forget a thing or two? Besides, who here forgot to order himself some nails last week, hmm?"

Roy jiggled a low branch, releasing a stubborn apple. "Hank, do you need anything while we're there?"

Hank pulled off another apple and tossed it in the not-rotten-yet bag, as Wallie called it. That bag needed the bad spots cut before the good sections could be used. "Just check the post. I know it hasn't been too long since you sent off Miss Wagner's letters, but there might be one back."

Roy looked between Mr. Lamson and Della. Finally, he raised his brow at Alice. "Her letters?"

"The ones about her next teaching position."

All three boys stopped collecting apples and stood.

"I didn't mail any teaching letters," Roy said.

Mr. Lamson crossed his arms, looking aggravated. "Why not?"

Roy pulled on his shirt as if he wore his itchy Sunday best. "Never found any."

Everyone turned to Alice, who placed her hand on her chest. Her concerned gaze sought Della's. "I never saw any letters, either."

Mr. Lamson set down the apple bag he'd hoisted onto his back. Gone was the fun they were having. He looked like she'd dumped his apple pie on the ground.

"I put them on the desk in the front room."

"Maybe they slipped off somehow," Alice offered. "Wouldn't be the first time that's happened."

Mr. Lamson rubbed his jaw. "You promise you actually wrote them?"

His doubt stung, but she forced herself to meet his eyes, unflinching. "Yes, I promise."

His stare bore into hers. "Then I think it best if we go search for them."

With nothing to hide, she refused to lower her head. She'd never lied to him. Once they found her promised letters, it'd further prove her dependability. And maybe he wouldn't have any reasons left to replace her with another teacher.

Edward sat on the tree swing Pa had made by slinging two ropes around the maple's lowest branch with a board fastened between them. However, Edward wasn't swinging, just pulling sections off a leaf and leaving only its stem. He rolled the bare stem against his thigh before flicking it off and picking up another leaf from the pile on his lap.

Hank placed his boot on a raised root and shuffled the bag of apple cores in his arms. "What're you making?"

Edward released the leaf and watched it float to the grass. "Grandma told me to sit outside."

"You don't have chores or lessons?"

He ripped off the points on the newest leaf victim. "My belly hurts."

Hank set the bag in the dirt, wiping his hands on his pants before placing his palm against Edward's forehead. It didn't feel especially warm. Hank squatted and Edward's brown eyes followed his movement. No glassiness to his gaze, and his skin wasn't pale. Maybe, just maybe, God was looking out for his family this time, and there wasn't illness to contend with.

"Grandma already did that." Was his voice scratchy sounding?

Hank steadied himself by grabbing ahold of the rope swing. "Is it only your belly? Or does your throat hurt, too?"

Edward shook his head. "Just my belly." There was a pause, and then he added, "You shouldn't have gotten upset with Miss Della after she looked for her letters."

Was that the cause of the stomachache? Worry caused the body to do all sorts of ornery things. Perhaps Edward wasn't sick, only concerned about Miss Wagner's feelings. Though he wouldn't say he'd actually yelled at her, but he had gotten a little steamed. Still, she'd deserved his sternness this afternoon. There should be consequences for breaking a promise.

The wind stirred the leaves, and a squirrel flitted its tail then scurried higher into the tree. Hank took a seat on the ground, leaning his elbows on his knees. "You know I don't tolerate lying." He sounded like his boys, giving an excuse for his hurtful actions. But Miss Wagner had started the trouble by promising him she'd written the letters when she obviously hadn't. He was being more than fair by giving her a second chance to write and send them.

Edward pushed the leaf crumbles off his pants. "It wasn't her fault Grandpa didn't find her letters."

Hank waited for Edward to say more, but the boy seemed utterly absorbed in pulling on a string on the edge of his pants where Miss Wagner had sewn a patch. A sign the boy was hiding something. "Edward, you know you'll be in less trouble if you tell me the truth now than if I figure it out for myself later. And if you're covering for your brothers' sake—" or even for his folks "—it's just as bad as if you did the deed yourself."

"I did."

Finally, the truth. "Okay. You did what?"

Edward grabbed ahold of the ropes and rested his head against one. "I hid Miss Della's letters."

"You…hid them?" Hank stared at Edward. Miss Wagner wrote the letters like she claimed? "Why?"

He shrugged. "Didn't want her teaching other kids. Robert said that you were making her leave when she found other kids to teach."

So there really were letters. Meaning he'd been cross with Miss Wagner for no good reason. Hank closed his eyes. Why did he have such a hard time trusting?

"She laughs at Robert's jokes. Even the ones that aren't funny, and she gives Wallie piggyback rides, a-and she lets me…be the leader sometimes." He shrugged again.

"You want her to stay?"

"If I give you her letters, do you have to make Grandpa post them? Can't she stay longer? She knows bigger words than Grandma and doesn't have to squint at the books when she's reading. I like how she sings Grandma's song. And she smells like flowers even when there's none around."

She did always seem to smell like roses. Hank couldn't pretend he hadn't noticed. He gathered the bag of apple cores. "You'll give me those letters. Then you must apologize to Miss Wagner." And he'd need to, too. "Tomorrow you will help Grandma wash the breakfast and dinner dishes. And you'll sweep the coop and add fresh straw on top of your other chores and lessons."

Edward straightened on the swing. "Then she can stay?" The boy didn't even seem upset about the punishment—he just kept coming back to that question.

Hank shook his head in weary resignation. "Thank you for telling me the truth. But you can't take something that isn't yours just to get your way. When you're older you'll understand why a different teacher needs to replace Miss Wagner."

Edward sank back against the rope. "So when I'm bigger I'll understand why you don't like Miss Della?"

Hank sighed. The scent of apple cider drifting on the breeze did nothing for the twist in his gut caused by his son's frown. Edward may never understand why Miss Wagner should leave. It was not because Hank didn't like her, but because everyone was starting to like her being around a little too much. Including himself.

His family had faced enough heartache already, and Miss Wagner was a special kind of lady, one who wouldn't remain unattached forever. He feared especially for Wallie's soft heart when she decided to leave them in a year or two. If Hank didn't protect the boys from potential hurt, who would?

Chapter Twelve

From Hank's spot in the field, the cloud of dust billowing and the amount of thundering hooves beating in the distance signaled trouble approaching—something worse than when his typical woman visitors approached. The women came one at a time. This appeared to be a whole posse of people headed his way. He'd thought the men had taken it a little too calmly when he'd fired a few of his oil workers for misconduct. There'd been some grumbling, but they hadn't put up a fight when they were escorted away. He should have taken their revengeful murmurs seriously, especially when the offenders had been known to play faro with outlaws.

A low tree branch swatted his face as he hopped over a pile of logs, yet he didn't slow down. Ma, more than likely, would be in the house. Pa was probably in his wood shop. Where were his boys? Not at the big maple tree. Back at the red barn? Where had Miss Wagner mentioned having lessons? She'd said something about the sunshine, hadn't she? How it might be one of the last chances to walk the creek before fall fully kicked in. Now would be the only time he'd be glad if the boys had disobeyed his orders and gone down to the old bridge. The bridge wasn't completely trustworthy anymore, but at that stretch of the creek, they would be out of the way if attackers came. If the boys had gone to the *new* bridge, however…

Hank's gut cramped and not because of the distance he was running. If they were at the new bridge, they'd meet whoever was arriving first. He swung his arms faster, forcing himself to pick up speed. Everyone's safety was on his shoulders.

"Papa?" Edward waved his arms over his head to draw attention to where he stood, near the water pump closest to the house.

"Thank You—" Hank bit his tongue. He was not about to thank God for protection when He hadn't bothered to save Evelyn.

Hank rested his hand on Edward's shoulder and sucked in air. "Where are your brothers?"

"Wallie's inside with Grandma. Robert's with Grandpa. Miss Wagner sent me to—"

At least she'd gotten them away from the potential danger. She was resourceful and remained composed enough to keep the boys calm, too. Edward didn't appear the least bit worried about the incoming trouble. "She's in the cabin then?"

"Grandma, yeah."

"No, Miss Wagner?" When Edward squinted, Hank knew the answer. "Edward. Where is she?" Was that a shout from the intruders or a neigh from one of their horses?

"She's in front—"

Hank sprinted for the front yard. The thundering horse hooves were too close. There wasn't time to grab his gun. He had to get to Miss Wagner and protect her before his vengeful ex-workmen reached the top of the hill.

Miss Wagner stood before the porch steps. As she turned with the broom gripped in her hands, her eyes narrowed with concern. He skidded to a halt in front of her, keeping her safely behind him.

With his back a mere breath away from Miss Wagner, he felt her shift her feet, but he reached his arms back to bracket her between them. His chest heaved and his lungs pulled tight. He'd arrived in time to protect his family. Now, if only he could handle the angry arrivals with wisdom, they might all get out of this encounter alive.

"What's going on?" Miss Wagner whispered from behind him.

"I'm protecting you."

"… From a preacher?"

Hank's arm slacked in surprise. "What?"

Miss Wagner pointed over his shoulder to the approaching wagon. "Isn't that him?" She tried to walk around him, but he stepped with her, keeping her behind him. "Did Edward not tell you? Alice has prepared some treats for his visit and didn't know if you'd like to join us."

That didn't explain why the preacher was traveling so quickly in a wagon. He normally visited on horseback. Plus, Hank had been certain there'd been more than one rider heading their way.

"Howdy-hey." A much deeper voice than Reverend Miller's made Hank move closer to Miss Wagner. A wagon, pulled by four horses, crested the hill. Two strangers sat aboard, neither of whom were the preacher.

Nor were they the men he'd fired. Was the driver one of their outlaw acquaintances?

The stranger raised his hat, revealing dark hair with white streaks peppered throughout. He hollered at his team and after the horses steadied, the man helped a woman off the buckboard.

Surely, if this man had brought his wife, he wasn't looking for a battle. Were they new neighbors to the east? There was talk of Pinkerson allowing a few homesteaders on his property. However, that didn't explain why dust was still rolling up the trail. There *were* more horses thundering toward his family. He hadn't been mistaken after all. Could this couple be a decoy to allow the coming troublemakers to sneak up and surround them?

Why couldn't his employees behave properly? Then he wouldn't have had to fire them, which had caused this strife in the first place.

Miss Wagner nudged him and whispered, "Didn't you hear him? He asked if you were *The Mr. Lamson*."

How had he missed that? Hank stepped forward. "That's me. What can I do for you?"

The man stroked his mustache with his hand. When he smiled at the lady beside him, a slew of wrinkles mapped his face and proved there to be quite the age gap between the couple, given that the woman looked quite young—more a girl than a woman, really. "We've moved to the area recently, and we heard about you, Mr. Lamson. Thought we'd better try before we lost the chance."

A chance at what? At Pinkerson's land? Or possibly a job with his oil crew? The man tipped his hat again, and the sun reflected off the gun on his hip, making Hank inspect the man for more clues of his intentions.

Hank rotated enough to glance at the cabin, while keeping an eye on the strangers. He and Miss Wagner were about three paces from the porch. If things turned ugly, he could provide enough cover for her to make it inside.

"Heard you're a father. I know you appreciate wanting the best for your young'uns. We share that in common, see. We faced all kinds of critters along the Texas border and I decided that was no place for Rosie. No siree." He shook his head and patted the lady's hand next to him. "We're starting over here in Missouri. Bought the tailor shop. It's only a skip away from the train depot. I want to be near my kin. Future kin, too. And after only being in town a few weeks, every time your name's come up, well...let's say the West needs more men like you, Mr. Lamson."

"All right?" What else was he supposed to say? Normal men didn't go around handing over their past, present and future to strangers. Hank's heartbeat was trying to return to a slower rhythm. This sure didn't *seem* like an attack. The stranger either was no threat to them or was an excellent hustler.

Hank studied the man's horses and wagon. Nothing out of the ordinary, except there were so many. The man kept ahold of a grin, as did his Rosie beside him, appearing to be harmless. But outward appearance could be misleading. He looked closer, searching for any signs of deceit or a vicious agenda. Where the man had dark eyes and hair, the woman had blue eyes framed by light brown hair. His nose was the first thing you saw, whereas hers was turned up at the tip. The only thing they shared was the purple-colored fabric of his shirt and her dress and a close-lipped smile.

Rosie whispered in the man's ear. He took off his hat and came forward. One step. Two. Rosie marched right with him, her hand on his elbow, neither one reaching for a weapon.

"Now." The man stretched out his hand. "I know Rosie here looks young, but she's a sweet girl. Her mama taught her well. She's quite good with little ones. And I dare say, she makes the best corn bread this side of the Arkansas River. Have you ever had it Texas style?"

Up this close anyone could tell why Rosie might be good with kids. She looked like she belonged in a schoolroom herself. If this was the man's wife, he was a cradle robber.

"Corn bread or not we hoped you hadn't made your final decision yet." The man checked over his shoulder. His team of horses hadn't stomped or moved an inch, yet more dust arose from the valley and another full-speed wagon dashed between some trees, climbing the last little hill before the cabin.

A bit of tension left Hank's body when it proved to be only Miss Vogel, with her brother beside her. Hank hoped his peach and pecan trees survived their usual shortcut through his second orchard. If that accounted for the dust of more horses that he'd seen in the distance, then maybe this wasn't an attack by ex-workers after all.

Miss Wagner's nearness felt warm through his shirt. She must think he was a fool. She didn't need him to stand before her and protect her from any danger. There wasn't any. He'd panicked for no reason—again.

She picked a loose piece of string off his shirt. "I'm

going to check on Alice. I believe she's unaware of the extras arriving."

While Miss Wagner's words dropped to a whisper, Hank found himself leaning into her voice—until he was jarred by a question coming from in front of him.

"Would you consider it, then?"

Hank turned back to the uninvited man. "Consider what?"

The man returned his hat to his head, and his boot spurs jingled with each step. "Marrying my daughter, Rosie."

Hank blinked at the girl holding on to the man's elbow. On the one hand, it made sense that she would be the man's daughter, not his wife. But on the other hand…they couldn't be serious, could they? Why would he marry a girl he'd never laid eyes on before?

"I understand you have another potential candidate with the preacher called out here today and all, but…" The man eyes grew wide. "Oh? Is this the lady? I thought she was one of your children being shy behind you."

Miss Wagner stepped beside Hank. "Good morning. If you'll excuse me. While you all finish discussing the future, I'll go make sure Alice doesn't need any help with the refreshments."

"Miss Wagner." Hank pleaded with his eyes for her to remain. If she stayed by his side maybe the man would think he was spoken for and Hank would be spared having to come right out and say that he didn't want a marriage to a schoolgirl.

"Perhaps I heard wrong in the shop. Are we too late? Have you already chosen a wife from the mail-order ad? Did we miss the preacher? I could have sworn we beat him here."

"How did you hear—"

"Sir, if you're referring to the confusion about me, you should know that I'm…" Miss Wagner's cheeks shaded red as she placed her hand on her chest, and dipped her head. "I'm only the boys' teacher."

Hank wanted to argue. She'd become much more than that.

"There was a bit of a mix-up over the want ad."

Rosie released the hold on her father and curtsied. Her dress revealed more skin than Hank would have allowed his own daughter to show if he'd had one. Flowers were tucked into her dull hair that hung around her shoulders.

"Excuse me." Miss Wagner nodded at the man and turned.

Hank blocked her way. "Where are you going?"

She sent him the reprimanding expression that she used on his boys. "To help Alice. You don't need me out here," she said the last part without meeting his eyes.

Oh, but he did.

"Do you have any of them almond cakes?" Miss Vogel's brother called from their now parked wagon. He hopped down, leaving his sister to settle their horse. Clyde nudged Rosie's father's shoulder when he joined them. "It's the only reason I agreed to make a trip out here today. You really should move closer to town, Hank."

"Clyde." Miss Vogel's jaw locked around a clenched smile.

Miss Wagner paused on the front porch. "I can check.

Be right out with some tea. I imagine you're parched from your long journey."

"You better believe it. Dodging those low-hanging tree branches is no easy matter." Clyde winked at Della, running his fingers up and down his suspenders. His grin slipped when he noticed his sister's wrinkled nose. "What? If she's only the teacher, then we both got a shot at being hitched."

Hank cleared his throat, but it didn't soothe the sudden burning sensation in his chest that had nothing to do with the possible damage the Vogels had done— yet again—to his fruit trees. Clyde was no match for Miss Wagner. She wouldn't become strapped to Miss Vogel's lazy brother, not if Hank had anything to say about it. It would be his duty to protect her. This time the threat was real.

Miss Vogel inspected her brother as if he was an animal ready for auction. "I think she'd be a better fit for Mr. Klement." She wagged her finger in the air. "Or maybe William."

"The old inn owner?" Hank found himself asking with a sour taste in his mouth.

"Well, his son. Yes. I think he'd be better equipped to handle a woman like her." She raised her brow toward her brother. "You heard she was a teacher?"

"I ain't stupid," Clyde hissed. "Momma told you to stop calling me as such."

Miss Vogel parted her thin lips and hissed something else at her brother. Hank wiped his hand over his face. If he wanted to hear squabbling siblings, he'd allow his boys to behave poorly.

"Mr...." Hank gestured toward Rosie's father.

"Bransky."

"Mr. Bransky. Your daughter… I'm certain she'll make someone a happy husband one day further in the future. But she's…"

"She's entirely too young." Miss Vogel faced Mr. Bransky, fully set on redirecting her distaste from her brother to someone else. "For goodness sakes, he doesn't need another child. He already has three."

When Clyde shrugged, he nearly took Rosie out with his shoulders. "Three's too many if you ask me."

Hank ground his jaw. He *hadn't* asked him. Hadn't asked for anyone to arrive in the middle of his work-day, ruining the progress he had made this morning with Mr. Precious. "Mr. Bransky, you and Rosie are invited to stay for a bite before you head back into town. Welcome to the area." Hank extended his hand and Mr. Bransky hesitated before shaking it. "I hope your shop does well."

Miss Vogel and Clyde waited, expectation painted on their faces, but Hank only nodded. They knew the drill. Ma would feed them, and Hank would try his best to remain scarce. Of course, usually he did his best to avoid interacting with them at all during their visits, but their normal routine flew south when he tried to protect Miss Wagner and only managed to become a part of the welcoming committee.

"Hank." Miss Vogel clung to his elbow, digging in her fingernails like a hawk latching onto its prey. He didn't know which he disliked more, her claiming his arm or her using his given name as if she'd earned the right to be so familiar. "I'm in need of apologizing. I'm entirely sorry."

She opened a fan with her free hand as if to bat away all of Hank's logic. "I haven't been here in a few weeks. I…" She fluttered her lashes and fanned her face. "Well, I misunderstood what your ma said about Miss Wagner. It really was silly what I assumed." Her fingers tightened around his arm, and it almost felt like she was squeezing them around his throat.

"But then I overheard Nicolas in town yesterday. Nicolas Davidson—you know, he's one of your work hands."

What kind of boss would he be if he didn't know who he employed? "I know Nicolas."

"Did you know he's sweet on little Mary Poe? Don't you think they'll make a fine pair?" When Hank didn't reply she looked to her brother. "Don't you think so, Clyde?"

Clyde rolled his eyes.

"Anyway, Nicolas mentioned that you weren't engaged to Miss Wagner at all. That she was just a teacher for your boys, and that she'd be leaving soon. A true miscommunication if I'd ever been a part of one—and to think it all started with your folks placing that want ad, going behind your back to order you a stranger for a bride. So when I heard your mother had sent for the preacher, I knew I had to get right out here to save you from another one of her schemes to try to force you into marriage with someone *she's* chosen instead of the person you want." Her lips puffed, and she dragged her finger along his chest, making Hank cringe.

"How could she have overlooked what we share? Well, today's the perfect day to set everything back on track. If you're about to visit one of your oil pumps, I'd love to tag along. Maybe Alice or Miss Wagner could pack us a picnic? Then we could spend even more time together." She fanned her face and almost poked herself in the eye. "I won't let your mother trick me into going away. Never again."

"Wait!" Everyone turned to find Miss Appleton struggling to make it up the hill. "I'm here." She rested her hand on her stomach and bent over beside the two waiting wagons. She looked exhausted, as if she'd run all the way from town, but she still managed to gasp out, "Don't choose the mail-order bride or Miss Vogel. I'm here."

Hank glared skyward. Why on this green earth was another lady here?

Mr. Bransky left Rosie's side and gave Miss Appleton his arm to lean on. Yet his kindness was met with a scowl once her gaze discovered Rosie.

"Don't you think your girl there will get in the way of the affections Hank and I share. We've a history together. You might as well head on home."

When they were in line with the rest, Miss Appleton straightened her light blue skirt and forced a smile. She too wore ribbons in her hair like Rosie and Miss Vogel. A bundle of flowers were clutched in Miss Appleton's hand. Back when the women first started visiting, they'd bring Ma a bouquet, but these ones were different. The ribbons tied around the flowers matched each woman's corresponding hair ribbons.

Hank pulled his shirt collar away from his skin, taking in Miss Appleton's appearance. Then Miss Vogel's. Rosie's. All dressed in their Sunday best. More than enough ribbons and ruffles to go around, looking ready to be brides. They'd all misunderstood why Ma had sent for the preacher, assuming there was to be a wedding. One they planned to stop, and swap themselves in as the bride.

He didn't know the true reason why Reverend Miller was coming, but he knew it wasn't for a wedding. Hank struggled to figure out how he could explain the situation to an audience who wouldn't allow the truth to reach their ears.

"My pa's wagon wheel broke before the bridge. He told me to hurry along before you chose." Miss Appleton gripped the flowers in both of her hands so tightly, the stems bent. "Don't worry. He'll get here. He wouldn't miss walking me down the aisle to you."

"So you really are choosing a bride today?" Mr. Bransky said.

Hank massaged his temples. He chose for everyone to return to where they came from. He'd liked the morning better when all he had to worry about was Mr. Precious pulling him through the mud.

"I know you needed time to grieve, but—" Miss Vogel rubbed his arm in a soothing gesture, oblivious to the fact that her touch only made his skin itch like he'd rubbed against poison ivy. "I can help you stand up to your mother. Telling her who's perfect for you so we can have more time to court, or I'm ready to marry you now if you want today to be our special day."

"Me, too." Miss Appleton lurched forward, narrowing her eyes at her assumed competition.

Miss Vogel wrapped her other hand around his arm. "We're in this together. Everyone will see. I'll just keep visiting like I used to before I misunderstood what your mother said. Every day I'll visit just to be here for you, if that's what you need. But I'm ready. Now. My brother's here. He can give me away. Why should we wait on our future? I'll make the best Mrs. Hank Lamson."

"How, when you don't even know his real name?"

Miss Appleton raised her chin higher. "You'll never regret choosing me, Hiram Robert Lamson."

Hank would have pinched the bridge of his nose if his arms weren't practically pinned. What he regretted was not going with Isaac to the pumps far, far away today. When he opened his eyes, Reverend Miller and his horse had reached the parked wagons, his bushy eyebrows lifted, taking in the gathered group. The reverend often visited with his folks and was aware of Hank's feelings on God. Sometimes, that put them at odds. Today, he could become Hank's best friend if the man would help him get rid of his guests who had upped their tactics to see themselves hitched to him.

Reverend Miller slid from his saddle. "Howdy, folks, what a pleasant sight to see so many here."

"More than enough witnesses for the wedding, don't you agree, preacher?" Miss Vogel demanded.

"Wedding?" Reverend Miller pressed his Bible against his chest gawking at Miss Vogel.

"As long as it has the proper bride." Miss Appleton batted her lashes while Miss Vogel leaned close enough to lay her head on Hank's shoulder.

"Well, I didn't come quite prepared for a wedding. Alice and Roy sent for me because they had some questions on a few passages in Romans."

Miss Vogel patted Hank's chest and released a cackle. "Oh, what a wonderful mistake this time. I feared you were sent here to marry off Hank." Miss Vogel's carefree laugh couldn't disguise her greed or make palatable her earlier undertones against Ma. "Then Hank, you're free to take me on a quiet ride. Just you and me of course, so we can make plans for our future?"

"No, he'll be taking that ride with me," Miss Appleton spat out.

Reverend Miller coughed. "Well, now, everyone is welcome to stay for our Bible discussion. Hank, will you be studying with us today or taking one of these ladies out for a ride?"

The back of Hank's neck itched. These women would never leave him alone. Next week there'd be more of them returning to their usual rotations of trying to call on him. Ma's dropped hints that he was engaged to Miss Wagner had worked for several weeks. What peaceful days they'd been. Yet now there were additional women joining the hunt for a wedding ring.

He wiped his palms on his mud-splattered pants. They would never stop their visits until he married one of them.

The front door whined opened and Miss Wagner walked onto the porch, a tray in her hands, looking more at home than he felt in this situation. Her focus on Hank seemed to be asking whether he was going to invite them over or if she was supposed to. Her inner beauty shone far brighter than any of the other ladies standing near him. He never got annoyed at her voice, or her laugh, or the way she argued with her brother, not that they were around to argue with, or how she didn't seem to notice that he had money.

All Miss Wagner worried about was taking care of his family, including him. Even when he'd jumped to the wrong conclusions, she'd proved herself trustworthy, good with his boys, and easy to talk to. He couldn't pinpoint when she'd become the perfect fit for his family, but she had. He'd spent far too much time creating excuses why Miss Wagner wasn't the right fit to see that she actually was ideal all along.

"Would everyone like to rest under the shade of the porch?" she called. "I'd imagine it's quite warm in the sun."

"Here." Clyde ran up the steps. The first board bowed under his weighted footsteps. "Let me help you with that."

Miss Wagner gave Clyde a smile, and Miss Vogel blocked Hank's view. Had it been the one with her dimple? Clyde swept his hand across Miss Wagner's as he reached for the tray and the hair on the back of Hank's neck rose.

When Miss Wagner laughed at something Clyde said, Hank spun around. "Reverend, this may shock us both, but I think I'll stick around for a while." He had an idea that might protect both Miss Wagner and himself from future trouble.

Chapter Thirteen

As Miss Vogel's brother, Clyde, took the tray, Della rewarded his kind gesture with a smile, but placed her hand behind her back and wiped it on her dress.

"Did you make any of these? If you're half as good of a cook as Alice then that would be enough to make me happy." Clyde slanted the tray and the dishes clinked against one another, sliding to the edge. "Where's Alice's almond cake?"

Della leveled the tray, saving the four slices of pie, bread, cheese, and apple butter from tumbling to the ground. Considering more people had arrived, with barely any notice given, Della thought the spread was more than adequate. Mother would have simply served tea or coffee.

Clyde frowned, making the mole hugging his nose appear to grow larger. His broad shoulders towered over her, and he eyed her fingers that was lifting the tray as if they were as appetizing as the desserts.

She hid her hand back behind her once more. "I've yet to try one of Alice's almond cakes, but I can attest that the apple butter is delicious."

Alice's jaw had dropped when Della had delivered the news about the extra visitors. "At least it worked for a while," she'd muttered before tasking Della with slicing up some bread.

From the corner of the porch, the boys watched their guests with scowls. Mr. Bransky and Rosie stood beside another man and woman Della hadn't met. Presumably, the man was the pastor Alice had originally invited, which had started the whole miscommunication with the others.

No wonder Hank had first assumed Della arrived to marry him. It appeared all of the ladies in the vicinity were eager to wed Hank at the drop of a hat.

Wallie slipped his hand in hers, and she tried not to stare at Miss Vogel as she nuzzled her head against Mr. Lamson's shoulder. Did Hank have feelings for the woman?

Alice bumped the porch door open with her hip while the tea pitcher sloshed in her hands. Her gaze focused first on Della and then widened when it switched to Clyde.

Clyde crowded Della and sniffed her hair. "Mmm. You smell pretty." His breath was hot against her neck and she wrinkled her nose at the hint of soured milk. "I'd be glad to take you for a walk, Del—"

"Clyde," Alice said, her tone stern. "Why don't you set the tray on the arms of the rocker there."

"You didn't make any almond cake."

"Yes, well, why don't you go let everyone know the treats are ready?"

"Everything but my almond cakes," he mumbled, doing as asked with less willingness than that of the boys upon the news they had to pick apples. Thankfully, Clyde's manners were none of her concern.

Alice moved the plates around and checked the pocket of her apron with her free hand. "Goodness. Didn't I put a knife on this tray?" She tapped her finger against her cheek.

Mr. Lamson took the porch steps two at a time. "Can I help do something? Anything?"

Alice surrendered the pitcher and pulled him aside, whispering loud enough for Della to hear. "It's starting again. And you wondered why we did what we did, bringing Della here. Those ladies are not a match for you. The newest addition's a mere child. What are we going to do? Because it's making me tired already, and their visits haven't even officially begun again."

He stared into the tea pitcher. "I'm working through an idea."

At least he wasn't seeking comfort from any of the other ladies. Not that it should bother Della if he did.

Alice rose on tiptoes and peeked around him. "What's caused them to visit all at once?" Her attention landed on the latest arrival. "I'm guessing it isn't to share in our devotional time?"

Hank groaned. "Miss Vogel overheard about your mail-order ad and that Reverend Miller had been sent for. She assumed he was to perform my wedding. She's determined as ever to become your daughter-in-law."

Miss Vogel led the guests to the porch and Reverend Miller shuffled forward and introduced himself. He smiled at the dwindling desserts Della offered, and waved her on to the next guest.

Each of them settled in around the ledge, leaning against the columns and enjoying the shade, except

Clyde, who made himself comfortable in one of the two chairs. If any of the boys had been sitting there, she would have reminded them how a gentleman would have offered the rocker to one of the ladies. Apparently, Clyde's generosity in carrying the tray earlier used up all his manners.

He scraped his plate clean and pointed his fork at the tray. Food rumbled around in his open mouth. "Will we be able to try some of that cheese soon?"

Alice's grin looked forced. "The quicker you get a knife, the faster everyone can get through their treats." She sing-songed the words near Mr. Lamson's ear.

Hank handed the tea pitcher back over to Alice and held open the front door. "Miss Wagner, you coming?"

"Oh." She didn't know why he needed her help finding a knife. She'd seen him on multiple occasions locate one himself. Was he rattled over all the guests and the idea of remarriage? She waited until Alice had filled the glass she held with tea, then rested it onto the tray balanced on the rocker. He probably needed more hands to help prepare additional food. She could search for something else for Reverend Miller to eat besides bread.

However, inside Mr. Lamson walked past the counter where the knives were tucked into a block of wood and marched right out the back door. He paced on the other side of the screen, occasionally pausing to shake his head. Did he not handle large crowds well? Her oldest brother, Johnnie, was like that.

Della grabbed a knife and another helping of apple butter.

Mr. Lamson reentered the kitchen. "Miss Wagner." His eyes explored her face, and then he took the items from her hands. At his light touch, a tingle danced along her skin where his fingers joined hers. He placed the items down and leaned against the table as if unable to stand on his own.

The front door opened, and Wallie poked in his head. "Grandma's wondering if you ran away with all the knives?"

Mr. Lamson didn't move. His back remained toward her. Della reached around him and handed a knife to Wallie.

"I'll hide a piece of cheese under a napkin for you," he promised in a confiding whisper. "But you better hurry. Grandma says Clyde has a hole in his stomach. He may go hunting and find your cheese."

Could Wallie get any sweeter? Especially with his missing tooth, the occasional whistle only adding to his character. How was she ever going to survive saying goodbye to him? To them all? "Thank you, kind sir." Only six years old, and he had better manners than Clyde. "Carry the knife carefully, please."

He gently tucked it into his palm. "I'm no baby, 'member?"

Della went back to grab more apple butter and discovered Mr. Lamson stooped in the same position, gripping the corners of the table. "Mr. Lamson? Are you ill? We can handle the guests if you want. Why don't you go lie down?" Had he gotten too much heat? It seemed the sun had forgotten that today had planned on being fall.

When he didn't move, she pulled out a chair nearest him. "Why don't you sit?"

He fell into the chair and dropped his face into his hands. "I'll get you some water and a piece of bread, too," she offered. "Might help settle your stomach. Or do you need anything else?" Had the idea of remarriage frightened him that much? It wasn't like anyone was forcing him to go through with picking one of those ladies.

"I think…" His face planted in his palms, muffling his words. "I need you to marry me."

Della's hand shook more than the pump when she shoved the handle down. The water ran over the rim of the glass, dripping down her wrist in a cool, steady stream. He hadn't said what she thought she'd heard, had he?

She wiped up the puddle on the floor and found herself drinking from the filled cup instead of handing it over. No, Mr. Lamson wouldn't have asked her to marry him. Despite what his parents had originally planned, he was very clear about his stance on the matter. Did he perhaps want her to *carry* him?

She peeked at him through the half-empty glass as she continued to drink. The view distorted his profile. Maybe he was truly ill. Or tired. Or both.

With the last of the water drunk, she lifted the handle to refill it. "I'm sorry, what did you say?" If he wished for her to carry him, she'd find Roy. She could shoulder some of his weight if Mr. Lamson spread his arms on them both.

She set the full glass in front of Mr. Lamson. The only noise in the room was the chatter drifting from the porch. He stared at the table. His face was quite pale, indeed. Even more so than when he had read the want ad his parents had placed. Yes, she had to find Roy. After they got Mr. Lamson into bed, she'd fetch a rag for his head, and then start on some broth. Make some tea, and maybe find some crackers.

"Della…" His voice halted her in front of the back

door. When she turned to face him, she saw his eyes were packed with an emotion she couldn't read. The same one they'd housed when he'd placed her on the porch away from the snake.

He stood to his feet, steady for the moment. "Marry me." He took another step. "Please."

The kitchen air grew thick in her lungs.

"You will, won't you?" They both startled at Wallie's excited question. He stood in the doorway, a napkin filled with a piece of cheese in his hand, and a huge gap-toothed grin on his face.

"I—I…" She rubbed her chest and inhaled. She'd come to care for this family. For the boys, Alice and Roy. Even for Mr. Lamson, but marriage? He'd seemed so set on her leaving. So why on earth would he want to marry her now?

Wallie jumped through the house, rattling the dishes in the hutch, and wrapped his arms around Della's waist. "You get to be Momma Della. I told you it was a good idea." Wallie squeezed out whatever air and common sense were left inside her, a hug equal to that of Roy's strength. "God answered my prayers like you said He would."

Della brushed his hair across his forehead. She had told him to pray, that God would listen and answer, but marriage wasn't exactly what she encouraged him to pray about.

"Wallie," Mr. Lamson's voice hitched. "Go on outside until we've finished talking."

"Yes sir, Papa." He hugged Mr. Lamson, then lifted his chin and grinned at Della. She ran her fingers absentmindedly through his hair that needed a haircut. "Please say yes, Momma Della. I'll be good forever if you do. Promise." He embraced her once more before bouncing away with equal enthusiasm. If telling her he'd save some cheese hadn't taken her heart, calling her Momma Della sealed the deal.

"Miss Wagner... Della... I... They won't stop. I mean..." The weight of Mr. Lamson's sigh displayed the depth of his frustration. "Those women will keep coming out here. I thought if they believed Ma's story about me courting you, then they'd stay away. But they're back, and there's more of them."

If Mr. Lamson truly was asking her to marry him, he was doing a horrible job. Even Tom had sounded more genuinely committed to sharing a life with her and in the end, he claimed he never actually loved her.

"If we were married, they'd have to stop coming out here. Right? Then maybe my peach and pecan trees would actually produce. Every time Miss Vogel drives out here, she takes a shortcut through that orchard and gets her wagon spokes too close to my trees, harming the bark. They've practically stopped growing. And... and... Miss Appleton's father wanted to see how soft my sheep's wool was and he left the gate open on one visit. The sheep wandered away and we never found three of them."

He took a quick breath and held out his hand. "And when the ladies from town are visiting practically every day of the week, Ma has less time with the boys and runs out of flour faster than a frog eats a fly. And... and...you don't irritate me."

If she wasn't so confused, she might have laughed. She didn't irritate him? That's why he was offering his hand in marriage? That and some misfortune with trees, sheep and flour. She blinked, waiting for him to add something else. Anything else, to say that he cared for her or wanted her to be part of his family. But he didn't. "You want to marry me because I don't irritate you?"

"Well, yes."

Della put her hands on her hips. "Then no."

"No?"

Why did he seem shocked? Love. That's why she'd accepted Tom's offer. Turned out she'd been a fool to have loved him, but she had at the time. Della realized not everyone was awarded with such a marriage, however that's what she craved. Prayed for. She sure wasn't going to get married to a man simply because she didn't irritate him.

Hank crossed his arms. "Why not?"

"Because you don't love me." She said this with more volume than she'd intended; fortunately none of the guests on the porch seemed to have heard it.

Mr. Lamson turned, his boots thudding against the floor. The dishes in the hutch didn't only rattle, they quaked inside the cabinet. She bit her lip. He was going to leave her standing there like Tom had when he'd broken their engagement. Broken her heart. But her heart wasn't on the line this time. It couldn't be.

Mr. Lamson pushed the front door closed, softening the conversation outside, and propped against it. "You're right." He didn't say more until she met his gaze. "But it's clear by your actions that you love my folks. You love my boys. And they love you. You could stay for them. For their love."

"I could also stay if you allowed me to keep being their teacher."

"As their teacher..." He pointed toward the porch. "They will continue to flock here. And do teachers stay forever? Despite the miscommunication and the deception that brought you here, I...think..." He shook his head. "I know I can trust your intentions. Never could I trust those women out there. They don't have my family's best interest at heart. They're only here because they want my money."

Della understood what Hank was explaining better than he knew. Tom had wanted more wealth. A status she couldn't provide. But those women may want to spend their lives with him for reasons beyond his wealth. "You don't know that for sure." Except her words failed to even convince herself.

"What I do know is I don't want to marry any of them."

Della's heart thumped in her ears, blocking out everything else except Mr. Lamson. She held her breath, waiting, but what did she want him to say?

He nodded as if understanding her hesitation. "I'm sorry I can't offer you love between us. A marriage to me would simply mean you'd have my name, and you'd love my family. Couldn't that be enough? I can even build you your own house if you wanted space away from me. You're great with the boys. And it's plain that they adore you. You don't want to leave, right? This way you'd never have to. It's a fail-proof plan."

A noise whacked at the window. Wallie pressed his cheek against the glass, cupping his hands around his eyes, obviously struggling to see around the parted curtains.

Mr. Lamson watched Wallie for a moment. "They want you to stay." Wallie couldn't have heard Mr. Lamson's barely audible words, but he gave Della a thumbs-up sign and disappeared. Mr. Lamson was right, she did love that boy. Each of his boys. And Alice. And Roy. And he was spot-on at least for part of his crazed scheme—teachers don't stay forever, but mothers do. A position she'd dreamed of having.

Roy's words rang in her mind. *Just trust. It'll all work out. He's gotten you this far. Hasn't He?*

Della closed her eyes. God had. Even when Della had rushed from Indiana without praying for wisdom.

Lord, is this why I've grown to love this family so much, because I'm supposed to be a part of it?

Did she really need a husband's love, when she had the rest of the family? And if she said yes to his offer, she wouldn't have to return home or fret over an unknown future. Wouldn't have to say goodbye. "Okay," she whispered.

"We're getting married?" Mr. Lamson said it like a question. One he didn't know the answer to. "Okay. Yes. Well, there's a preacher outside—"

"You want to marry me right now?"

"You're right. I didn't think… I'm being selfish enough as it is. You probably want a large celebration with family and friends. A special dress. Flowers or whatever else women want or think they need."

No, she didn't desire all of that. Not after Tom had ruined her other preparations. Mother would probably laugh at her if she told her parents she was getting married to the man who'd hired her. Or worse, assume she'd done something sinful that had forced the need for her to marry quickly. Even Freeman would doubt her marriage announcement after the letter she'd sent him just the other day, saying she didn't know how long Mr. Lamson would allow her to stay.

"Hello, Hiram?" Miss Appleton opened the front

door, shoving Mr. Lamson out of the way and snapping Della back to the moment. "Oh, there you are, darling." Della didn't know why the woman's fluttery lashes made her stomach tighten. "I was wondering if you'd have time for our ride now? Or a quiet walk?" She glared at Della then sent another round of flirtatious smiles toward Mr. Lamson. "Alone. Out to one of your numerous oil pumps, perhaps?"

Hank looked at Della, his plea obvious. His family wanted her, and he was offering her a chance to stay. She wouldn't have to return to Indiana when no other teaching positions desired her. Did it matter what her family thought of her decision? She could love Mr. Lamson's family as if they were her own. Because they would be. Forever.

God had indeed worked out everything.

At Della's slight nod, Hank actually smiled. "Sorry, Miss Appleton. The only woman I'll be escorting on any walks or rides from here on out will be Della."

He wore happiness well, and Della found herself smiling, too. Mr. Lamson... Hank couldn't offer her love today, but maybe in the future he'd learn to love her as his family did. As Roy had said, God brought her this far. Couldn't He bring her the love she'd prayed for, too?

Ma lifted her hands into the air as if the stove was on fire. "Today is not fine."

This wasn't the reaction he'd expected. "You're telling me that this isn't what you wanted? Did you or did you not go behind my back and order Miss Wagner, I mean Della, for me to wed?"

The strain in Ma's brows released as she sought Della, who paced in the corner. "Of course, but—"

"And now you don't want me to marry her?" He should have encouraged Della to wait outside with Wallie. Were those tears in her eyes? Hank stepped toward her, feeling a tug to offer the comfort she deserved. This mess wasn't her fault.

"Hiram Robert Lamson, you're putting words in my mouth. I've wanted Della Mae in this family since the moment I read her letter. It was you who didn't wish to remarry. Why now? I won't have you playing with her emotions. Not my sweet Della's."

Della blinked and the sadness disappeared. Hank fisted his hands. She didn't need him to coddle her. She'd showed time and time again that she could take care of herself. He must remember his remarriage wasn't the real kind he was used to. "Those women will not stop coming until I finally cave and marry someone. Della's agreed to stay. She'll continue to help with the boys. Help you."

Ma glared. "That doesn't sound like a marriage to me." She lifted Della's hands into hers. "Dear, is this what you truly desire? As much as I want you to stay, I'm not convinced this is the best option for you."

"Wallie overheard." Her lip quivered, and she pushed out a sigh. "He called me Momma Della—and I've come to love this family."

"And we love you." Alice brought Della against her chest, matching the embrace she'd given her on the day she arrived. "It doesn't have to be today. Don't you want your family here? You need a wedding dress. You wouldn't have to make one, but Hank can pay—"

"No one has to buy anything extra. Really it's fine." She stared off in the distance. "My family wouldn't be able to leave the newspaper anyway."

"Well, you're near Evelyn's size. You could wear—"

"No," Hank said.

Ma stepped in front of Della as if she needed protecting. Hank knew how untrue that was. "You know Evelyn wouldn't mind. In fact, she'd be pleased."

"I said no." He didn't need Evelyn's wedding dress stirring up any unwanted emotions.

Ma unstacked the dirty dishes from the tray and came back for the cups. "It's plain to see that Della treasures the boys. Otherwise I'd not understand her willingness to marry a man who doesn't even attempt to meet her needs."

Now who was putting words in whose mouth? "I'll meet her needs."

"You're not even giving her a special day. She deserves a fine and proper celebration. Don't give her a wedding like I had."

"What do you mean like you had?" Ma hadn't ever mentioned a negative thing about her wedding. Not that an elaborate wedding reflected how a marriage turned out.

Ma waved him off. "Never mind. This isn't about me. This is about Della. How do I know you'll take care of her if you're rushing through what will be your first day as man and wife?"

Was she seriously doubting her own son? Picking Della over him? "I gave her my word. I even promised to build her her own house if desired."

Ma stopped pumping water into the sink and turned, her eyebrows raised. "Where you, her and the boys will live?"

Was she hoping to have a house with just her and Pa again? If so, why did she never bring it up? It looked like he'd be building two houses. "Where she could live alone. I understand I'm not always the easiest to live with."

"Oh, Hank. No." Ma pressed her hand to her stomach, water seeping onto her dress. "This is not what I prayed for." She pointed a finger at him, sending droplets splattering, and shook her head. "A marriage. A real one." She returned to the dishes, scrubbing with more energy than she'd used in a while. "That's what I prayed for."

Hank rubbed his knuckles into the kink in the back of his neck. He unfortunately knew that prayer didn't always work. "I'm offering what I'm able. Della, if you don't want to..." He swallowed the bitter taste of pride. "I understand. Or if you require a dress, let's go order one."

The front door sounded like it fell off its hinges as Pa burst through, with Reverend Miller and the boys right behind. "Wallie says you're getting married?"

"Yep." Wallie skipped under Pa's and the Reverend's arms.

Roy gestured to Della, a sparkle in his eyes. "To Della?"

Wallie slid his fingers around Della's and swung their joined hands back and forth. "See, I told you. Praying for Momma Della to stay worked."

Why did it seem like God always answered everyone else's prayers, except Hank's?

Chapter Fourteen

❧

Yesterday's heat had been all but forgotten. The only proof that it hadn't all been a dream was Hank's new wife sitting near him on the buckboard.

"Boys." Wasn't like them not to beat him to the wagon, or for Wallie not to have arrived hand in hand with Della.

As Della rearranged her skirt, her elbow bumped his and warmth blazed up his arm and settled on the back of his neck. They hadn't been this close since they'd released hands after the wedding ceremony.

Hank arched his stiff back. It felt like they've been waiting for the boys forever. He glanced at Della and gripped the reins tighter. He really ought to say something to her this morning besides *please pass the salt.* Would it be conceited to ask if she liked her gift? Not that a single picked rose was much of a wedding present, but since she didn't have any of her favorite flowers at the ceremony—or really anything she might have dreamed of for her wedding—he'd left it on her dresser after breakfast.

Yesterday Wallie had tied a bow around Mabel's neck

to fancy her up for the ceremony. Edward had picked a bouquet that included more weeds than flowers. Robert mentioned searching for roses, but Hank's unwelcomed guests were already growing restless. Probably due to the fact that Hank wasn't marrying any of them.

Surprisingly enough, Hank had actually been glad they were there, in the end. The more witnesses to his wedding the more proof to all the other greedy ladies that he was officially, one hundred percent off the bachelor market.

For someone preaching about God's goodness, Reverend Miller sure was sly, saying he'd only perform the impromptu wedding if Hank and Della would come to service the next day, something Hank hadn't done in a while. Nonetheless he could make it through a service to further show any other scheming ladies in town that the rumors were true. He was in fact wed.

Della faced him, pressing her mouth into a tight, hesitant smile. It was a little disconcerting to know for a fact that her lips tasted like honey.

You have to kiss her, Papa. Don't he, Reverend Miller? Wallie had pleaded during the wedding. Della had given him a true smile after their chaste kiss. Reliving the moment, Hank frowned, wondering if that dimpled smile had been for him or his son. Either way marriage had looked perfect on Della in his favorite green dress. Modest, yet beautiful. Her eyes had been the last thing he'd remembered before he'd finally fallen asleep.

He shook his head. What he needed to do now was locate his boys. "Robert. Edward... Wallie."

Della rested her fingertips on his arm, and his rebellious body leaned toward her. She really needed to stop touching him if they were to have an in-name-only marriage. "I'll go search for them."

The heat from her touch moved into his chest. "Miss Wag—" Hank watched Della's smile fade. He'd accidentally called her Miss Wagner at breakfast, too. If she was anything other than Della to him after their *I do*'s, it would be Mrs. Lamson, but he wasn't ready to call her that. Even if it was her new name.

He cleared his throat. "Della, thank you, but I'll get them."

He hopped down before she could argue. His legs could use a stretch from being curled to the edge of the seat. It was going to be a long ride into town.

Inside Ma greeted him with a wrinkled brow. "Why haven't you left?"

"Been waiting on the boys." His folks weren't riding along with them to service. Pa offered a Scripture reading for the hired men every Sunday. Not many came and listened, however Pa always said that if even one showed, it was worth the effort.

Ma busied her hands with dishes in the sink. "I'm so glad you're going to the service."

She was probably claiming that as another answered prayer. "You know why I'm going." He marched to the back door and yelled again for the boys. "Where are they?"

"I told them to go lie down." Ma stirred the pot on the stove and began to hum that song of hers. Della's song, too.

"Ma?"

"Hmm?" She paused, rubbing her wrists.

"Why did you send the boys to bed?"

"Oh, that. Well, it seems that they required a bit of rest."

"They were fine at breakfast. Do they have fevers? Sore throats? Or is it their stomachs?" Please let it not be stomach. The last time all three of them had stomach troubles, the house was out of commission for over a week.

She dusted the already clean hutch. "I'm sure they'll be better by the time you and Della return home."

He should have known. "Ma, enough with the lying. All to create some ruse again. I don't need alone time with Della."

"I did not lie, Hiram Robert. The boys were more than thrilled to go rest for a while in exchange for not having to clean out the chicken coop tomorrow. Rest will do them good. They were squirmy last night, all excited. Pa and I heard them moving around in their beds until the wee hours. And Wallie knocked on Della's door before the rooster announced the day. And you do need alone time with her. Every newly married couple requires—"

"We are not an ordinary wedded couple. Della will remain here with us like you wanted, and I won't be bothered anymore by Miss Vogel and her band of ladies. It's a good solution for all of us. Why aren't you satisfied with how things are? You got what you prayed for. You get to keep Della."

Ma placed her palm on his cheek, her hand cool against his skin. "But you are throwing away her love."

"You can't throw away something that you don't have—that wasn't offered."

She let her hand drop. "Even if that were so, neither have you tried to gain it. I understand that life hard-

ened your heart, but only you can be the one to decide
to let go of the past. Della has proved she's special, or
you wouldn't have wed her. And no, she isn't Evelyn…
but…" Ma's voice grew soft and there were tears shining
in her eyes. "I miss her too, yet I think she'd approve of
you loving again. Don't you think God brought Della
here for just that reason?"

He didn't want to rehash who had actually brought
Della here. "If God wanted me to love, He would have
saved Evelyn. I'm not the bad guy. And you were there
when I decided to try to love again, with Miss Smith.
That not only cost me another piece of my heart, but a
portion of my money. Our family's security."

"Della isn't like Miss Smith."

He knew that, or he never would have married her.
But Della wasn't the issue here. *He* was. "I've offered
Della all I can, and she accepted."

"She's worthy of more."

Would they argue about this every time he ventured
into the kitchen? He was starting to think he might want to
build a second house—for himself. Della could stay with
his parents. It was obvious they liked her better than him.

As he neared the wagon, Dorothy stomped and the
clouds appeared grayer than before, but it was Della's
gaze filled with concern that made Hank stop short. Ma
was right. Della deserved more than what he had offered
her, except the last two times he allowed a woman to
take up room in his heart, he wasn't left with much to
spare. He couldn't give Della love he didn't know how
to feel anymore.

Della couldn't decide which was worse, receiving
scowls from a quarter of the women of the church con-

gregation, or Hank squirming away from her while she'd held their shared hymnal. Was he already having second thoughts about marrying her?

When her arm brushed against his and he'd jerked, it felt like Tom was right there beside her, telling her he didn't love her all over again. But she was being ridiculous. She'd agreed to a marriage of convenience. So why was she upset that her husband wasn't affectionate? What had she expected?

When she'd found the rose on her dresser this morning, it'd been an encouragement of why she'd married Hank. There *was* love for her here—even if it wasn't from her husband. The boys must have gone out before breakfast and found it for her because they knew how much roses meant to her. She had the love of five others to make up for the absence of Hank's affection. Their love would be enough, wouldn't it?

Reverend Miller blocked their exit after the sermon. Della hoped he wasn't about to request her opinions on the Scriptures because she'd have to admit that her mind hadn't been as focused as it should have been during the service.

"Now, Hank. It would be a mistake to turn down my wife's smashed taters. They're the creamiest you'll find anywhere. And trust me, I'm in a position to know— I've been invited to more than my fair share of dinners. There're more perks to being a preacher than spiritual blessings. Like Mrs. Tyler's oat cookies." He rubbed his stomach. "Somehow sharing the Good News means I keep my belly full. Probably how the Levites felt about the portions of sacrifices they were allowed."

Della liked the idea of sharing more time with Reverend Miller and his wife. He reminded her of Pastor

O'Ryan, the pastor back in Indiana who'd shared Christ with her, yet she really wanted to get home and spend her first full day as a married woman with the reasons she'd become Mrs. Lamson—with her boys.

Hank's eyebrows lifted as he searched her face. She wasn't sure how to answer without sounding rude, so she offered him a half smile.

"Thank you, Reverend Miller." Hank shook his hand. "Though, I believe we need to be on our way. The sky's looking a bit perturbed at the moment and the ride home will take us a while. Perhaps another time?"

"Yes. Perhaps." Reverend Miller's tone made it clear he didn't believe another visit to the church would be coming anytime soon. After the pastor said his good-byes, Hank lingered in the churchyard and greeted all who peered their way, repeating several times in a bellowing volume how Della was his new wife. Finally, he led her to the wagon, but paused as he started to help her into the buckboard. "This is what you wanted?"

Did he worry she was having second thoughts about their wedding? While it was true that it wasn't the kind of marriage she'd always dreamed of, their marriage gave her the thing she had wanted most—a way to stay with his boys. She was satisfied with that. It's not like they could get unmarried now anyway. "Yes, I like being a part of the Lamson family."

He blinked at her. "No, I mean, you didn't want to stay and have dinner with the Reverend and his wife, right? I thought that's what your smile meant."

He got all that from her half smile?

"We can still accept his offer for dinner if that's what you prefer," he rushed to offer, "however, I was being truthful about the clouds. I really do believe a storm will keep us here longer than we want if we don't leave soon. But still, it's up to you."

She readjusted the hat pinned on her head and watched the trees swaying in the wind. So far Missouri's late summer, early fall season had been comparable to Indiana's. But she'd heard stories of terrible storms out this way. She had no desire to get caught up in one.

"I'm ready to go home with you. I mean, I wish to spend the day with the boys."

The sound of thunder rumbled from behind them and Hank studied the sky. "So much for hoping we'd be far ahead of the storm. We can make it, however we're going to have to take the shortcut." He narrowed his eyes. "Promise me, you'll never use this way unless I'm with you. It's not been completely reliable since the last big storm."

The concern on his face was mesmerizing. Tom had never looked at her like that. Like it mattered deeply to him to ensure that nothing bad happened to her.

"Della, do I have your word?"

She managed a reply and pulled her gaze from Hank's. The shortcut meant retracing their way along Main Street. This time around she didn't have to worry about any females glaring her way as they rumbled past. The alley gave way to a weeded road that petered out slowly until only a grass path lay ahead, bowing in the threatening storm.

"Maybe you could pray the shortcut will be quick enough to get us home before the worst of it hits," he shouted over the wind, driving Dorothy at a breakneck speed.

Why couldn't he pray, too?

Once the first drops of rain hit, Hank wrapped his

arm around Della's shoulders, moving toward her instead of away as he'd done earlier at church. "I've been meaning to fix the old bridge over the creek, but the work kept getting delayed by other ranch needs." He shook his head. "It will hold our light load, especially when I walk Dorothy over." He pulled his feet up higher on the wagon, moving the position of the reins.

Thunder rumbled, drowning out the relentless pounding of Dorothy's hooves and the screeching wheels. Tree branches bent around them, creaking almost as loudly. Lightning flashed and icy rain dripped onto Della's face, slowly at first and then peppering down.

"Hang on." Hank slapped the reins, and when a bump lifted her off the board, Della reached for something to hold her steady and ended up latched onto Hank's leg. Except she didn't have to worry about falling out because he was already tucking her tighter against him.

"The bridge is right around the corner. There's no time to walk Dorothy over. We're going to have to ride the wagon across. At this speed it will only take a few seconds. I don't want you out any longer than necessary in this mess. It's not safe under these trees."

A descending bolt of lightning lit the sky and illuminated the old bridge, giving her her first glimpse of it. Old, indeed. Ropes made up more of the bridge than the worn boards. How he expected an entire wagon to cross and not land in the rushing water and rocks below, she hadn't a clue.

Hail started falling from above and somehow, Hank wrapped both arms around her and still managed to hold the reins. She pressed her forehead against his chest and prayed for safety.

"I've got you, Della." He urged Dorothy on faster, and his muscles flexed under Della's grip. "Here we go."

The planks on the bridge complained under the wheels and the ropes pulled tight. Hank's teeth chattered either from the vibration of crossing or from the chill of the rain, seeping through his shirt as he shielded her. Or both.

The back row of the wagon's wheels cleared the structure, and Della peeked behind at the quivering bridge, stunned that it was still standing.

"We'll arrive at the hay barn first. When I stop, you hop off and run inside."

"What about you?" Her throat ached from the force it took to be heard over the pouring rain, now falling sideways around them.

"I'll be there as soon as I release Dorothy from the wagon. I can't let her run off in panic. Don't want her breaking any legs."

Della pushed a sopping piece of her hair off her face. Her hat was long gone, lost somewhere along the way. "If I help, it'll go quicker."

The hail had eased, but the wind hadn't. Raindrops had settled on his eyelashes as he glanced down at her hands wrapped around his stomach. "Sorry." She released him, but she wasn't sure he heard her.

"Della, when we stop, I need you to hurry inside the barn. I'll deal with Dorothy. Please. I need you safe."

"But who's going to keep you safe?"

Pushing a scared Dorothy through the narrow barn door was a painstaking ordeal that resulted in the rain not leaving a dry spot on Hank. At least Della would be sheltered from the storm. That was more important than him and Dorothy getting pelted.

Despite Hank's instructions, Della came and took ahold of Dorothy's halter, stroking the horse's nose. "Come on, girl. We'll be safe through here."

Dorothy broke from her fearful stubborn streak much quicker than Mr. Precious ever would have and stepped fully into the unfamiliar barn. Hank removed her bit and secured her in the corner where she could eat the stored hay.

As Hank turned to thank Della, his heel slipped on something slick. There wasn't opportunity to wonder whether he had a leak in the roof or if his boys had been up to no good again. He was falling—hard.

Except he never hit the ground. Instead, the smell of roses surrounded him as Della managed to catch him. Sort of. It was more or less a softening of his fall, with the end result of landing on her instead of on the ground.

She released a muffled moan, and he hurried to remove the burden he hadn't meant for her to carry. "Della!" Clumsily, he rolled over and held out his hand to help her up.

"I'm sorry. I thought I was…" Her hand slid into his and despite the chill of her skin and his drenched clothes, he couldn't recall the last time he'd felt this content. Although the storm threatened to blow through the barn, it didn't have near the power that seemed to be pulling him toward Della. Her hair looked as if a bird used it as a nest, but somehow, she'd never been more beautiful.

"Thanks for helping with Dorothy."

"I'm the one who should…"

He drew closer, intending to remove a piece of straw

sticking in her hair, but instead his fingers brushed her cheek. Her breathing hitched at his touch, and the storm faded into the dimness around them, leaving just him and Della.

Her eyes sought his before drifting to his mouth and then back. He didn't need her to smile to read the questions she held. They matched the ones running through his mind. To answer them, he rested his forehead against hers, erasing what space there was left between them.

"Della." He didn't know why he was whispering. All he knew was that he was trying to think of a reason not to kiss his own wife—and he wasn't able to find a single one. Especially since her fingers were laced between his. Would her lips taste of honey again?

Someone cleared their throat. "I see that I was wrong." Isaac's voice opened a flood of panic through Della's eyes and provided the shock Hank's body needed to let her go.

Reluctantly, Hank backed away. "It's not what you think."

"Boss, it's none of my concern what married folk do together."

True. They were married, but he'd offered an in-name-only marriage. Heat crept around his soaked collar. "We're not... I mean..."

"Again. That's none of my business."

"Hank fell." Della licked her lips and pointed at the barn floor as if it had offended her.

Isaac wore a smirk. "It usually starts with someone falling." While Isaac's gaze bounced between Hank and Della, Dorothy took it upon herself to announce her feelings on the matter of Hank's embarrassment by releasing a heavy snort.

Isaac caressed Dorothy's nose, and Hank squeezed his now empty hand into a fist. Had he or Della let go first? "Saw the wagon racing this way through the bunk's windows. Thought you might need help. It appears my timing was off. However, the rain sounds like it's dying down. So you and the missus should get to the house and out of those wet clothes before you catch something. Or not."

Could Hank fire someone over too much smirking?

"Either way, I'll see Dorothy safely to her own barn."

As always, Isaac was full of valuable advice. Not just the idea of warm clothing, but getting out of the dark barn and away from the temptation of kissing his wife. A wife he hadn't promised his love to. Yet what if he could? Dare he open his heart to a real marriage again? Was it safe to even think about?

Chapter Fifteen

❧

"Della, about our wedding…"

Della secured her grip on the hoe and willed her stomach not to tighten at Hank's words. Alice said he had been absent from supper last night because he was surveying the damage from the storm. That hadn't explained why he'd avoided her this morning. She'd thought they'd shared something while alone in the barn, however it wasn't the first time she'd misread a man. He could be here to admit that he'd rushed into marrying her and now regretted the decision. Should she promise to stick to the original terms of their arrangement—a marriage in name only? She'd say that, if it was what he wanted to hear. And she'd mostly mean it. If only her heart wouldn't keep replaying their almost kiss.

She was surprised Hank's neck wasn't raw considering how much he was rubbing it. He picked up another hoe the boys had left at the end of the garden and marched toward her. "You didn't get to be a bride in the way you probably pictured. Your family wasn't here." He let his hand drop to his leg. "Your dress, you probably would have wanted something different. Not that

I'm saying that green dress on you wasn't… I mean. It was pretty. You were…" He produced a sigh that left no doubt that he wanted to be anywhere else. "I guess I just wanted to say that I'm sorry I ruined your special day."

Della took the hoe from Hank and headed for the shed. Hadn't they been over this already? "The wedding was fine. I didn't need anything more." Why rehash something that couldn't be changed?

Hank followed her and opened the shed's door. "Ma argues differently. You deserve a better wedding gift from the groom than what you've received." Della wasn't sure what he meant. What gift had he given her? Was he talking about getting to stay with his boys? That alone was a treasured gift. "I wouldn't know what to give you," he admitted. "Not something you'd actually want. So I need you to be plain and tell me what it is you'd like."

After she put the tools away, she turned, not realizing he'd drawn closer.

She shook her head to keep from ogling his freshly shaved jaw and his crooked smile.

"Please," he whispered.

There was nothing she needed that he hadn't already given her. "I have the boys and your family. I have all I need." Besides a husband who might love her, but she couldn't blame him for not delivering that.

"Della." Hank said her Christian name slow and deliberate as if it remained a struggle to not call her Miss Wagner. "Our marriage is…different…"

That was an understatement. It would also be the complete opposite from his last. He had loved Evelyn— Della knew that without ever having met the woman. He wore the loss in his eyes, carried it on his shoulders every day.

"I wish to see you happy. There has to be something you'd enjoy. If they don't have it in town, we'll have it ordered. Would you like to have one of those sewing machines? Or some new books? A new dress? Or five? I do also want to get you some taller boots, too."

"Truly, there is no need."

"I'm afraid I won't let this matter rest."

No, *Alice* wouldn't let this matter rest. His mother was the one who had told him he should get her a gift. She was certain the thought never would have crossed his mind. Two birds flew in the sky, sparking an idea about the perfect wedding present. The old steeple blended ahead into the fluffy clouds above. What she'd like to do was see inside the church again. Had the seedling of the tree grown? Had any more of the building been damaged in the storm?

Alice had told her Hank's report of the property damages. A portion of the sheep's fence was smashed, along with a hole in the old barn's roof, a few fallen tree branches and an uprooted peach tree. Considering all the wind and rain and hail, they were blessed to have been largely protected from the storm.

From the distance, the church appeared much the same. Such a waste as it sat now, no longer holding services, only a statue of ruined memories. If the building were cleaned and cleared it could be so much more. It could house Roy's Scripture readings for the hired hands every Sunday. Be the boys' school during the week, even a schoolhouse for the whole region, open to more children who were outside the Lamson family.

Perhaps she could convince him that the old church could be so much more. "How about a walk?"

He studied her and then said, "With just me?"

"Are you the groom asking me what I want?"

"Yes, but…" His swallowed and turned so she couldn't read his face. "I suppose a walk will give you a chance to determine what it is you really want." Hank offered his elbow. "Since I thought we might have to go into town, Ma volunteered to take care of dinner and the boys. So we don't have to rush back."

She could feel the strength of his arm under her touch, reminding her of how safe she'd felt when he'd held her close during the storm. "I'm sorry you haven't had much of a break since you've arrived. You've done so much more than just teaching. I hadn't realized how much Ma was roping you into."

She readjusted her arm near his side, relaxing her shoulders. The wind held the edge of yesterday's weather and the browning grass crunched under their shoes, filling in the silence when their conversation lagged. Yet the stretches of quiet between them were peaceful and felt more natural than when Tom used to pack every moment of their outings with his voice.

Once they traveled down the hill, Hank directed them along the path that led to the creek with the new bridge.

"Actually, let's go this way." Della didn't wait for an answer, only used her hand on his elbow to steer him in the opposite direction. When the angle twisted her wrist slightly, another thought occurred to her. "Has Alice ever mentioned having pains in her wrists?" she asked.

Hank's frown gave Della her answer.

"Would she say anything, if she did?" Della pressed. "She rubs them after rolling pie crusts. It's why I first offered to make the pies. And then there's the mending. When I sewed a patch over one of the boy's pants,

I found she'd hidden clothes that required the simplest of stitches. Piles and piles of them. With the contents of her sewing basket, I know it wasn't because she didn't know how to make the repairs." Every needle inside had thread looped through and knots ready to be used. The spindles had half their thread gone, proving that someone had done a lot of sewing, just not lately.

"I'll never believe for one second that Alice is lazy and simply didn't want to mend the boys' clothes. She's one of the hardest workers I've ever met." Della moved her wrists up and down, thinking through the motion. "I believe it's the movement of threading and stitching that hurts her. It would be the same when she's rolling dough."

"I *have* seen her rub her wrists, now that you mention it."

"I'll be glad to help more when they're hurting. That is, if she'll admit to her pain. It will probably take both of us together to get her to, though."

"Guess it's a good thing I kept you around."

Della offered a tight smile. "I'm glad, too."

She inhaled, taking in scents of persimmon and cedar. She was someone's wife. It remained a bit surreal—which might be why she had yet to write to her family about becoming Mrs. Lamson. Though she'd started a letter three separate times, none of the words had come out right. She wasn't sure what she could say that would forestall Mother picking apart her decision. Or criticizing her new family.

Della pulled her hand away from Hank's arm and lifted her dress to free it from the grass. The fabric had already snagged on a sticker bush, and there were several more dotted along the incline toward the old church. When she walked on, Hank didn't move from his spot beside a pine tree.

"I thought we could finish our walk by going to the old church building," she called back to him.

He took a step. One away from Della. Away from what she desired.

She stopped, and turned to look at him. "You asked what I wanted for a wedding gift. I want to see the old church."

Hank shifted, crossing his arms. "You only said you wanted a walk."

"And *you* said a walk would give me time to think on what I truly desired." She understood the place held bad memories for him, but she couldn't approve of the way he was allowing the past, something he couldn't control, to determine his choices in the future.

She smiled and slid her fingers around his like she'd done in the barn. The spark his touch created filled her with courage. "Please, Hank?"

His gaze locked on to hers at the sound of his name. This time he followed when she started for the church.

"It's the most beautiful building I've seen in a long time." Yes, it was covered in ivy, paint was peeling off the outside and there were boards nailed over the front door. None of which exactly seemed especially welcoming…but she knew in her heart that this building was meant for greater things.

Just like her.

The tinted windows shined in the lowering sunshine. The purple hues of the sunset mixed with the red and blue stained glass that only made the cross in the center of the design all the more noticeable. It was as if God was proving He'd been with her the whole time.

Della led the way as if guiding a resistant child behind her. "Not much farther," she encouraged over Hank's clumpy strides.

When they reached the back of the building Hank wiggled from Della's grip. "There. We walked to the church. Now we'd better get back and see if Ma needs help with supper. Especially with her wrists hurting and all."

Hadn't he just said something about how they didn't need to rush? But she sensed it was his haunted memories that were speaking. He still carried so much hurt from the past and something inside her wanted to be a part of his healing.

"One small peek and then we'll go."

Hank blocked her way to the back doors. "We're not going in."

Della sank back on her heels. As much as she wanted to see the growing tree inside, she could tell that he wasn't going to budge. All right, then—she could explain her plan from here. "Hank." She rested a hand on his chest. Unlike yesterday, he stiffened under her touch, and his eyes grew wide.

Her face heated and she withdrew. It was one thing to take his elbow when he offered, or to tug him along up the hill, but to touch his chest? It wasn't like they were trying to endure a storm. She was getting too used to being near him.

She focused on what she needed to say. That was what was important—not how she'd interact with her husband. "This building could house your father's Scripture readings on Sunday."

"Pa's no preacher."

"It would be a great place for the boys to have their

lessons, too. We could get them some desks and a real chalkboard. I'm sure Roy could build—"

"You already have chalkboards."

"Not ones bigger than a plate. Didn't your teacher have a schoolhouse and a large board where she showed how to work out how many apples are left if Dorothy had fifty-eight and Mabel borrowed twenty-three for her owner's apple pie? A room full of fun and books and maps."

There he went, rubbing his neck.

"And what if we got more than three desks? For more kids."

He stopped rubbing and swallowed. "Della… That would mean… If…" His eyes sought hers, and for a moment she almost reached for him again. "If our marriage remains…different than normal…" He licked his lips, glancing away. "Then there won't be any… There will only be…" His hands clenched at his sides. "The three boys."

Her face was on fire, and she suddenly had the desire to rub the back of her own neck. She'd only meant that they might open the school to other families. But the way he'd replied…it wasn't just the old pain of knowing that she'd never mother a babe of her own. There was also the way Hank's eyebrows pinched together, like the idea of being united with her was less appealing than mucking out Mr. Precious's stall. Another rejection, after a lifetime of them. Hank saying that there would never be a future where he would love her.

Fine, then. If his friendship, and a partnership when it came to caring for the boys, was all they would share, she would be fine with that. Friendship with Hank would be enough. She'd vowed as much. She'd put away her wish to be loved by her husband. Clearly that was never going to happen.

"I could teach other kids that aren't…that aren't ours. I believe you mentioned at least one younger child that lives nearby. Once that girl is old enough for schooling, I'd imagine that family is probably too far out to allow their child to make the trip to the town schoolhouse, like your boys. Our boys." Because whether or not he wanted to believe it, by marrying her, his boys had become hers now also. Della loved the idea of claiming them. "I can teach not only our boys, but the other families who live out here."

"Della." Her name came out in a huff.

"The boys' lessons are even more important to me now that I've become their mother."

"You aren't their mother." Hank seemed to regret his words as soon as they were spoken, but the apologetic expression he produced didn't soften the wound he'd given.

"I will never replace Evelyn," she said softly, tears threatening, "But Wallie already calls me Momma Della. Hank, when I agreed to marry you, I promised I'd help take care of them. You have to know me well enough to understand that I'm not trying to replace her." She spread her arms open at the church. "Making sure they get their lessons and learn skills before life gives them something they can't handle is one of the reasons you wanted me to stay. Isn't it?"

"The place is evil."

She felt like stomping her foot. Instead she lifted her chin. "There's no such thing as an evil place. Places can't choose what happens in them. Only people can do that. We have a choice as to what happens here—

and I want to choose for it to be a place for faith and education. You said I was a good teacher, and I'd like to help other families too if we can. Here would be a perfect place to do it all at." She motioned once more at the church. "Please. Just think about it."

Before Hank could answer, Della marched around him and opened the back door. "This place can have new memories, if you'll allow it. Look at the windows, Hank. They're exquisite. And do you see that there?" She pointed, smiling. "There's a tree growing on the inside. Have you ever seen such a thing?"

Hank didn't cross the threshold with her, but he watched her every move. "It's ruining the floorboards."

Della touched its yellowing leaves. They were soft and the ends jagged. Funny how he cared that the tree ruined the church's floor and yet didn't want the building being used. What did it matter if the floor was destroyed when it wasn't being put to any other use?

She scooped up the hymnal papers off the lonely pew. What else could she say to convince him? His hand on her elbow stopped her before she could further her case.

"Look, Della. We walked. You saw the church. I listened. It's all you said you wanted."

This moment might be all she had, and she was failing to convince him. Della felt the defeat from her shoulders drift to her toes. Or had her foot actually bumped something?

She squinted. Please let her not have broken off an edge of the pew. It was dim, but light enough to see what she'd felt against her boot. She clenched the broken hymnal against her chest while her breath caught in her throat.

It would have been better if she had damaged the only standing pew.

A coiled snake raised its head, and Della's heart rattled as a silent scream rang in her mind. This was not a harmless snake like the one she'd seen in the Lamsons' garden.

Even in the shadows dancing under the pew the danger was clear. Slanted eyes, diamond-shaped head, the exact coloring pattern of a venomous snake. The memory of Father whisking them away from a pile of rocks during their last family picnic came to mind. This was not a friendly snake. And she'd been the one to antagonize it.

A board came smashing down, snapping her out of her thoughts, and pinning the snake to the floor.

"Get out of here!" Hank repositioned the board in his hands, restraining the danger, and stepped in front of Della. "Della. Back. Away." His arms shuddered more than his words.

"I'm not leaving you." She could help, they made a good team. That was when she remembered not to panic. "D-do you want me to get another board or something and—"

"Della…" His rapid breathing pulled his shirt tight against his chest. "If you want to get me a wedding gift, you'll get as far away from this church as possible. Then tell Pa to bring me my matches."

"Why?" she asked, afraid that she already knew the answer—hoping against hope that she was wrong.

"Because I should have burned this place down years ago."

Chapter Sixteen

One hundred and four questions. That was how many it seemed Wallie had asked him, seated beside him with his legs swinging under the buckboard. Hank nodded as Wallie yammered about something else. The boy hadn't taken a breath since the trees cleared at the bottom of the hill, bringing the cabin into view.

A single column of smoke drifted from one of the chimneys, the haze mixing in with the clouds above. Hank spit out a wad of sunflower seeds he'd purchased in town. If he'd gotten to burn the old church building like he wanted last night, there would have been remains of smoke from the west.

The rain had ruined that plan. Why had God chosen then to send the showers? Didn't God know that no one else needed to get hurt from the evil that place held? If Hank hadn't acted quickly, Della would have gotten her foot bit. Like Evelyn. And then, she'd be gone, too.

To the left, the steeple peeked through the thinning leaves while the rest of the building remained blocked by the trees and brush. If Hank's to-do list allowed, he'd set it on fire tonight. Then come tomorrow he'd be free to begin fixing the old bridge. It was past time, especially after how much it had swayed when he and Della rode over it. What good was it to have a shorter route into town if they couldn't use it safely? Especially now that he was no longer in danger of any more greedy women discovering it.

"And Mabel said she loved that idea. Do you?"

A wagon wheel hit a mud puddle and sent Wallie a few inches into the air. Hank put his hand on Wallie's knee, anchoring him through the rough bouncing. "What idea was that?"

Wallie groaned and crossed his arms. "Weren't you listening? My idea about the corncobs."

Hank slapped the reins, encouraging Dorothy to trot up the incline, and to provide him opportunity to wrack his mind for what his son had said during their one-sided conversation. Corncobs? How had those even come up? Hadn't Wallie been talking about the sock puppets Della had made? Before that he'd pointed out clouds in the shape of a bear. A pancake. Even a boot. Had he seen a corncob-shaped cloud?

After searching the sky and Wallie's face for any help and finding none, Hank went with a whitewashed answer. "It might be. Mabel always likes your ideas."

As soon as Hank set the brake, Wallie hopped off. "That's because she's a good listener." His tone gave weight to his unspoken meaning, that a chicken was a better listener than his father. So much for giving Wallie individual attention.

Della suggested taking only one of the boys on his occasional business trips into town. She said her brother Freeman often felt overlooked because he was stuck in the middle of all the children, meaning he never got time alone with his parents. His boys had jumped on the idea of alone time, and Wallie ended up with the smallest piece of straw starting off the rotations.

For having not been a mother before, Della had a surprisingly sturdy grasp on how things worked for children. Sometimes parenting appeared more natural for her than it did him. She wouldn't have let Mabel beat her by being a better listener. It wasn't a pleasant feeling to know that Della was becoming a better parent than him—their own father. Which was probably why his big mouth had blurted out that she wasn't the boys' mother. Jealousy had made him lash out.

Hank reached into a crate in the back and held up a fat envelope. "Don't forget to give Miss—Della her letter."

Wallie ran back and snatched the envelope. "I hope Freeman sent us more stories this time."

"Don't believe it's from Freeman." It had given Hank comfort to find out Freeman was Della's brother weeks ago, and that she wasn't filling the boys' heads with stories from an old flame.

Wallie tried pronouncing the name on the return address, but failed. He scrunched his nose. "It's more family, right? Good thing you married her before anybody else heard how great of a teacher and momma she is. They might have married her for her pie. Clyde looked like he wanted to."

Hank wouldn't argue with the pie comment. Nor could he pinpoint when the switch for the boys happened, when Della turned from simply being their teacher into something more. For him, especially since the storm, he'd been drawn to her more and more. But had it started earlier? Perhaps from his proposal, when she'd willingly surrendered her wants for his boys' sake? Nailing down his feelings—and even figuring out when they'd started and how they'd grown—had proven surprisingly tricky. He didn't have many successful experiences in following his heart instead of his head. Last night, he'd allowed Della to lead them into the church, leaving behind his better judgment, and it had almost ended with Della getting bit. The thought of no longer having her in his life had frightened him almost as much as the snake.

Hank touched his pocket where a gift rested to help him apologize to his wife. She hadn't deserved his burst of anger. "I'm guessing it's from her ma."

Margaret Wagner was printed on the envelope in bold crisp lettering. It had to be her ma's name because Della hadn't talked about having a sister. Not that he'd ever asked her much about her family. He needed to change that. A husband should know his wife's folks' names. This Margaret was technically the boys' grandmother.

Ma was right, newlyweds required alone time. Perhaps he'd ask Della to sit with him on the porch after supper. He could also explain his compromise about her desired wedding gift. He'd still burn the old church, but he'd build her and the boys a different school in return. He could also use their time together to give her the thimble he'd purchased for her and to apologize.

He'd seen the thimble while Wallie was picking out his candy and the roses etched around its rim reminded Hank of Della, serving almost as a sign that they could make this marriage work together. They'd just have to watch out for the thorns.

Wallie balanced the envelope in his hands like a

scale. He brought it to his face, peering down the length of the envelope with only one eye open. Before Hank could wonder what the boy was doing, Wallie tossed it into the air and watched it float to the ground.

"That's gravity. You want to know what I learned about gravity?"

Hank unhooked Dorothy from the wagon, and paused, stuck between wanting to listen and wanting to start on his to-do list so he could have the satisfaction of seeing smoke rise from the west sooner rather than later.

The need to be a better papa won. He patted Dorothy and turned to listen fully. "What, buddy?"

"That all things, they have to fall. See? Like the letter."

Hank wanted to sigh at the depth of Wallie's uncovered wisdom. Like gravity, all good things in life would eventually fall, coming to an end. Hank didn't want to think about what was going to fall next. He'd already buried too much.

"Can I give Momma Della her present that you bought for her when I give her the letter? I want her to love me more than she does Robert or Edward."

Competition ran deep through all his boys. "She'll love you all the same."

Wallie made a face. "I know that's what she's *s'pposed* to do, but she may not know all the mothering rules yet."

Hank also needed to apologize for how he'd said she wasn't the boys' mother. "Then just in case, why don't you only give her the letter."

Wallie cocked his head and dropped his gaze to

Hank's pocket. "Are you trying to make her love you the most? Is that why you want to give it to her yourself?"

Hank fished out the new thimble and rolled it around. It was too tiny to fit on his fingers, but it would protect Della's. He'd pictured Della giving him her dimpled smile when he'd surprised her with it.

Was he hoping this gift would open the door for possibly more between them?

Before he could rationalize why he'd truly gotten Della a present, Wallie snatched the thimble and dashed up the steps. "Last one in doesn't get one of Momma Della's hugs."

It was probably best if Wallie gave her the thimble. That would give Hank time to ponder his apology and choices. Keeping Della here was supposed to make his life less complicated, not more. But here he was, tied up in knots over how he felt about her. It would be simpler if he didn't care at all. But hadn't she proved herself over and over again to be worthy of his trust? Would it be a good idea to see if they could grow their relationship?

After releasing Dorothy into the pasture, Hank climbed on top of his white horse, Pete. His oil crew should be preparing for their newest location. Checking it out didn't need to happen today, but heading out would give him something productive to do and stop him from obsessing about his beautiful, frustrating wife.

The combination of the briskness in the air and the speed of horseback stung his face. The weather finally decided to turn into fall, all except the beaming sun. The ride was quiet—too quiet. It sounded odd without the hum of the steam engine moving the walking beam on Father Abraham's rig. And the silence wasn't helping him stay away from examining any potential emotions concerning Della.

The closer Hank rode to the drill site, the stronger the smell of sulfur, and the more it looked like his men were standing around. He'd thought he and Isaac had finally weeded out all the slackers and troublemakers after the last set of employees who had been fired. Apparently not.

When his men spotted him, someone jumped on a horse and headed Hank's way with dust clouds thundering behind. When he was close enough for his face to be visible, Hank realized it was Nicolas.

"Where's Isaac?" Hank asked when they met in the middle of the field near one of the old wooden barrels.

Nicolas jerked his chin back toward a trio of trees. "Under the shade. He...well. Sir." Nicolas blinked twice. "When we were disassembling Father Abraham, a beam landed on his head. He says he's all right."

"How bad is it?" Hank asked. Nicolas squirmed in his saddle, and Hank's stomach knotted at the hesitation. "Come on, man. Spit it out. How bad is it?"

Nicolas tightened his grip on the reins. "There's been some blood. Or a lot. Depends on who you're asking."

"I'm asking you."

"Plenty. Sir."

Hank nudged Pete into a gallop and soon arrived at the retired drill site where Isaac lay sprawled on the ground. A saddle had been turned into Isaac's pillow, elevating his head and neck. His shirt was off and pressed to his forehead. Bright red stained his once clean work shirt. The other men were squatted around, gawking at the ground as if waiting for help to sprout out of the earth.

"Does anyone want to tell me how the man who got hurt is the one who gave up the shirt off his back to stop his own bleeding?"

"Leave 'em be, Boss." Isaac licked his chapped lips. "It was far quicker to do it myself than to start barking directions I didn't feel like giving at the time." Isaac's eyes remained closed, and his voice was hoarser than normal.

That explained Isaac's actions, but did nothing to justify all the other men standing around and doing nothing. Why couldn't Hank hire men who held any gumption? He couldn't even claim Isaac. He'd been hired by his father-in-law. Hank knelt and lifted Isaac's bloodied shirt. A nasty gash above his left eyebrow ran into a lump above it. Hank gently set the shirt back to keep the seeping blood from dripping into Isaac's eye.

"I'm sure it's better than it looks," Isaac muttered and readjusted the rag before resting his other hand on his stomach.

The man was too pale. Someone should have ridden to the cabin for help. "Have they at least given you something to drink?"

"I'm fine, Boss. Really. Just needed to rest a bit. I'll be ready to work in a few."

He thought Hank was going to let him go back to work? Hardly. "You are not working today or for a long time."

Isaac's eyes popped open. Hank expected them to be glossy from pain and blood loss, but they bore a heated glare Hank wasn't used to receiving from his laid-back foreman. "You're firing me?"

There was no denying now that the man had hit his head entirely too hard. "I'm not going to fire you, Isaac.

Why would you think that? I have a feeling once I learn the story of how you got yourself lying on the ground, it will be anything but your fault. Even if it were, you know me better than to believe I'd fire you over one mistake. Plus, you can't leave. This place would fall apart. However, it's my beam that landed on your head, and I'm here to tell you, you're taking days off until you're healed."

"I'll be right as rain in a bit."

"I'm serious. You're taking a break. You're not going to hurt yourself worse by jumping back in too quickly."

"You know this little cut isn't your fault."

It wasn't a simple cut, and in a way, it *was* his fault—or at least his responsibility. Everything that happened to the men while they worked on his land was his responsibility. "Seven days. That's how long you'll be resting. Maybe longer. It will be a good opportunity for Nicolas to test his leadership capabilities." Or lack thereof. "Especially if he'll be wanting a raise now that he's got marriage on his mind."

"Ah, so the rumors made it to you."

Hank grunted an acknowledgment. Miss Vogel had been the one to mention it. For once one of her visits had been useful. His father-in-law had often reminded him of the importance of staying up to date on their crew's personal lives. What went on in their off-duty hours affected how they worked and would trickle into Hank's family's lives, too. Which was why he'd panicked the day he married Della and assumed his fired employees had returned to seek revenge.

"I can handle the crew while you're resting. If the newest site goes well, I'll put the men on barn roof patching duty." That should work for most everyone.

His men would still get paid. Isaac would have much overdue rest and be back in time to check the reassembled new rig.

"Don't want to rest. I'll be fine by morning." Isaac lifted his shirt, now a makeshift rag, and his face slackened as he noticed the amount of blood that had soaked through.

First he'd claimed that in a bit he'd be well, and now he'd extended it until the morning. If that wasn't proof enough of the seriousness of the situation, Isaac's lack of color revealed the truth. It would be a poor reward of Isaac's loyalty to put him back to work while he was still healing. The man could have left when Hank's father-in-law passed, but instead he'd stuck around and mentored a very green oil land owner. If he needed time off, Hank aimed to see that he got it. "I'm sending Nicolas on back ahead of the wagon. Ma will be ready to fix your noggin when we arrive." He hoped her wrists would feel up to it, because he knew Della could sew, but wounds were not her allies.

Hank grabbed his canteen from one of the pockets in his saddlebag and lifted it to Isaac's mouth. "A week. I mean it, Isaac. You deserve a break." Even if that meant his own plans for the church, bridge and talks to get to know his wife had to wait.

Hank stared at his plate of food and tried to scrounge up the energy to eat. All he could focus on was how much Isaac needed a raise. It had only been a couple days of running the oil crew by himself, and Hank wasn't sure if he was coming or going.

Another light joined his in the quiet kitchen, and Della's smile chased away more of the room's darkness.

"Did I wake you?" She was still in her day dress, but her hair was unpinned and flowing around her shoulders.

"Couldn't sleep and wondered if you'd rather have some warm oats instead of chilled leftovers?"

Her kindness made his jaw slack. "Please, don't feel like you have to do that."

"No one wants cold food when they've been working so hard," she said as she readied the stove, oats and pan.

"It's my own fault for not being on time for supper." He could have eaten with his crew. Yet it was like something was calling him to work straight on through so he could hurry home afterward. "And you're probably more tired than I am after herding the boys all day."

"I doubt you enjoy oil work as much as I love spending time with the boys. Hardly fair to compare." She opened the hutch and grabbed a bowl. "How do you want your oats?"

What he wanted was for her to sit and for him to provide her with the compassion she was always handing out to his family. He stood and blocked her way to the butter and milk. It was time he showed her how grateful he was for all she was doing for his family. He opened his mouth to say as much—but something else came out instead. Words that had been hovering on the tip of his tongue for days now. "Sorry for snapping at you at the church." He reached for the bowl, and she didn't move when their fingers connected.

"It's okay."

It wasn't, not really. He never should have hidden behind his work instead of talking with Della. Despite his overdue apology, he wasn't quite ready to explore the depth of fear that came from the idea of losing her. But he wasn't ready to be alone for the night, either. "Want to stay and eat some oats with me? Might help you fall asleep faster." He leaned around her for another bowl. "Butter and sugar or milk?"

He heard her swallow, and she didn't move until her lips pulled into a smirk. "Actually, I prefer to use a little of all three plus a secret ingredient." She raised her brows as if to challenge him.

He shrugged. "If you can best Ma's pies, I think I can trust your cooking."

"If you're sure." She smiled fully with her dimple close enough to kiss. "Though I must warn you, it's the best. Once you try it, you won't want them any other way."

Everything about Della was the best. That's what made it so hard to shield his heart from falling for his sweet, caring wife.

"Hiya, Isaac!" The boys waved as they passed.

"Good morning, Isaac," Della called as she trotted a few steps behind them on their way to their next study spot. "How are you feeling?"

The man usually gave her a warm greeting, but today, his smile was missing. She wondered if it was pain from his injury that had dampened his spirits. The cut above his eye was healing, but it still looked decidedly uncomfortable with the purple bruises that circled the knot on his forehead.

Isaac closed the barn door. "Same as I did four days ago, Mrs. Lamson. Fine enough to go back to work. Your husband is entirely too stubborn." He tipped his hat and headed for Roy's wood shop.

Mrs. Lamson. Della repositioned her hold on her

teacher basket. Isaac wasn't the only one to call her by that name. Each time she heard herself referred to as such, it felt more and more real. Especially after sharing oats with Hank in the kitchen. And yes, her husband was entirely too stubborn.

He hadn't been around much since taking over Isaac's job, and he'd looked so worn-out last night. But Isaac's injury held some hidden blessings. For one, it meant that Hank hadn't had any time to burn the old church building. God had been watching out for His church. And for her with the snake. Neither had Hank brought up building her that separate house he'd offered during his proposal. She understood the intended kindness in the gesture, but she didn't want to live all by herself. Alone.

What she prayed for was a husband who wanted to be near her. Who loved her, not just for how good she was with the boys, or for how she helped Alice, or made him pie. She wanted to feel accepted and valued as a wife instead of just a stepmother and daughter-in-law.

Last night when Hank asked her to stay and eat with him, he looked like he wanted to kiss her again. So why hadn't he? How did she go about removing the wall between them? This was her home now, her family. She wanted to do whatever it took to make things work— because she was certainly never going back to Indiana. Not to stay, anyway.

The letter from home she'd received days ago proved that Mother only valued her when it was to her own benefit. How could she have asked Della to send her money? Everyone knows a teacher's income wasn't much more than what they could live on. Not that she really wanted her money. She wanted Della to return home and work for Father at the paper for free, just like she always had. It seemed Mother finally realized the importance of all Della had done around the house and at the newspaper. The backhanded acknowledgment of her contributions didn't bring the satisfaction Della had once believed it would.

She switched the basket into her other hand and observed how the boys walked in a line, oldest to youngest. Funny how they did that even on their own. Wallie lagged behind with his head tilted, gazing at the clouds. He hadn't asked her to call him Wallace anymore once she admitted to liking his nickname.

When he tripped over a stick on the ground, she caught his arm and Wallie gave her his toothless grin. "Thanks, Momma Della. I was watching a ship sail across the sky." He nodded to a rectangular cloud. "Do you think real ships are as big as that?"

"Have you never seen a steamboat before?"

Wallie shook his head. "Just the steam engine at the pumps." His big brown eyes displayed his disappointment on the matter.

"We'll have to change that, won't we? And yes, they are as big as that cloud."

Wallie skipped away, hollering at his brothers that they were going to go see a real steamer-ship someday. Back in Indiana Della and her brothers had gotten to see the boats. She hoped eventually Hank and the boys would travel with her for a visit back home. The boys would love meeting Freeman. And she missed him. Together they could share with the boys their once favorite spot for catching frogs. Take them to the paper, not because she wanted to show them off to Tom, but because Edward would enjoy reading a freshly printed edition. She'd teach them how to blow on the ink so it wouldn't smear.

But would they be welcome at the paper if Della failed to give in to her mother's demands? Della felt bad that Father's newspaper was struggling, but what could she do? Even if she wanted to, she couldn't return and help. Her job now was to help raise the boys. And she didn't have any extra funds to send.

How was the paper in the red anyway? It hadn't been before she'd left. And it shouldn't be, with a new partner who'd married for money. Why not ask Tom for the money instead of the daughter who'd fled to get away from that man's greed and hard heart?

Wallie turned around as if he knew something had upset her. She gave him a smile to reassure him that she was fine. And she was. God had provided her with a loving family, even if it wasn't the one she'd been born to.

Robert and Edward stopped in front of a pine tree at the bottom of the incline that led to the old church building. When she arrived, Edward reached for the blanket in her basket. "I can spread it out for you, Momma Della."

She blinked away tears. "Thank you, Edward. What a gentlemanly thing to do." He had never called her momma before. Wallie had, but not the other boys. Oh, how she loved her new job. Teaching. Motherhood. These boys—her boys. If Wallie looked again at the shapes of the clouds, she wouldn't be surprised to discover her heart floating there because it'd leaped with joy.

She treasured these moments all the more because of the contrast with other parts of her life. Della expected more mail from home any day, and she couldn't fool herself into believing her family would have anything kind to say—even to the news she'd shared via her latest letter about her marriage.

She had a feeling Mother would somehow find a way to disapprove of her marriage to Hank. And Father would side with Mother to keep her happy and prevent her from turning her sharp tongue and biting criticisms toward him. Not that Della blamed him. She used to aim to do just the same; except she'd never landed the target. For as long as she could remember, she'd been her mother's favorite object to berate. The latest letter from home showed how that had not changed.

To say Wallie's gifted thimble was a welcomed comfort after her mother's letter was putting it mildly. The roses engraved on the side proved how much he cared for her, knowing her favorite flower.

She and the boys had settled in on the blanket when she noticed Isaac walking down the hill from the cabin. He veered toward them instead of heading to the creek, surprising her.

Wanting to speak to him away from the boys, in case something was wrong, she handed the boys their chalkboards. "Let's start with locating our memory Scripture for the week and writing it on your boards. I'll be right back."

Robert opened the Bible and began the search for the first book of John.

"Is everything all right?" Della asked when she met Isaac.

His thumb itched a spot above his brow. "Yes, everything's fine. Sorry to worry you. Have you seen Roy?"

"Roy? I think he and Alice went to visit Reverend Miller."

"Oh. He did. All right. I'm sorry to bother you then, Mrs. Lamson." He tipped his hat and turned to walk away, but she called out to stop him.

"You're not bothering us. Are you sure everything's okay?"

He toed a clop of weeds, much like the boys did when they were trying to procrastinate tackling a chore, and glanced back at the cabin. "Yesterday I assisted Roy with a woodworking project, that's all. Was hoping to feel useful again. I don't think Boss realizes that sitting still isn't good for my soul."

She understood the desire to feel needed, but also saw the reasons for Hank's concern. "I'm sure he only wants you and that wound to heal. Everyone needs a little rest now and then."

"I rest on the Lord's Day. Hank doesn't realize that I can't be…" He wiped the back of his hand across his mouth. "Idle. Nope. Can't. And all the animals have been fed and watered. Brushed even. The barn mucked. All of them. The coop, too. I've run out of tasks, and I'm in need of something to keep these hands busy." He held his palms out and narrowed his eyes at them as if they required punishment for not having a task already. "With Roy gone…" He dropped his hands to his sides. "You wouldn't have anything needing done, would you?"

Her gaze automatically lifted to the old church on the hill, the steeple the only thing within view. She'd explained to Roy about her idea. He, unlike her husband, loved it, and had encouraged her to keep praying about the situation, reminding her God could change hearts.

He could, but whose heart would He be changing, hers or Hank's? In the end, she'd prayed God would show them His will for the old church.

There had been no clear sign either way, yet every time she was outside, she thought of how the stained-glass windows were being wasted not being gazed upon. And each time the boys were stuck doing their studies at the kitchen table, distracted at every turn by whatever meal Alice was preparing, she wished they had a special place to go where they'd know that their focus wouldn't be interrupted.

Della bit her lip and looked from the steeple to Isaac and back. Hank had apologized for how he'd reacted at the church. Maybe if they cleaned the place up, they could help him look past his ideas of the church. If Isaac was willing… Was God providing help to keep this project moving forward?

"Isaac, what are your thoughts on snakes?"

Chapter Seventeen

The sun streamed through the bottom panel of the windowsill much higher than he was used to seeing it. Hank rubbed the morning from his eyes before kneading the ache in his lower back. Was the rooster sleeping in? Maybe the old bird was feeling the long week, too.

Hank checked his pocket watch on the bedside table and squinted at the dial in disbelief. The rooster wasn't the only one who'd slept in. After throwing on his work clothes, he bumped into Ma in the kitchen.

"Mornin', sleepy head," she said, sounding far too amused.

"Why didn't you wake me?" he grumbled.

"It appeared that you needed rest. Not sure how you achieved any with the rooster carrying on like he did, though. I was beginning to wonder if he'd ever quiet down. Wallie counted six crows while we were sitting at breakfast."

Hank tugged on one of his boots, sending shards of dirt along Ma's floor. He usually woke to the rooster's crow so automatically that he was out of practice getting ready in a rush. "What I need is to make sure George doesn't hurt himself or anyone else again." Would Nicolas lead the men to the drill site without him? It would show initiative, which would be a positive sign for Nicolas—but it would also mean that the men would risk getting hurt without him there to supervise.

"You know you don't have to worry." Ma finished sweeping the floor, probably for the second time. "Isaac will watch them. He always does."

Hank took the broom from her and tucked it back into its corner. She shouldn't be cleaning the mess he created. "Isaac is supposed to be healing and relaxing."

Ma mumbled something and worried her fingertips in her apron. Never a good sign. "Ma?"

She grabbed a mug out of the cabinet. "You're hungry. Let's get you something in that belly. Coffee's on the warmer, and I'll whip you up some eggs real quick. The boys ate the ones Della fixed this morning. They must be in a growth spurt. Never seen them polish off so many."

The boys were always in a growth spurt, they were boys after all, but their egg eating may have something more to do with being in the honeymoon stage of bending over backward to please Della. As Wallie had proven, there was an ongoing competition to be her favorite. That wasn't surprising. It was the other part of what his mother had said that snagged at him.

"Hold on the eggs. What's going on with Isaac?" Was he more injured than he let on? If he was, it would be all Hank's fault for not protecting him.

"You know that man is a hard worker."

That wasn't an answer, and she knew it by the way she fled to the stove. "Ma?"

"Ahh, Hank." She cracked an egg into a skillet and

the grease popped. "That man doesn't have a sit-still bone in his body." Ma squeezed her wrist before cracking another egg. Ever since Della had mentioned Ma rubbing her wrist, he'd noticed her favoring them. A lot. "There's nothing to tell. I went to bring him a treat late yesterday." She fluffed the eggs with a fork. "He wasn't resting in the bunkhouse is all."

The knot in Hank's stomach eased a bit. Isaac was going to heal then. There was no permanent injury to feel guilty over. That was a relief, even if it was obvious something else was going on that he'd have to figure out. "And?"

Ma shrugged, adding seasoning to his breakfast. "That's all I'm certain about. Didn't want to find out where he was because then I'd have to tell you he was back to some kind of work."

He rolled his shoulders to release the tension in his neck. Of course Isaac wasn't resting like he was supposed to. Would the man ever learn he was not required to work himself to death? It wasn't like it was his property. The responsibility wasn't his to bear. It was Hank's. However, at the moment, Isaac wasn't the only one needing correcting.

Hank gave Ma a stern glare. "Are you lying again?"

Ma clucked her tongue. "Not hardly, Hiram Robert. I didn't know where the man was—or what he was doing—and I didn't go looking. Like you said, he is supposed to be enjoying his time off. Maybe he was doing so in a different location than the bunkhouse. I only chose not to chase him down. He is a grown man who is capable of making his own decisions." She aimed the end of her fork in Hank's direction. "Like telling you when he's well enough to return to work."

She left the stove and gathered a pile of clothes off the table. "Here. Do you mind taking these and laying them on Della's bed?" She'd phrased it as a question, but it was clear that the only acceptable answer was yes, given the way she shoved the boys' pants into his arms without waiting for a reply. "I'll get your breakfast finished. Need to put some coffee in you yet. That way, whenever you do find Isaac you won't be entirely grouchy."

"I'm not…"

Ma was back into her mother role full force, stopping him with a single, powerful look and the judgmental slant of her head. "You are. Now shoo." She directed him toward the stairs as if he were Mabel in need of her coop.

Della's door was already propped open, but Hank knocked anyway, not wanting to overstep any boundaries. He stared at the carpet bags in the corner, uncomfortable with the way they reminded him of when she first arrived. How she'd made it obvious that she was no mail-order bride and had no desire to marry him. And how he'd encouraged her to accept his proposal later on because of his boys. For Ma and Pa. Not for himself. He'd been protecting his own heart, but had he damaged hers in the process?

The ring on his finger was a weighted reminder of how he longed to be a part of a pair again. Having someone to talk to before drifting off to sleep. Not feeling alone when dealing with life's stresses. A built-in best friend. A helpmate. Yes, his folks pitched in so much, and he was unendingly grateful for them, but marriage provided a different kind of support. One that he missed.

The scent of roses and honey in Della's room brought the memory of how her lips had tasted when they sealed their wedding vows. He shook his head harder. What if she wasn't ready to be fully married? What if he upset her by changing the terms of their marriage beyond what she'd agreed to? It would be safer, wouldn't it, to think of her as the boys' caretaker and teacher and not in that green dress? Not as a wife—his wife?

He needed to get out of her room. His heart shouldn't get fully involved if there was any chance that hers wasn't. Though if she wasn't ready yet, would she agree for him to court her? Ease into the idea of forming a true relationship, based on mutual love?

He pondered that idea as he placed the pants on her dresser. With his errand completed, he turned to leave when something crunched underneath his boot. Thankful it was nothing breakable—just a piece of note paper, covered with writing in an unfamiliar hand. He went to place it on Della's bed, but his gaze caught a word of the handwritten script.

Money.

He gripped the paper tightly in a futile attempt to stop the shaking of his hands. The penmanship was small and slanted, nevertheless the word *money* hopped off the page in multiple places. Hank threw the paper down and backed away, his shoulders bumping into the open door.

Someone in Della's life was asking for money. His money.

His lungs clenched in his chest, squeezing tighter with each determined step away from her room. But in that moment, he felt as if there couldn't be enough distance in the world between him and another woman he'd misjudged. Especially since this time, he'd married her, which was a mistake he couldn't undo.

Had Della fooled him just like Miss Smith? If it really was all an act, he had to congratulate her on her skill—and thoroughness. Instead of pretending to love him, Della had done it to his entire family.

But was it truly all an act? Yes, the letter hinted that she might be like all the other greedy women of town… except her actions with his boys—with him—had felt genuine. He prayed it was all a misunderstanding. Like the one that brought her here.

Hank left a confused Ma in the kitchen. The smell of breakfast and the sound of her questions drifted out the back door after him as he let it slap shut. He couldn't stomach either. Not when his stomach was twisting into knots over this new trouble that money had brought into his life. It had already stolen and ruined so much. Would it ruin his marriage, too?

Wallie had his tongue pushed against his cheek with one of his eyes closed, concentrating on writing the perfect *w*. Edward's groan drew her attention. "Here comes Papa. I hope he's not coming to give us more chores."

"Can't we stay and do lessons instead?" Robert's comment caught her off guard. She was pleased that he was enjoying his lessons, but she hoped he wasn't using them as an excuse to get out of his chores.

"I'll have to talk with your father."

"But you're Momma Della now," Robert argued. "That means you can tell him no."

"Parenting works better if your father and I are allies."

"Oh!" Wallie raised his hand. "That means friend."

She rested her hand on her chest, feeling her pulse getting carried away. Was Hank coming because of chores? Or because he wanted to see them—see her? She'd tried to wait up for him again last night to offer him more oats and conversation, but had fallen asleep by accident, not stirring until morning.

She'd continue to pray that she could be Hank's friend who would become worthy of his love one day. She had no expectation that today would be that day, but she still hoped that she'd at least have a chance to spend time with him and grow their relationship.

She searched for her husband while he disappeared behind one of the trees along the path. When he came back into view, she lifted her hand in a wave, feeling herself flush as he drew nearer. Was it silly to respond so strongly to the approach of her husband? Especially when their marriage was still in-name-only? Did Hank ever think about their moment in the barn, or did his heart ever race when she was near? Or did he find himself longing to discuss his day with her?

Wallie tugged on her sleeve. "I reckon he came to hear your story and to see us since he's been busy 'cause Isaac got hurt. Do you think he'll notice you lowered our ears?"

"Even if he doesn't, you boys made me proud with how well you sat still and waited for me to finish cutting your hair."

Wallie jumped to his feet, and after Hank embraced him, Wallie took hold of Hank's hand. "You're just in time for the story! It's gonna be a giant story. A giant is someone who's really tall." Wallie stretched his free hand high about his head, rising a bit on his tiptoes. "Even taller than you, Papa. Right, Momma Della?"

Della nodded, studying Hank's rigid stance and the tense lines spread across his forehead. Why wouldn't he meet her gaze? When his stare strayed beyond her, toward the church, the stone-like weight in her chest buckled her knees. He must have found out about Isaac cleaning the building. And for him to look that angry about it, she could only conclude that his heart hadn't been changed.

Della licked her lips, hoping it would give her a moment to think of how to explain.

"Boys." Hank's voice was gruff. "Pa needs you at the barn."

"Ahh." Wallie dropped his hold of Hank. "But Momma Della was going to read."

Hank gave Wallie a stern look.

"Yes, sir," Wallie whispered, letting his head droop along with his words.

"We'll read it in a bit." She couldn't help the waver in her voice.

Hank watched his two older boys chase each other back on the path for the house. Behind them, Wallie was dragging his feet. He kept peeking over his shoulder as if he'd noticed the tension between her and Hank and wanted to run back and fix it. The boy was too observant and kindhearted for a six-year-old—or for any age, for that matter.

Once out of the boys' sight, Hank crossed his arms and set his gaze on her. Della swallowed, liking it better when he was inspecting the church. Her fingers gripped each side of her skirt. How could she have been so foolish? She hadn't fixed a problem; she'd created a larger one.

She released her skirt and smoothed its imaginary

wrinkles. She knew that she should have told him before recruiting Isaac to help clean up the church. Yet he wasn't around, and Isaac wanted something to do. It wasn't like she had gone back inside the church. On the contrary, she'd stayed away, like Hank had asked. Yes, she'd peeked in after Isaac had removed the barriers from the front door and proclaimed it snake free, but then she'd left without stepping foot inside. And Isaac said *he'd* never promised Hank that he would stay out of the church building—only that he would stay off ladders during his time off work. So technically, no one had broken any promises.

Della rubbed her hands up and down her arms, the self-soothing action providing little comfort for her nerves. "I'm sorry. I should have come to you first. But I didn't want to push. You said you needed time to think about the whole school thing, but then after the snake, you seemed so upset, especially when you mentioned burning it down, and when Isaac said—"

"Wait." Hank's glare softened into confusion for a moment. "Isaac? What does he have to do with this?"

"It was his boredom, really. He wanted a project to tackle, and I told him about my idea for the old church. Actually, I told Roy…"

Hank stepped to the side and squinted up the hill. With the boards removed, the front doors to the church were open, giving Isaac the fresh air and sunlight he needed as he tackled his cleaning project. Technically, *their* cleaning project. She thought God had okayed her desire—that He had sent Isaac to help her as an indication of His approval. It wasn't like she had searched for Isaac's help. She'd prayed. Waited for a sign. Hadn't one arrived? She thought if the old church was cleaned,

Hank would finally be able to visualize the potential the beautiful building still contained. She didn't want Hank fearing snakes or only seeing evil in the place that caused him and his family pain.

"You mean to tell me Isaac's working *inside* the old church?" He placed both his hands on the top of his head.

Della drew in a breath, suddenly worried. He wouldn't fire Isaac, would he? As Hank turned for the hill, she reached for him, but he shrugged off her touch. The rejection stung, as usual, but she pushed her feelings aside to focus on what mattered. "Don't fire Isaac. Please. This is my fault. Not his. He only wanted to help. That's all I want to do."

Hank glared at the spot where she'd touched him. "Did you plan this from the start? I have to say, you were smart. It's clear you did your homework. You knew just what to say, what to do to hook me and my family into loving you."

Had he meant that? Did he love her? But if so, how could he also be so cruel, accusing her of manipulating him and his family?

"Della...were you even going to stick around after you found the money? What about the boys? Are their broken hearts a part of your scheme, too?"

She crossed her arms at the mention of the boys—her boys. "I'm not leaving or breaking any hearts. Hank, when have I said I needed or even wanted your money? Are you talking about money to fix up the church? I hadn't planned anything beyond cleaning it." Where was this coming from? Had one of the town women spread a lie about her to Hank to try to sabotage their marriage? "Did Miss Vogel tell you I was after your money? Do you really believe her over me?"

"Your letter told me."

Her letter? What letter? Had he read the letter she'd written to her family before Roy had mailed it? But why would that letter have upset him? All she did was talk about marrying him and how happy she was in Missouri, but...

A second later, the penny dropped. Mother's letter... which had asked for some of her teaching money...had been out in her room. Had Hank seen it? Did he think the greedy, mercenary nature her mother displayed in the letter was reflected in Della as well? Della placed her palm to her cheek as the ground felt like it disappeared underneath her. It appeared misunderstandings would be a battle they'd never stop fighting.

If only he'd read the letter in context. "There's been some miscommunication. Again. My mother didn't know I married when she sent me her letter. And she for sure couldn't have predicted you had money to give, whether or not I was willing to ask for it. I don't even know how much money you had or have, and I don't care. In the time I've been here, you've proved to be a man who loves his family and takes pride in seeing to their needs, so I trust you to provide for me." She stepped closer, fisting her hands in her dress so as not to reach for him. It was clear by his expression that her touch wouldn't be welcomed. What could she say to get through to him?

"I'm never leaving the boys. I love them. They are *my* boys now. You all are my family. Including you. Reread the letter. My mother didn't say anything about your money. She just asked me to return home to work at Father's newspaper so my parents could save their own money rather than hiring someone to replace me." Shaking her head, she muttered under her breath, "As if blaming me for the end of my engagement and offering a partnership in the newspaper to my ex-fiancé wasn't bad enough." She pushed the thought away. "Let me get the letter. You can see for yourself—"

Hank widened his stance and opened and closed his mouth. "End of your engagement?"

She held her chin higher. She would not cry over Tom. Never again. "You aren't the only one who has been hurt by thorns of life."

Hank rubbed the back of his neck, strain lining his forehead. "If what you say about the money and the letter is true, then why did you break your promise about the old church? You know how I feel about that place."

Of course she knew. He hated it because it was where his wife had been hurt. The wife he had actually loved.

How had she believed cleaning a building would wipe away the disgrace of its past? Like her, it wouldn't have a new beginning. A tear slid down her cheek, falling to the ground where her hope for a marriage that was more than a convenience lay trampled.

Chapter Eighteen

As Alice wrapped Della into a hug, the last bit of her restraint seemed to break and the tears finally came. How had Alice gotten her to spill what she'd kept buried? Della shifted on the bed, wanting to throw the beloved quilt over top her head and will time to turn back. But to when? It wasn't like her problems had only started when she'd married Hank. Even before she'd come to Missouri, she'd had a lack-of-love problem, thanks to her parents and Tom.

After letting her cry herself out, Alice slid a handkerchief into Della's hand. "Come on. Let's wipe away those tears."

Della dabbed the offered cloth on her cheeks. She shouldn't let Alice see her like this, all red, blotchy and burdensome. When Tom had ended everything, she'd locked herself in her room. Mother hadn't even bothered checking on her. Alice, however, had taken one glance at her and followed her up the stairs, matching her pace, and pushed the door open when Della tried to keep her out.

"There we are. There are those beautiful eyes." Alice

patted Della's hand. "Why don't you go enjoy God's creation? Fresh air for a fresh perspective. Take a walk. Talk to Him. Hmm? Life doesn't always go as we hoped. You may have planned to have a different future, but I'm so glad the Lord had us lined out for you."

"Me, too." And she meant it. She loved Alice and Roy and the boys. Treasured being a part of their daily lives, being a teacher. A mother. She had almost everything she dreamed of. Everything except love and trust from her husband.

"Roy and I cherish you," Alice assured her. "Oh, dear one, we do. So much." Her voice was in soft harmony with Della's waves of sniffles. "We loved you before we even set our eyes on you. But it won't be enough. Neither will the boys' love. But there's more waiting for you—I'm sure of it. Not just Hank. I believe one day, Hank will see what we already know. Yet even his love won't be enough."

Alice touched Della's wet cheek, running her knuckles up until she pushed back part of Della's hair that had escaped its pins. "No matter whose devotion you gain, it will never be enough. King Solomon searched the world for contentment and happiness, never finding it in gold, or knowledge, or in earthly relationships. My Roy offers me his heart daily, but it isn't his love that completes me. It's God. He alone can satisfy this hunger to feel loved."

Alice wiped at her own watery eyes with the edge of the apron she wore on Della's first day—the one that matched the window curtains. Della had arrived to teach some children, but she had been given more than simply a place to run away from her embarrassment over Tom. She'd been given a chance to find herself, and figure out what she truly needed to be happy. As much as she wanted Hank to love her, she held no control over his heart. Only her own. And she must keep that heart focused on God, because Alice was right, He would always be enough.

Alice opened Della's Bible, turning to a section in the middle and marking the place with the very letter that started another round of mix-ups.

"Now up with ya." She tugged Della to stand with barely any trouble and adjusted the collar on her sweater. "Here, take this," she said, handing over the Bible. "You can't trust God to work if you're hiding in here fretting. Go talk to Him." She gathered up Della's shawl as well, passing it over. "And don't forget this. Winter's chill is moving in on the wind—but you should be fine for the little while you'll need to get yourself sorted. Then go speak to your husband again. Enough miscommunication. Marriage is full of discord. Someone has to be the first to reach out, and it's usually not the stubbornest."

"What about the boys' lessons?" Della released a wobbly breath, trying to control her emotions. "I promised Wallie I'd read David and Goliath. Then there's—" She pointed to the pile of clothes on the dresser, waiting to be mended.

"There will always be a to-do list. Sometimes we must take care of ourselves before we can care for others. Especially us mothers." Alice winked at Della. "The boys will be more than thrilled to play for the rest of the day. And I'm pretty sure I can take care of reading one of my favorite Bible stories."

Alice guided Della down the stairs and out the back door. With a wave, Alice closed the door behind her. Della hugged her Bible to her chest. Where was she supposed to go? She could have very well wrestled with God in the safety of her room. What if she ran into Hank? She wasn't prepared to face another manifestation of his anger and disappointment.

The wind tugged at her sweater and sent a shiver coursing through her body. She wrapped her shawl around her. The air had cooled since she'd run from Hank. Mabel stood at a distance watching her as if she, like Wallie, sensed something troubling her. The rooster strolled beside Mabel and flapped his wings, making him appear twice his size, startling Della so much that she nearly missed the bottom porch step. Wherever she went, it wasn't going to be anywhere near that rooster.

The big maple's rope swing teetered back and forth as if calling for the boys to come and play. The sight of it reminded her of the grouping of trees where she'd given the boys, or rather tried to give the boys, their first lesson.

No, she didn't want to go there. The red barn was full of animals—and most especially animal smells. She wrinkled her nose and looked across the thinned garden. The boys would probably be jumping from the hayloft in the large barn before the hour was up.

Della craved a visit to the old church building. She was sure Isaac had cleaned it up quite a bit before Hank stormed the hill, and since Isaac had said it was definitely snake free, a visit should now be safe. But she wouldn't break her promise. Having Hank find her mother's letter and learning that she was fixing up the church building all at once had been disastrous.

Without any more thinking, she walked, not really paying attention to where she was going other than noticing that it was away. Away from the rooster, away from the baaing of sheep. Far from the hammering in the wood shop. She didn't stop until she reached the water as it tumbled against the creek banks. Up ahead of her was the old bridge Hank had brought them across on the day of the rainstorm. Its boards groaned in the breeze as if someone was marching across. She should have brought the boys to this part of the creek for their lessons during the warmer days. It looked to be a lot deeper than the section they had visited. They could have enjoyed swimming in the water, and the shade along the creek would have been perfect for their studies. It was more sheltered than along the other bridge.

A few water droplets splashed upon her cheek, yet she was far enough away to enjoy the view without getting too wet. There was time to go swimming and have lessons here next year. She wasn't going anywhere. No matter what Hank believed.

She spread her skirt on the cool grass and opened her Bible where Alice had marked.

"Let us hear the conclusion of the whole matter: Fear God, and keep His commandments: for this is the whole duty of man."

Her job wasn't to try and make her husband love her. Wasn't to strive to be enough for him, for his boys or for his parents. Or even for her parents. God simply asked that she honor Him. Love Him.

With all the worries surrounding her the past few months, she hadn't been doing a very good job of trusting or obeying. A bird sang overhead, the chirps combining with the melody of the water and creaking boards. Della waited with her eyes closed, listening to the music of God's creation. A smile tugged on her lips as Pastor O'Ryan's departing words came to mind.

Too often we're not still long enough to read God's Word to find what He has for us. The verse found in Psalms 46 was a part of the last sermon he'd given before she boarded the train for Missouri.

Why hadn't she sought God's Word with all that had been troubling her? She reread the marked verse, putting the words to memory. It didn't matter how much she had failed in the past. Now she would truly start digging into and applying the truth.

The Bible pages on her lap fluttered in the wind, and it almost sounded as if she heard her name.

"Momma Della!"

Della stood, her Bible and shawl dropping to the ground at the urgency of Wallie's cry. She looked behind her and across to the other side of the creek. There was no sign of her little boy in sight.

Where was he?

"Momma Della, help!"

"Oh, Wallie!" Her son was on the old bridge, leaning over the teetering rope railing.

Hank didn't knock on the door of Pa's wood shop, instead he traipsed in and started rummaging through drawers. "Where have you hidden my matches? It's beyond time one of the ruined things around here gets fixed. Today, the old church finally pays for its past."

"I believe your wife has a better plan for the church's future that doesn't involve any matches," Pa replied calmly.

"Yeah, well, my wife..." He leaned against Pa's workbench, needing something solid to give him support because his own strength was failing. Had been for a while. "Has spent far too long making plans. She..."

She'd been slipping past the walls he'd carefully built around his heart and look where that had gotten him. Again.

Pa's hand was on his shoulders directing him to the far wall. "Why don't you try out the newest rocker? Isaac helped attach the armrests."

"I wouldn't bring Isaac up. I'm none too happy with him, either." Hank ran his palms along the wood and jerked his hand when a splitter caught in his skin. "The rough spots need to be smoothed out."

"Rough spots, indeed. Afraid that's a common problem going around. I'll agree to the no Isaac talk. However, those wrinkles on your forehead point to someone upsetting you, and I'm pretty sure I saw her running into your Ma's arms not long ago. So are you going to give me the story the easy way, or am I going to have to carve it out of you?" Pa smirked as he lifted one of his wood planes.

Hank didn't feel like laughing. "Your daughter-in-law may not be as perfect as you'd hoped." He explained about the letter and the church, though he also included Della's explanations, which he grudgingly admitted mostly made sense. What didn't make sense was his fear.

Pa remained quiet until Hank finally locked on to the splinter stuck in his skin. He pulled out the sliver, leaving a tiny flesh wound behind. It was amazing how much pain a thorn-size problem could produce.

Pa handed him a rag. "I can guarantee that you and Della will have your fair share of arguments. Even if she was—"

"She was supposed to be safe." Hank rose and tapped

his fist on the wall. Could anything be safe when God was in control instead of him?

"Safe?"

"Nothing. Never mind. Where are those matches?"

"Help me understand. That's why I'm here. We're around to help. That's why your ma and I got Della to come in the first place—so you wouldn't be alone if anything happened to us. No one lives forever, you know."

"That wasn't you being helpful. It was you getting your own way. You wanted me to marry. So you took it upon yourself to see it done." They took away his control, and he hated feeling so weak.

"Yes, and look what has become of it." Pa's grin made his eyes shine, and it irritated Hank.

"Are you seeing the same thing I am? What is there in all of this to be happy about? And did you know she was engaged before? What if there's other things about her past that we don't know?"

"Did you tell her that after Evelyn died you were engaged once, too? There's no shame in a past engagement. The main reason you're so untrusting about the letter is because someone did steal money from you. But Della's not Miss Smith. That woman never loved any of us."

Pa was right. Yet Miss Smith had played her part well. Hank sure had believed that she loved him. Or maybe he'd just wanted to believe it, in the hopes that a future with her would fill the emptiness that was in his heart. "You shouldn't have brought Della here."

"The boys and you and your ma are better because of your marriage to Della. And if you allow yourself,

I think you will be, too. Talk to her. Share your fears with her. More importantly, share your fears with God."

"I'm stuck in a marriage to a stranger. What was I thinking?" When all those women had gathered from town, he'd thought Della was the best of the bad options. The safest option. Part of that safety had been because he never expected to love her. He thought his heart was protected from future hurt. But it sure was hurting now.

"You're only stuck, because you're stubborn. You and Della can have a wonderful marriage—"

Hank held up his hand. "Della and I aren't like you and Ma. You both were—"

"More like you two than you understand." It was Pa's turn to sink onto the rocker. "Our marriage. Your ma…she came from Indiana."

"I know. She traveled west after her father died."

"She held little hope for a decent future." He sat up straighter and scrubbed his palms on his pants. "I'd just gotten back from the war."

The sun must have gone behind the clouds because the room darkened as if to match the somber tone.

"All that awful fighting." Pa rocked forward and back three times before he spoke again. "It taught me that life is short. When I returned, I was ready to settle down. However, I didn't have women traveling to my cabin, begging for my hand like you. Heard a rumor how some couples were finding each other through the papers. So, I paid for an ad, and your ma, well, she answered."

Was Pa saying what Hank thought he was? "Ma was a mail-order bride? Why haven't I ever heard about this?"

"A relationship is hard enough when two sinners come together and live in the same house. We didn't want others' opinions on our union to hinder the hurdles we'd already be facing. So, we kept the information quiet. We placed a want ad for you, because it worked for us. We used the same newspaper and everything. Yes, we were strangers at the time, but we were filled with hope and determined to put God first. Are you willing to open your heart to trust and accept God's guidance? Hardships will still come, but so will the blessings. And one of those blessings is Della. She loves you. It's in her eyes when she looks at you. It's in the way she treats your boys. It's in the way she's going to stay even though you accused her of being after your money. Are you truly against the idea of loving and trusting your wife?"

"But how do I know I can trust her?" Hank argued.

"How do you know you can trust anyone?" Pa countered. "Have you idealized your marriage to Evelyn to the point where you think the two of you never had any disagreements or misunderstandings?"

Had he put Evelyn on a pedestal? Was that another thing he'd done to keep himself from falling in love again? Could he let that go—let go of everything that was protecting his heart? "I can't." Even Hank strained to hear his own words. What if he allowed Della in all the way and she died, too? "I can't let God take more of my heart away." He'd have nothing left to offer his boys but bitterness, and he yearned to be a great father.

"God doesn't work that way. I won't argue that bad things never happen. We live in an evil world. That doesn't mean God sits around rubbing His hands wondering how He can make life more miserable. He wants to take your burdens. Aren't they getting heavy?"

"He had the power to save Evelyn, but He didn't. How can I trust Him?"

"In the war…" Pa swallowed, his eyes turning misty. "We were ambushed." His gaze danced along the ceiling, as if he was seeing the past unfold. "Both of the men beside me lost their lives. Gone before I could even plead with God to save them." He tapped his chest twice and his next words were weighed down with emotion. "It could have easily been me instead of either of them. There're some questions we'll never find answers to on this side of heaven. Doesn't mean God's not in control. Let Him show you His love. It will be enough to cover all your anger, questions, hurt…"

Hank couldn't glance away from his father's gaze.

"…and the fear to love again."

Chapter Nineteen

What was Wallie doing up on that bridge? Della picked up her skirt and sprinted over until she reached the edge of the first board. "Wallie." Her word went out like a question and a prayer. She wanted to run to his side but she was terrified that her weight would further destabilize the bridge.

"I—I thought you went across." Wallie licked his lips as his arms shook, clinging to the rope. "Papa doesn't want us on this bridge, and I didn't want you to get in no heap o' troubles. I wanted to find you because you looked sad and…and my boot's stuck. Momma Della, my boot's stuck."

Wallie tried to lift his leg, and the movement made the whole bridge slant toward the water. Wallie cried out.

"Momma. Help me!"

How was she going to get him safely off the bridge? She whispered a prayer, even though she understood that simply trusting and obeying God wouldn't mean that He'd keep Wallie from harm. She'd ask for His blessing—and then she'd do what she felt in her heart was right.

She lowered herself to her hands and knees and crawled, carefully balancing her weight on each board. How had she and Hank made it over this thing in the wagon? Wallie tugged his foot up and down, trying to break free of the board's hold. Panic was readily apparent in his movements and on his face.

Della dug her nails into the nearest wooden plank. His panicked struggles were putting him in more danger. She had to find a way to calm him down. "Wallie, honey…" She began singing to him, the very song she'd heard Alice sing to him at bedtime—the one she'd sang on his birthday. She wasn't sure how much Wallie heard over the thumping of Della's heart, or the water thundering below, yet he settled and color reappeared on his cheeks.

His bottom lip quivered. "I'm stuck."

Della nodded and continued singing as she crept closer. Wallie's foot had slid farther down through the hole. Only the top of his ankle could be seen. She needed time to plan, except a snapping sound from the other end of the bridge told her that her time was up. Only one thought filled her head—she must protect Wallie at all costs.

With a lunge, she wrapped her arms around her son. The boards beneath them gave way. This meant they no longer had to worry about getting his foot unstuck, but another problem surrounded them—or rather didn't.

As they fell, she tugged his head against her, trying her best to shield him from the worst of the upcoming impact. The slap of the creek's water made her suck in a breath. All she could take in was cold—until she noticed that the creek had turned red around them. She pushed the thought away, knowing she couldn't do anything about it in that moment. She kicked her feet to keep them floating, directing them toward the shore. Somehow she'd lost a boot, and she felt rocks scrape against her bare toes, her knee, her head.

She heaved herself and Wallie out of the water. Blood seeped through a cut hidden in his hair. She eased Wallie's hand away from his head, telling herself sternly that it would not do to get ill at the sight of his injuries. Not when he needed her.

She tugged off her drenched sweater and placed it under Wallie's hand. "Press down, Wallie." Water dripped from the sleeves and joined the flow of blood down his cheek. "Can you hold this here? Please hold this on your head, tight as you can."

Goose bumps rose below her short-sleeve shirt, but numbness and adrenaline worked like a temporary coat of armor.

"Don't leave me!" Wallie's arms flailed as he reached for her, ignoring her instructions to put pressure on his wound. More blood spilled down his face.

"Oh, honey. I won't leave you. I promise. Now, don't forget, you need to press. Okay?" She showed him with her hand as she pressed over his, ignoring the throbbing at the back of her own head. "Does it hurt anywhere else?"

Wallie shook his head and leaned further into her.

Della looked up, praying to find help standing before them. Anytime since her arrival when she'd ever been in danger, either real or not, Hank had been there. But this time, he wasn't. No one was. Except God.

And He was the only one she needed.

Wallie shivered in her arms. She had to get him warm. Della nearly tumbled on her trembling legs, trying to get to her dry shawl. She wrapped it best she could around him. "Are you pressing down, Wallie? I need you to keep pressing that on your ouchie. Can you do that for me, please?"

She scooped him into her arms and prayed that God would provide strength to make it back home, because she couldn't do it alone.

Hank was only positive of one thing: he was exhausted. When he stomped his muddy boots on the back step, glad to be done for the day, Pa came out and blocked his way into the house. If Hank were in a better mood, he might have laughed. Had Ma sent Pa out as a guard to protect her kitchen floors? Or worse, to extend their wood shop conversation?

"Wallie's fine, son, but—"

All humor and mud forgotten, Hank shouldered past Pa and took the steps three at a time. Pa only called him "son" when things were bad. Really bad. His breath caught in his throat. Why hadn't anyone gotten him before now?

On numb legs, he braced his hand on the doorway and then plowed forward. He didn't know what he expected to see, but it wasn't Wallie looking normal, kneeling beside his bed. His little hands were folded, and he was mouthing silent words.

He was really fine as Pa had said. Hank crushed him up into a hug and rubbed his hand through Wallie's hair until his little head jerked back. Only then did Hank see the cut near the top of Wallie's hairline.

"What happened?" He stroked the side of Wallie's face, careful not to get near his wound.

Wallie didn't answer. Tears filled his eyes, and Hank wanted to both hug him and demand answers.

Lord, please let him be okay. The prayer came out less grudgingly than usual. He was starting to hope that maybe God would listen.

"He's all right," Pa said from behind him. "Head injuries bleed more than they ought. His scratches were deeper when he stuck his hands into those rosebushes."

"What happened, Wallie?" Hank asked. "Did you jump out of a tree? The barn loft?"

Wallie's lips remained sealed. "Wallie, son…" He'd used the word *son* like Pa had earlier. Hank touched the other side of Wallie's forehead. "Tell me what happened so we can check to make sure you don't have any more injuries besides this one."

Wallie shook his head, the dread Hank felt daily in his heart mirrored in his son's eyes.

"Truth sets us free," Pa whispered.

Wallie rested his cheek against Hank's shoulder, gripping the sleeves of his shirt. "I didn't mean to. I thought she crossed the bridge."

If Hank glanced down, he'd expect to see his gut plunge to the wooden floor beneath him. "Which bridge?"

Wallie took in a gulp of air and held it in for a minute before he mumbled, "The one we aren't supposed to be on."

"Wallie, you know—"

"Momma Della was sad. I wanted to cheer her up. Then I thought I saw her cross the old bridge."

"Della was *on* the bridge?" That woman. As if the

church wasn't bad enough. She'd promised him she wouldn't go on that bridge without him. Was she trying to ruin his trust completely? Wallie could have been killed.

"No! Momma Della wasn't on the bridge. It was me. I was stuck, and she… Momma saved me. My foot." Wallie's lips quivered, and he wiped the back of his hand against his cheek. "It got caught. She had to come after me. And then the board broke, and she…" He wrapped his arms around his chest. "She saved me."

"We believe she protected him when they fell."

"What do you mean they fell?" Wallie's eyes grew in size before looking at Pa for what Hank could only decipher as help. "Off the bridge? You fell off the bridge?" Into the water. Into the cold water filled with rocks.

Wallie tilted his chin down. Hank cradled his son's head to his chest, taking him in. His smell. How small he felt, and how powerless Hank truly was to protect anyone.

Wallie had fallen off the bridge that Hank should have already fixed. Except he hadn't. He'd failed to protect his son…and God had stepped in, sparing the lives of his son…and his new wife.

"Is she all right?" Hank clenched his nails into his palms.

"She…had a difficult time," Pa hedged. "She positioned herself to take the brunt of the fall. And then, soaking wet, Della carried Wallie all the way home. Ma is tending her." Pa's tentative tone made Hank grip Wallie tighter.

"Can I see her yet?" Wallie asked plaintively. "Papa, Grandpa wouldn't let me see Momma Della. Did you know the wind wasn't cold on my wet clothes? Her shaking hugs were warm. She sang Grandma's song all the way home. Except when she fell by the trees two times. Then she was praying instead of singing. But God heard her, because we made it up the hill, and Grandma came running for us. That's what Momma Della asked for. Help. God gave her what she needed even though I caused all the bad to happen. I disobeyed, not Momma."

Wallie's eyes filled with tears. "I prayed for her like you told me to, Grandpa. So can I see her now?"

"I'm so glad you prayed." Pa's smile only pulled up on one side of his face. "Why don't you go visit with Mabel first? Give her another scoop of her special feed. If your brothers come around with grumbling bellies, show them where to get their snack until we figure out what to do about supper."

"They know where the bread is, Grandpa."

"Right you are." Pa held out a finger. "Though sometimes we need help with the things we already know."

Wallie hugged Hank and gave a matching one to Pa. "God is good. Right, Grandpa?"

"That He is, even when it doesn't look like it."

Hank felt his father's gaze on him, but instead of meeting Pa's eyes, he focused on calming his fears by watching Wallie leave. There was a spring in his son's steps as if he assumed God would make everything okay. Only when he was out of earshot did Hank turn to his father. "How's Della?"

"Your wife's body seems to be nearly as wounded as her heart is bruised from your last conversation."

Hank drug his hand over his face. "How bad?"

"Her heart?"

Hank glared at Pa.

Pa sighed. "She's feverish. By the time she reached the house, she was soaked, shaking and exhausted. It wasn't exactly an ideal day to take a swim or earn quite a few cuts and bruises."

"They could have…" Hank shouldn't have procrastinated in fixing the bridge or his marriage. If he was honest, all the blame for their injuries could be laid on him. It was as if he was reliving his worst fears even after trying so hard to protect his family and his heart.

"Oh, thank the mighty Lord." Ma came around the corner with her sewing basket in hand. "You're home. If you want your wife to heal quickly, you'll march in there and convince her that all this isn't her fault. She won't listen to me telling her that the blame is mine, not hers. It was my idea for her to go walk and pray. And then I took a nap, and by the time I woke up, Wallie had disappeared. Never would I have guessed he'd go to that bridge."

It seemed the entire house was loaded with guilt, and it began because he hadn't trusted Della. Or God.

"And whatever she says don't let her fool you, she's not to mend anything while she's in bed. I'm hiding this downstairs so she can't bribe the boys into bringing it to her."

The day was a mess. How was he supposed to fix everything? Hank stood. "Do you think she'd want some tea?" If only there was a blend that offered instant healing and forgiveness. No, he had a better idea. "I could make her some oats, or go to town and order some—"

Ma's hand rested on his. "Just go sit with her. Love and forgiveness don't need anything fancy. Talk. Pray."

Hank crept down the hall and knocked on Della's ajar door.

"Della?" When she didn't answer, he imagined the worst and cracked the door further open so he could peek inside. The last quilt Evelyn had sewn was tucked around Della, as if embracing and blessing her replacement. The beautiful woman lying beneath the quilt was fast asleep.

Footsteps up the stairs made Hank turn as he stood in her doorway.

"Ah, man." Wallie pouted. "Are you going to read to Momma? It's supposed to be my turn first."

"No, Wallie, I wasn't… I don't think…she needs to rest." She had to get better so he could apologize for all his shortcomings.

"She told Grandma we could read to her. See." He opened the door wider and pointed to a few books beside the bed.

Always a teacher. The thing that started this new adventure. No, he should call the want ad mix-up what it really was—a blessing in disguise.

Wallie sighed and held out a book to Hank. "Go on. You better read first. I want your heart to be happy." His son must have seen the question on Hank's face because Wallie pulled the sides of his lips down with his fingers. "Your mouth is like this."

Hank ruffled Wallie's hair that Della must have trimmed. Amazing how seamlessly Della had become a part of their family, strengthening him in his weaknesses. Wallie looked up at him expectantly.

Should he tell his son why his heart hurt? Hank had always preached honesty. "My heart hurts because… Have you ever been afraid?"

Wallie nodded. "Don't worry. Momma doesn't care if you read slow. She still loves Robert's reading."

Hank chuckled. "That's not why I'm worried."

"If it's because of today, Grandma says I'm fine and that Momma's going to be fine. She gots to be because…" His lips quivered. "Because I got to tell her thank you and…and that I love her. I should have told her that already."

"You love Momma Della?" He waited for her title to feel strange, but the wave of guilt never came.

Wallie nodded, climbing on the bed beside Della before Hank could stop him. "My heart doesn't hurt when she's around. Instead, it feels like I'm landing in a big pile of hay. Not because she has squishy hugs like Grandma, but because of right here." Wallie reached his hand forward, drawing closer to Della.

"No, Wallie." Hank whispered as loud as he could. "We shouldn't—"

"Yes, we should." She told me anytime I'm afraid I can always pray, and I can also hold her hand. She said we can pray anywhere and anytime." He pointed to Della's hand in his. "You want to try holding her hand?"

Hank's fingers twitched at his side, remembering how it felt when she'd slid her fingers around his in the barn. "I will. Later." And he would, right after he figured out how he was going to apologize for not trusting her.

Wallie smiled and crawled off the bed. "I'm going to go find Mabel. She always cheers Momma up."

Hank didn't have the energy to tell his son chickens don't belong in the house and instead sat in the chair pulled next to Della's bed. No matter what brought Della into his family's lives, Pa was right—his boys were better for it. He was better, too.

God had known what he'd needed all along. Hank

pushed back the strand of Della's hair that had fallen across her beautiful face. Even while Hank was mad at God, He continued to work in his life. Hank may never understand why Evelyn died, but he'd clearly been granted a second chance at love.

But would Della forgive him for pushing her away? For not trusting her? Was he too late to offer his love? Hank glanced at Wallie's open Bible on Della's dresser, his gaze locking on to another single word: *love*. Something far more valuable than any sum of money. *"We love Him because He first loved us."*

In his hurting, Hank had allowed himself to assume that God no longer cared about him because his life hadn't gone as he'd planned. Hank was also afraid that he'd run out of room in his heart. But that wasn't true. He could always show love no matter what he received back. What better way to start appreciating his wife than for him to mirror the One who loved us despite ourselves?

He took her hand in his. "Della, I'm sorry," he whispered, wishing she would open her eyes, but knowing she required rest. He needed to put God first, her second, and what she needed was…to not feel so warm.

He gently pressed the back of his other hand to her forehead, confirming what he'd discovered. She was burning up.

Wallie appeared at the foot of the bed with Mabel in his arms. "Did you not read to her yet? Your face is still scrunchy."

"Wallie, your momma needs cool rags, blankets and…" What if he was too late to fix this mess between them? What if Della didn't recover? What if—

Wallie slipped his fingers around Hank's hand.

"Don't worry, Papa, God's always with us. In the good and bad."

Taking his cue from his son's childlike faith, Hank prayed for healing. For a chance to tell his wife he was sorry, and that he was ready to love and trust not only her, but the One who'd never left him through it all.

Chapter Twenty

Della didn't know which woke her, an accidental kick in her knee from a bed-hogging Wallie or the piles of blankets crushing her chest. How cold did the boy think she was last night?

Wallie's shorter hair stood straight up around his healing wound. She sent up a silent prayer of thanks that God had supplied the strength to get them both home safely. Why hadn't she noticed Wallie was following her? If she had, he wouldn't have been on the bridge. And if she hadn't misunderstood Alice and Roy's mail-order bride ad for a teaching position, Hank wouldn't have offered to marry her—a choice he obviously regretted.

And yet, despite all that had happened—all the mistakes and misunderstandings—she wouldn't change any of it. Perhaps it was selfish, but she treasured being here surrounded by those who'd earned a place in her heart. Even if she never felt loved by her husband, Alice was correct. God had always been all she needed and would always provide the love and acceptance that she craved.

Careful of her bruise on the back of her head, she

fluffed her pillow and spotted one of her chalkboards placed on the nightstand. The boys must have practiced their memory verse to surprise her.

"We love Him because He first loved us."

Yes, God's love would always be enough. And with the certainty of His love, she allowed herself to believe that there was nothing wrong with loving her husband of convenience, too. She could risk her heart without worrying that another rejection would destroy her. Hank might forgive her one day. He might not. Either way, she couldn't ignore the fact that she'd fallen for him. That love was a gift, whether it was returned or not.

A sound came from outside her window, and she slid out from under the covers. Wallie rolled over and mumbled something before snuggling into her pillow. She tiptoed to keep the floor and her body from complaining, though the knot on her knee ached enough to make her grit her teeth.

She peeked through the curtains and saw that Hank stood beside the house with his arms crossed while Isaac petted the nose of his black horse, his faithful Stetson on his head. Della propped her weight against the wall for support, taking the pressure off her knee. If Isaac was still here, it meant Hank hadn't fired him over the work on the old church building. That was a load off of her mind.

Isaac was speaking, though she couldn't make out any of his words. Della pressed her cheek to the window, but all that accomplished was to fog the cool glass.

She continued watching as Alice came into view, her apron lifted at the corners carrying something—something which was revealed when Isaac gathered apples and bread from Alice's apron. He shoved the food into his saddlebags and received a long hug. After Alice let him go, she touched his cheek as if to give him one last…goodbye?

Della stepped away, ignoring the pain the movement caused her body. Hank was firing Isaac *right now.* She rushed around her room, trying to find a dress to throw on. She didn't bother tying up her hair or grabbing her boots. Despite the pain in her head, she had to stop Isaac from leaving. Her mistakes shouldn't cause such hardship to someone else.

She thundered down the steps, and hurried outside, the frosted grass crisp on her bare feet. "Hank!"

She limped toward her husband. "Please wait," she begged. "Don't fire Isaac. Don't make him leave because of the church…because of me. It was my fault. I'm sorry for everything. Please…"

How was she going to change Hank's mind when Isaac was already galloping away? Della looked to Alice for help.

The woman was grinning. How could she be happy about Isaac leaving? "I'll be inside," Alice announced. "You two won't need me."

Della and Hank both watched Alice leave. Della caught Hank rubbing the back of his neck, but her thoughts were mostly focused on the departing foreman. Where would Isaac go? Did he have any family? What would the man do for money? Food?

"You should be in bed," Hank said at last. "Aren't you cold?"

She didn't have time to thank about how nice Hank's hands felt along her skin. "Please don't fire Isaac," she repeated. "If…if anyone should be held responsible it should be—"

"Me." Hank's hands locked in place on her arms as he spoke. Darkened rings under his eyes hinted at a restless sleep, and he hadn't shaved this morning. "The fault is mine."

Hank rubbed Della's chilled arms, thanking God that her skin no longer held the fever that had worried him the previous night. "I'm so glad you're better. And please don't worry about Isaac. I didn't fire him."

"He quit?" She inspected him like he kept all the answers in the world.

All he could do was shake his head. He hoped Pa was right that she'd feel for him as he felt for her. But if not, even a sprout of love could grow if it was tended properly. And part of that meant opening up, sharing what had happened in his past.

"I had a fiancée," he said. He'd practiced what he wanted to say, if and when she'd healed, and this wasn't exactly it. But still, it needed to be said.

She checked over her shoulder, probably trying to determine what he was staring at, but there was nothing behind her but the cabin, the trees and the church's steeple in the air. She swayed on her feet, and he steadied her. "Do you need to rest some more?"

"No changing the subject and please no more miscommunication. I want this to get fixed. You had a fiancée other than Evelyn?"

He also wanted things between them fixed. "Yes, this was about a year after Evelyn passed. She… I thought… Well, I let my guard down." He glanced skyward, knowing God was there. Always. During the good and bad. "Her name was Miss Isabel Smith. I believed she'd fallen for me, but she only sought what I could offer her financially. I let it slip how I had a code word to access my account at the bank. That way Isaac or Ma or Pa could get funds they required for the ranch if they were in town."

He shook his head. "Like Samson, I was a fool. I trusted her with the code word, and she used it to disappear with quarter of that account. The highest amount that could be accessed by anyone other than me. After she left town, rumors spread about my wealth and my availability as a bachelor. That's when all the other ladies started making their way out here. It's when my bitterness put down deep roots."

"And you assumed I came here because of your money?"

"At first, until you proved genuine in your determination to be a teacher and in your affection toward the boys. And Ma and Pa." He watched her, soaking her in. She was beautiful. Inside and out. He'd always recognized it, except it was her inner beauty that truly made her a gift. "But then I saw that letter. I didn't even read it—I just noticed the word *money*, over and over again, and it sent me right back to that day when I found out Miss Smith had left town with a chunk of the ranch's account."

She stepped back and waved her hands in front of her as if she needed to plead her case. "Hank, I promise I had nothing to do—"

"I've let my fear cloud my better sense. I've done so since Evelyn's death. I was mad at God for not saving her." He wiped his palm over his mouth, shifting his weight.

"I'm so sorry," she said, her words filled with unmistakable sincerity. "For Evelyn. For having Isaac work on the church. He wanted something to pass the time, and I needed… I felt like it was the right thing to do. I hoped if you saw the place as I did—cleaned up, with its potential revealed—then you'd allow me to teach the boys there. That you'd see that despite the pain from the past, God could use it for good. I wanted the church to be an example of starting over. Like I was trying to do." She shrugged, hiding her fingers in her sleeves. "To be the rose during the thorns of life. I didn't want the boys to grow up never feeling comfortable about going into God's house. I never meant for Isaac to take the fall."

Hank stepped closer. He was beyond tired of being so far away from everyone. From her. "Della, I promise I didn't fire him, and he didn't quit. He's going to fetch your wedding gift."

"But I thought…" She pointed over her shoulder. "My gift was our walk. You took me to the church, and I messed everything up. I don't need that old building. I only need—"

He touched her cheek and her breath hitched. She didn't step away, either. Surely that was a good sign?

It was now or never. No more misunderstanding. He trusted God to protect his heart no matter how Della felt about him. "I'm far from perfect in all things," he admitted, "and a walk is no wedding gift for the gracious woman I married. Nor was a rose or a thimble or Scripture on a board."

She leaned into his touch. "I thought all those things were the boys' doings."

He slid a strand of hair behind her ear, enjoying how the rest framed her face. Liking how she fit next to him. A place where they could battle future struggles together. "You scared me last night. I was afraid I'd lose…"

"I'm so sorry about Wallie. If anything had happened to him—"

"No Della, I'm not talking about Wallie. I'd never felt hands as feverish as yours. Last night, I was scared I might lose you."

Della's legs were numb, whether from the cool air or Hank's words she wasn't sure. She tried to clear her thoughts, but it was nearly impossible to concentrate on anything other than Hank being so near. It felt so right, him beside her. Without realizing, she leaned into his palm on her cheek, closing her eyes. Had he stayed with her while she slept? Was that why he looked tired? Had he been the one to pile the blankets on top of her?

"You risked your life for Wallie. You loved my family from the beginning, and I hope one day I will earn your love, as well."

He withdrew his hand. At the loss, she opened her eyes to find him down on one knee. "I promise from now on I will strive to be the husband God wants me to be. One who isn't fearful of the things that are out of my control. Who no longer blames Him for the evil in this world. The one who desires to be everything you need me to be. I can still build you that new house if that's what you want, but if I may be honest, I want us all to live there together. I don't want you to only be the boys' caretaker or Ma and Pa's daughter-in-law." He reached for her and ran his thumb across her skin, igniting a warmth she never wanted to extinguish. "I want you to be my wife. This ring on my finger reminded me that I missed being married. Having a helpmate. And there's no one better for me than you, Della. You have what's left of my heart…if you want it."

A tear fell down her cheek, and Hank stood and wiped it away. "That's your happy smile." He whispered near her ear as his stubble on his face rubbed against her skin.

"How do you know?"

"The proof is in your dimples."

When they broke from their embrace, he pressed his lips to her forehead. "It worried me the first day when you arrived, that I could tell right away the difference in your smiles. I worried you were someone I could fall for, and I was scared to let it happen. Afraid what allowing someone in again would mean. Especially if I lost them. However, I must trust God with my tomorrows. I hope my wedding gift shows you how sorry I am for the way I've reacted. I don't want to push you away anymore."

She pulled back to read his face. Was he serious about loving her? Memories of his actions flooded her mind. Of him protecting her from both snakes. The time he'd looked at her on the porch and the way her heart had responded. His compassion during the storm and his kindness when he invited her to eat oats with him. Those little gifts she hadn't known he'd given, yet all of which showed that he'd paid attention.

However, most of all, how he treasured and cared for his boys and parents proved his words about love could be trusted. She'd dreamed of love and security like that. And though she'd realized that it was God's love alone that truly fulfilled her, she wanted to embrace all the blessings God had given her: this beautiful place, her wonderful sons, the most loving parents-in-law imaginable…and Hank.

"I only want my husband to love me as I love him."

"Pa claimed you did, but I… You love me?"

"You're kind of hard to ignore."

"In a good way, I hope." Hank nuzzled her neck. "Ma was a mail-order bride."

"Hmm?" she murmured, enjoying this affectionate side of her husband too much to truly take in his words.

He nodded his chin to the front porch where the boys were now watching them as Alice and Roy rocked on the rocking chairs. "They were strangers once like us." His gaze poured into hers. "I want us to have what they have."

She stepped forward, eager to be closer to him, and managed to land on a sharp stick. "Ouch."

His smile dimmed. "You're barefoot? How did I not notice that before? I keep failing you."

She shook her head. "It's not your fault. I just couldn't wait to get to you." She reached down to rub her foot. "I mean, there wasn't time… I had to stop Isaac. I thought—"

"I like the first answer best, Mrs. Lamson." He scooped her up in his arms, and she rested against him, smiling. Her true, happy one.

Chapter Twenty-One

Della tapped her piece of chalk on Wallie's board. He scrunched his nose, lifting the healing scar farther into his hairline, as he refocused on his school task. Robert had picked to study under the maple today, probably hoping to get a break on the rope swing swaying nearby. The air was colder than she would have liked, but with a blanket covering their laps it wasn't entirely uncomfortable. And it was definitely noticeably warmer than when she'd carried Wallie from the creek.

"Momma, what's this word?"

She checked the book in Edward's hands. "*Territorial.*"

His eyebrows lowered as he mouthed the word.

"Do you know what it means?"

Edward's face brightened with realization, but Robert beat him. "Like when our bull protects the cows. It's why we can't go inside the fence."

Wallie flicked a piece of dirt off the blanket. "Like how Papa is with you."

"With me?"

Wallie set his chalkboard to the side and sat up on his

knees. "Yeah, Papa says I can't sneak into your room at night no more. That's Papa being territorial." Wallie struggled to pronounce the word even though his understanding was correct.

Della covered her laugh by clearing her throat. Her room was also Hank's now, and yes, Wallie was once again very observant. Hank had become very territorial of their alone time. "I suppose you're right. Don't you think it's good that your papa wants to protect me?"

Wallie frowned. "Not from me."

Della spread wide her arms, welcoming Wallie into a hug. "You know I love you." She looked at each of the boys. "All of you." Before Wallie leaned into Della as he normally did, he sprang to his feet and ran off.

"Wallie?"

A moment later, she realized that he wasn't running away from her, rather toward two men coming their way. She shielded her eyes. Hank walked on the right, and she would have assumed the other to be Pa or even Isaac, who still hadn't returned, except the man was much taller than either of them. Della had pleaded with Hank to let her know what Isaac went after, but his lips had remained sealed. What type of wedding gift took so long to retrieve?

When Wallie reached the men, he didn't go to Hank but to the taller man. Was he a new oil crew member? Though Wallie hadn't made a habit of leaping into any of the workers' arms. Not even Isaac's.

The man's deep, throaty—familiar—laugh made Della shoot off the ground. It couldn't be, could it? Why would her brother be here?

Della chased after Edward and Robert. When she reached the men, they both stared at her, expectantly.

"Well, look at you." Freeman smirked. "You go off to become a teacher and turn into a wife instead. Mother was… Doesn't matter what she thought. Marriage looks good on you."

Della joined in with Robert, Edward and Wallie in wrapping Freeman into a hug, ignoring the part about her mother. "I'm still a teacher."

"And an even better wife," Hank said.

She sent the smile she knew her husband was after. "What are you doing here? *How* are you here?"

Freeman somehow managed to shove his hands in his pockets with the three boys hanging on him. The twinkle in his eyes that had gone missing the last several years made the hazel more like her own green eyes. "Sounds to me like you want me to return home. Is that what you're hearing, Hank?"

Wallie slid down to the ground. "No, Uncle Freeman! You just got here. I haven't shown you Mabel yet. Did you get my letters? Did Isaac give them to you? Did he, huh?"

"Mine, too?" Edward said.

Robert shook his head. "But you read mine first, right?"

Freeman clasped onto each of the boys' shoulders, one by one. "Got all of your letters, and Della, you should be proud of their penmanship." He let out a low whistle. "I can't wait to see the hayloft and to go check the oil rigs." He squatted in front of Wallie. "And to meet Miss Mabel." He thumped Wallie's nose. "Most importantly, I'm excited about my nephews. I've never had any before."

Wallie's mouth shaped into a small circle. "Never?"

"Nope. Any suggestions on what we should do first?"

Wallie sprung into the air. "Have some of Grandma's chocolate cake she made for Momma."

Della put her fists on her hips. "She made me cake? When?" Probably after Alice had booted her out of the kitchen when she'd offered to help with the dishes.

"After we promised not to tell you that Uncle Freeman was coming." Wallie grinned, the top of his new tooth visible.

She glared at Hank. "That's why you missed breakfast?"

"I figured Isaac's horse wouldn't appreciate carrying both him and Freeman, so I brought the wagon into town. Finally found a job Mr. Precious will do without throwing mud on me. He did quite nicely beside Dorothy. Who knew all the stubborn animal needed was the right helpmate?" He gave her his crooked grin she'd grown to love. "Hope you're not disappointed in your wedding gift. I like to make you happy."

She fell into the spot that seemed to be made for her along his side, and he tucked her against him. "You do. Thank you." She had to endure some of life's thorns, but her life had flowered beautifully after she'd married this wonderful man. "I love that my gift is Freeman. I've missed him."

Freeman rocked on the balls of his feet. "Who wouldn't?"

Della swatted, but missed a moving Freeman.

"All right, boys, lead me to this cake." Freeman rubbed his palms together. "I prefer to share in sweet moments that I can actually eat." Her brother winked at Della. "Last one to the house earns the smallest slice."

It didn't take the boys long to take off. Freeman grabbed a trailing Wallie and threw him onto his back.

By all of their laughter, Freeman wouldn't have to worry about learning how to be a good uncle. It looked like it came as naturally to him as mothering had felt for her.

Hank laid his chin against Della's head and seemed to breathe her in. He'd been doing that a lot lately, as if he couldn't get enough of her. She prayed he never would. "I sent Isaac with money for your father's newspaper, too."

She should have been more concerned with her parents' financial situation, but it had been all too easy to put it out of her mind. She hadn't wanted to remember all the hateful things Mother used to do and say, proving that she believed Della would never amount to anything worthwhile.

"You didn't have to give them anything." Her words were soft as guilt prodded her. His gift was more than kindness or a hope of happiness for her. It was an example of what she needed to do. Growing up, Della could never please Mother no matter what she did. Couldn't make her mother love her for who she was. Della bit the inside of her cheek. Hadn't she learned that her job in life wasn't to prove herself to anyone? She only needed to forgive, and trust God with everything.

Hank squeezed her fingers. "I wanted to. They're my family now. Your father paid off the debt he owed, giving Freeman the freedom to leave the newspaper without any guilt. He was happy to come here when I offered him a job. And what do I need all that money in that bank for when I have more than enough treasure right here beside me?"

"Thank you. But what's Freeman going to work on? He hasn't been trained in anything other than print work. How's he going to manage as an oilfield worker?"

Hank smiled, making Della's heart skip a beat. She loved how happiness looked on her husband. "That's the other part of your gift. He's going to help get the old church ready for next fall's school year."

Della blinked. Had she heard right?

"Someone very wise mentioned that old building should have a new start. God knew what He was doing when He brought you here, Della. He had a plan to reach this stubborn heart. And He of course was right—it too needed a new start."

She threw her arms around his neck and met his awaiting lips.

"Can we save the tree inside?"

"I did say I like to make you happy."

Della threaded her fingers into the hair on the back of Hank's neck, and he leaned toward her. But the back door slapped open, interrupting their moment. Alice was on the bottom of the porch steps. "You two better come get this cake before it's gone. Your brother has proved he's not shy when it comes to filling his belly."

The smell of sugary goodness hit Della as she stepped next to Alice on the porch. The sound of the boys playing around in the kitchen was even sweeter. After nodding for Hank to go on, she turned to Alice. "Thanks for praying for me. You know, even before—"

All the air disappeared in Della's lungs as Alice crushed her to her chest. Before her next breath, someone else was wrapped around both her and Alice. "Why are we hugging in the cold when we can do it inside while eating cake?" Roy asked.

Alice laughed and released Della. "I'm so glad the Lord brought you here and made you our daughter-in-law." Alice used the edge of her new apron—one that

Della had made—to wipe her wet cheeks. "Even if our plan wasn't entirely welcomed at first."

Hank handed her a plate piled with cake. "Since the whole mail-order marriage worked for you both, and it worked for Della and me—"

"I was a mail-order teacher."

"Sticking to that story, huh?" Hank took a bite of cake. How did his smile make her knees weak even with chocolate stuck to his top lip?

"Hiram Robert Lamson, what are you getting at?" Alice said as she snuggled into Roy.

Hank shrugged, eyeing the doorway where Freeman stood.

Freeman wiped his mouth. "What?"

"Well, you see, there's a winning streak to keep up. Don't you think, Della?" Hank kissed her forehead and smirked at Freeman. "I'm sorry. But you'll thank us later."

Confusion clouded Freeman's face. "For what?"

"It'd be for his own good." Alice nodded.

Freeman sent his hand through his shaggy hair. "For whose good? And why is everyone staring at me like I'm about to become plucked for dinner?"

Della leaned her head against Hank's shoulder. "Freeman… I think what everyone wants to know is… what are your feelings on ordering a want ad bride?"

* * * * *

LOVE INSPIRED

Stories to uplift and inspire

Fall in love with Love Inspired—
inspirational and uplifting stories of faith
and hope. Find strength and comfort in
the bonds of friendship and community.
Revel in the warmth of possibility and the
promise of new beginnings.

Sign up for the Love Inspired newsletter
at **LoveInspired.com** to be the first
to find out about upcoming titles,
special promotions and exclusive content.

CONNECT WITH US AT:

f Facebook.com/LoveInspiredBooks

🐦 Twitter.com/LoveInspiredBks

Get 4 FREE REWARDS!

We'll send you 2 FREE Books plus 2 FREE Mystery Gifts.

FREE
Value Over
$20

Both the **Love Inspired®** and **Love Inspired® Suspense** series feature compelling novels filled with inspirational romance, faith, forgiveness, and hope.

YES! Please send me 2 FREE novels from the Love Inspired or Love Inspired Suspense series and my 2 FREE gifts (gifts are worth about $10 retail). After receiving them, if I don't wish to receive any more books, I can return the shipping statement marked "cancel." If I don't cancel, I will receive 6 brand-new Love Inspired Larger-Print books or Love Inspired Suspense Larger-Print books every month and be billed just $5.99 each in the U.S. or $6.24 each in Canada. That is a savings of at least 17% off the cover price. It's quite a bargain! Shipping and handling is just 50¢ per book in the U.S. and $1.25 per book in Canada.* I understand that accepting the 2 free books and gifts places me under no obligation to buy anything. I can always return a shipment and cancel at any time. The free books and gifts are mine to keep no matter what I decide.

Choose one: ☐ **Love Inspired**   ☐ **Love Inspired Suspense**
              Larger-Print   **Larger-Print**
              (122/322 IDN GNWC)   (107/307 IDN GNWN)

Name (please print)

Address   Apt. #

City   State/Province   Zip/Postal Code

Email: Please check this box ☐ if you would like to receive newsletters and promotional emails from Harlequin Enterprises ULC and its affiliates. You can unsubscribe anytime.

Mail to the **Harlequin Reader Service:**
IN U.S.A.: P.O. Box 1341, Buffalo, NY 14240-8531
IN CANADA: P.O. Box 603, Fort Erie, Ontario L2A 5X3

Want to try 2 free books from another series! Call 1-800-873-8635 or visit www.ReaderService.com.

---

*Terms and prices subject to change without notice. Prices do not include sales taxes, which will be charged (if applicable) based on your state or country of residence. Canadian residents will be charged applicable taxes. Offer not valid in Quebec. This offer is limited to one order per household. Books received may not be as shown. Not valid for current subscribers to the Love Inspired or Love Inspired Suspense series. All orders subject to approval. Credit or debit balances in a customer's account(s) may be offset by any other outstanding balance owed by or to the customer. Please allow 4 to 6 weeks for delivery. Offer available while quantities last.

Your Privacy—Your information is being collected by Harlequin Enterprises ULC, operating as Harlequin Reader Service. For a complete summary of the information we collect, how we use this information and to whom it is disclosed, please visit our privacy notice located at corporate.harlequin.com/privacy-notice. From time to time we may also exchange your personal information with reputable third parties. If you wish to opt out of this sharing of your personal information, please visit readerservice.com/consumerschoice or call 1-800-873-8635. **Notice to California Residents**—Under California law, you have specific rights to control and access your data. For more information on these rights and how to exercise them, visit corporate.harlequin.com/california-privacy.

LIRLIS22

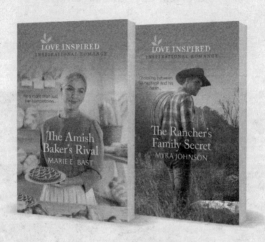

IF YOU ENJOYED THIS BOOK, DON'T MISS NEW EXTENDED-LENGTH NOVELS FROM LOVE INSPIRED!

In addition to the Love Inspired books you know and love, we're excited to introduce even more uplifting stories in a longer format, with more inspiring fresh starts and page-turning thrills!

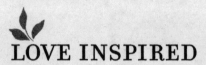

Stories to uplift and inspire.

Fall in love with Love Inspired—inspirational and uplifting stories of faith and hope. Find strength and comfort in the bonds of friendship and community. Revel in the warmth of possibility, and the promise of new beginnings.

LOOK FOR THESE LOVE INSPIRED TITLES ONLINE AND IN THE BOOK DEPARTMENT OF YOUR FAVORITE RETAILER!